WITCH'S FATE

Linsey Hall

DEDICATION

For Veronica Morris, an amazing friend and person. I'm so glad we found each other!

PROLOGUE

Warlock's Apprenticeship, Corrier's Home
Norway
1606 AD

"Oh my gods, you must be jesting." Sofia Viera gripped the armrests of the chair as her heart plummeted into her stomach. Kitty, her feline familiar, pressed against her calves, trying to comfort her. It didn't work.

"I'm afraid I am not." Corrier's voice was grave. Her mentor's white hair was wild as usual, his robes dusty. "You've done very well in the warlock's apprenticeship— many don't make it this far. But to complete the transition to warlock, you must become an Oath Breaker."

"Oath Breaker," she whispered. A person bound by fate to break any oath or promise they made. A rare curse. Corrier had taught them about Oath Breakers, but he'd never said that warlocks *were* Oath Breakers. To become one…

It would ruin her life. Every promise, every commitment she made would be destroyed—fate and magic would conspire to break them. It was strange, dark magic, but it was infallible. And an Oath Breaker could never love, because love itself was a commitment.

No love. No Malcolm. Her throat tightened unbearably and her hands trembled. She forced down the ragged sob at the thought of all she would lose.

"But why?" she bit out. Her panicked mind scrambled for a way around this. She needed a warlock's power to break the curse on her village. But if she became an Oath Breaker, she would lose Malcolm.

"A warlock's power is great. Near that of a god's. That kind of ability comes at a steep price. You're a powerful witch. Excuse me, Bruxa," he corrected himself, using the Portuguese title that her species of witch preferred. "It's what qualified you for this apprenticeship. But to become a warlock and reach your full potential, you must pay a great price to obtain great magic. Break your most important vow. Become an Oath Breaker."

She could see the terrible progression so clearly—and the havoc it would wreak on her life. "Why did you not tell me sooner?" she whispered. It seemed like an awful trick.

"It's a warlock's greatest secret. If others knew we were Oath Breakers... That's a terrible weakness. Apprentices are only told once they have become qualified to transition. We guard the secret well."

She swallowed hard. Of course. By their very nature, warlocks were shrouded in secrecy.

"Does Malcolm know?" she asked. Her heart pounded as a chill spread over her skin.

Corrier frowned. "I haven't told him because I haven't had to. His people are sorcerers. Dedicated to this path. He's known the price since he was a child."

Horror rose in Sofia's chest, a dark substance that threatened to strangle her from within. She shook her head. "No. No, he couldn't have."

The first bit of sympathy entered Corrier's eyes. "You've become close to him, Sofia. I'm sure he's told you about his people."

Tears burned at her eyes and she blinked them back frantically. *Become close to him?* Over the last six months, he'd become her world. They'd shared everything. Or so she'd thought. He'd mentioned his people, a small clan of sorcerers in Southern England who were dedicated to this path, but he'd never mentioned becoming an Oath Breaker. Oath Breaker's couldn't love. If they did, only tragedy would ensue.

"You understand that you must end whatever is between you when you transition." Corrier's voice was firm. "You remember Laira."

At the mention of her friend, horrified realization stole Sofia's breath. Laira had transitioned to warlock two months ago. She'd left the apprenticeship with Oliver, the man she loved and another warlock. Just last week, Corrier had told Sofia of Laira's death in a battle in the south.

"No." Sofia shook her head. "Her death was an accident. It had to be. It's not because she was an Oath Breaker."

Corrier nodded gravely. "An accident ensured by fate. I couldn't tell you the details before because you couldn't be allowed to know of the connection between warlocks and Oath Breakers. But after she transitioned to warlock, she didn't part with Oliver as she should have. So fate intervened.

3

Oliver was fighting for his people in a battle in Turkey. He mistakenly turned her over to the enemy. It was fate's way of ensuring they broke their oath of love to one another."

"I cannot continue the apprenticeship." She couldn't believe the words were leaving her mouth. She'd worked so hard for this. But it was clear to her.

"For Malcolm? You know that he might not make the same choice."

"He will." *He had to*. Panic threatened to strangle her. She rose from her chair, nearly shaking. "I'm sorry, Corrier, but I—I must go."

She whirled and ran from the room, Kitty on her heels. The stone-walled corridor of Corrier's large home flashed by and she sped down the hall. She had to find Malcolm. He couldn't have known this. He'd fallen in love with her too. These had been the best months of her life. It couldn't all be falling apart now.

She raced up the stairs and down the hall to Malcolm's room, then pounded on the door. Her little black cat scratched at the door, mirroring her distress.

No answer.

Outside. He had to be outside.

Without stopping for her cloak, she ran out into the cold Norwegian winter, followed by Kitty. She didn't even feel the chill as her feet sank into the snow. Normally, she'd be miserable. Her thin Brazilian blood couldn't take this cold. But now, fear and panic supplanted everything else.

She found him at the frozen waterfall where he practiced his magic. The chill wind whipped his dark hair back from his face as he threw a jet of flame at the ice, melting it.

The sight of him, so tall and handsome, draped in his black cloak, calmed her. Love swelled in her chest. This wasn't true. He didn't know about becoming an Oath Breaker. He hadn't lied to her all this time. He would choose her over magic. Of course he would.

He turned, clearly alerted by her harsh breathing. Concern swept across his beautiful face. The sharp lines, full lips, and golden eyes had become so familiar to her. Beloved.

"Sofia. Are you unwell?" His British accent reminded her of how different he was from her. But that was all right. He would make the same choice she would.

He strode to her and gripped her shoulders in his big hands. He loomed over her, nearly a foot taller than her own five and a half feet.

"I—I heard something terrible." She sucked in a ragged breath.

He swept his thumb over her cheek and only then did she notice that tears were pouring down her face. She glanced down, trying to get herself together, and caught sight of Kitty, who stared at Malcolm suspiciously. Her squinty eye narrowed even more than usual.

The sight of Kitty's suspicion sent a streak of fear through her. Kitty normally liked Malcolm. Did her familiar sense the truth? That he'd always known?

"What is it?" His deep voice was rough with concern.

"Oath Breakers." The words tumbled over her tongue as she looked up to search his face. "Corrier told me we're supposed to become Oath Breakers to complete the transition to warlock."

His brow creased, but it was the understanding in his eyes that sent a chill through her. He wasn't surprised or confused or upset.

"You knew," she whispered, her voice strangled. "You've always known."

He nodded and her heart felt like it would break her ribs. "You say you love me. Yet you didn't tell me about this? You've continued with the apprenticeship. You know that we can't become warlocks and stay together, so why continue?" Fear clawed at her, tearing at her heart.

There *was* no reason to continue if he knew what awaited him. If he'd chosen her, he'd have already quit the apprenticeship.

"Of course I love you," he said. The intensity of emotion in his golden gaze calmed her fear a bit.

He did love her. Of course. He'd told her so for the first time in this very place. She wanted to believe it so badly that she clung to his words, though her fear remained.

"But I have to become a warlock," he said. "You know that."

She stumbled back, out of his embrace. The cold finally hit her, both inside and out. "You can't. You know that if you become one, there's no hope for us."

As soon as Corrier had told her what she must to do to complete her transition, she'd known she could never become a warlock. She couldn't give up Malcolm.

"We can make this work." He reached for her, but she stepped back.

Horrified laughter welled in her breast. "You're jesting. You know that's not possible. Corrier told us what happens to Oath Breakers. Love is an oath. Fate will intervene. And

Laira?" Her voice rose in panic. "Corrier just told me how she died. That Oliver turned her over in battle. A mistake. One that fate engineered."

"He was stupid. Weak. I wouldn't do that."

She shook her head frantically. He was so stubborn. "Oliver wasn't stupid. Don't you see? You won't have any control. Or I might be the one to do something that destroys you. We cannot control it. You know how powerful fate is. If you love me, you'll abandon the apprenticeship with me. You promised we would be together. Right here, at this waterfall. You promised." Her voice broke. She wanted to grab him, shake him.

"And we will. Become a warlock. We're smart enough to avoid what fate has planned."

"Can you hear yourself? *Avoid fate*?" He was delusional. He wanted the power of a warlock so badly that he thought he could avoid fate? All Mytheans knew that was impossible. Mortals might not understand, but they also didn't realize that their myths were real. They didn't know that fate was an infallible power. But Sofia knew.

"You need to become a warlock, Sofia. Your village needs you. With the power of the aether, you can break the curse upon your village. Free yourself from being Protector."

A rush of desire swept through her at his words. It's what she'd wanted all along—the reason she'd sought out the apprenticeship. Upon her mother's death, she was expected to take on the role of Protector of Bruxa's Eye. She loved her village at the edge of the Amazon River and would dedicate her life to protecting it from the High Witches' curse.

Unlike most Mytheans, warlocks were made, not born. Most Mytheans took their magical power from the aether, that ephemeral substance connecting earth and their afterworlds. Their immortal souls absorbed the aether power like a sponge and they used it to fuel their magic. But, like a sponge, there was a limited capacity and then a Mythean had to wait to reabsorb more power. But a warlock could open a channel to the aether and fill up on nearly unlimited power.

"But not at this cost," Sofia said. "I love you, Malcolm. I love my village. Becoming an Oath Breaker would mean leaving you. Maybe even my village, too. I cannot do that. I will not! And if you love me, you will not either. It's not worth it."

The cold determination in his eyes sent a chill across her skin. Fear and loss threatened to overwhelm her, a cold force dragging her down. She was losing this battle. It was clear in his eyes. Sorcerers were cold, determined. His clan in particular. It was in his blood to do this.

But he was part wulver as well. His father's people, from northern Scotland, were wolf shifters. They were loyal and believed in the importance of bonds, of family. Of love. It's why she'd been able to overlook the coldness of his sorcerer side. But she'd never seen him turn into a wolf, nor had he mentioned it. Perhaps the fact that he was a half-blood meant that he couldn't. And perhaps too, he didn't feel emotion as strongly as his kin.

"I have to become a warlock, Sofia." His voice was hard. "I love you. But I have to do this."

"Why?" Her chest ached with loss.

"Because becoming a warlock is the greatest thing I can accomplish."

Pain hit her. "The greatest thing? Love is the greatest thing."

"We can have that too."

Something snapped inside of her and she screamed, "We can't! You know it. You've heard the stories. Our friend was struck low by the Oath Breaker's curse. Oath Breakers cannot love." She sucked in a ragged breath. "You can become a warlock, or you can have me. But you cannot have both."

"You're wrong, Sofia."

She drew her wand and shot a bolt of lightning at him. He deflected it with his hand and it hit a tree, felling it. His face hardened and her heart felt like it cracked at the sight of his beloved features twisted in anger at her. The bolt wouldn't have killed him, but she wanted to make him hurt as she was hurting.

She tried to harden her voice. "Those are my terms. You made a vow to me that we'd be together forever. If you break it, you're on the path to becoming an Oath Breaker. It's me or becoming a warlock."

"You would give me an ultimatum?" Shock and anger played across his features. Understanding dawned. "You will leave me if I become a warlock."

She nodded sharply, unable to open her mouth for fear that a sob would burst forth.

"You know what I choose," he said, his voice cold.

She nearly fell to her knees. The earth seemed to tilt on its axis. What had just happened? Had she really just lost everything?

She turned and ran.

CHAPTER ONE

Glencoe Mountains, Scottish Highlands
Present Day

Sofia stared at the exterior of Malcolm's enormous castle, unable to believe she was here. For over four hundred years, she'd stuck by her vow to never see him again.

Yet she was now standing on top of a mountain in front of his home, a sweeping vista of snow-sprinkled peaks and valleys stretching into the distance before her. Moonlight gleamed off every white surface.

Rage banished any chill she felt from the cold. It burned away the painful memories of their parting, memories that had torn at her insides for years.

"That bastard had better still have the Demon Blade," she said to Kitty. She'd used all her magic and the strongest spells she could find and he'd still broken in and stolen it. He'd been cocky enough to leave her a message in the chest where the blade had been locked. In her own home. *Come to me.*

Kitty hissed.

Harsh wind whipped across her cheeks as she stomped toward the huge front doors. Kitty led the way, her round little body stalking across the snow as if she too meant to make Malcolm pay for stealing the dagger. Sofia would see to it he did.

His home loomed before her, enormous. She scowled. Not only was he an immensely powerful warlock, he was now insanely wealthy, if the size of his home was any indication. But if he had the obscene amount of money it would take to own this place, why the hell was he stealing from her? Why was he back in her life at all? *He* was the one who'd destroyed what they had.

She shook the painful thought away and glared at his house. It was not a typical castle, made of great, ugly blocks with only a few narrow windows. No, this one was both stark and beautiful. Gray stone towers rose from the mountain and glass glowed with warm light. There was no exterior defense wall. There'd be no need, of course. Not with his power. Despite its beauty, it was somehow desolate. As if the person who lived within were as cold and dark as the night surrounding it.

But then, Malcolm was dark and cold and she knew it better than anyone.

She climbed the wide steps and raised her hand to pound on the door.

"Screw it." She lowered her fist and pushed against the door, sending a jolt of power blasting through his protection charm and forcing the door open. It smashed against the inside wall. He might be ridiculously powerful and wealthy, but she was no slouch herself.

11

And she was just pissed enough that she wanted to bust into his house and break a few things. Like his head.

She stepped through the now wide open door and took in the rich wood paneling and priceless art covering the high walls of the entry. A huge staircase swept up to the right and a large archway on the left led to a wide hallway. The sheer beauty of the interior was so great that it quashed her previous desire to break things.

Her skin prickled when she looked toward the hallway to the left, so she set off that way. She could almost feel herself being drawn to him. How was it possible after so many years?

Kitty stayed close by her side as she stomped down the hall, her footsteps thudding on the gleaming wooden floor as she made her way past closed doors. A glow emitted from the one at the end of the hall, the light within so bright it shined out from between the cracks at the edges. It beckoned her in the best and worst way.

Her heart pounded in her ears as anticipation fought with her anger.

Bastard.

She shouldn't want to see him after all these years, but she did. Her hurt over the past had faded some. What was left had turned to anger, which she stoked. She couldn't bear to relive that crushing pain. So she'd focus on anger.

But she couldn't help the anticipation.

She sucked in a deep breath and stepped through the doorway. The room within was dark, the only light coming from the large fireplace that was blocked by a man sitting at a desk. She could only make out his silhouette.

She ignored her pounding heart and took in her surroundings, searching for additional trouble. The room was round, the ceiling soaring high above. She must be in one of the towers. Books lined the walls, stretching up five stories to the domed ceiling. A wide walkway spiraled up the sides of the round room, making it easy to access all the books. Kitty pressed up against her legs, trembling slightly.

Satisfied no other lurked in the shadows, she looked at the man at the desk. Shadows concealed his face, but not the outline of his form. Despite the dark, she could make out the breadth of his shoulders and the fall of his dark hair.

Her heart threatened to break her ribs and a chill broke out on her skin.

Malcolm. Desire that she'd thought long dead rushed through her. Her breath came short. She hadn't even really seen him yet and she still wanted him. They'd only ever kissed, but memories of his skilled lips bombarded her.

He remained sitting, his feet propped on the gleaming wooden desk. A crystal tumbler of whisky sat in front of him. Firelight set the amber liquid aglow. Her insides tightened as her eyes adjusted to the dim light and she could take him in better.

The man—it really was Malcolm—lazily spun her Demon Blade in one big hand.

"This what you came here for?" His voice was as deep and rich as the darkest chocolate. No sweetness. Just a hint of the bitterness that followed a bite of the rich substance.

Fear suddenly shivered down her spine. She was a powerful Bruxa—powerful enough that she had no need for modesty—but she was also a smart one. And she was right to be afraid.

This wasn't the Malcolm she remembered. Of course it wasn't. He was now one of the most powerful beings in all of

13

the Mythean world. A warlock. Destruction and power personified. All bought by becoming an Oath Breaker and throwing her away.

The reminder sent anger through her again. A reminder of what she was fighting for. What she'd always been fighting for. Her village. And for the first time since her line had taken up the role of Protector, they were at risk.

Because of this man.

"Yeah, that's what I came here for." Her voice could have cut stone. "Now give it back."

He surged fluidly to his feet, his shoulders blocking out the light of the fire. For such a large man, he was incredibly graceful. He approached her, his gait smooth and long, and she stifled a gasp at his size.

Had she forgotten? Or had he grown? He was at least six and a half feet tall, his shoulders broad and his waist narrow. His sweater and pants were dark and expensive looking. He stopped just inches from her, looming over her.

His scent, rich with spice and darkness, wrapped enticingly around her. He bent his head, seeming to enclose her in an invisible embrace. His dark hair fell around his face. This close, she could make out the masculine beauty of his features. Dark brows and golden eyes, full lips that twisted with a bit of cruelty.

Otherworldly. She trembled as desire surged to the fore again. She might be mad at him. Afraid of him.

But she still wanted him.

"You don't care at all why I took it?"

Again, the rich timbre of his voice sent a shiver across her skin. Only this time, it wasn't entirely due to fear. It was there, of course, making her skin prickle coldly. But a surge of heat came with it. Desire fueled by fear. He was dangerous.

He raised a hand as if he would touch her. Anticipation streaked through her. *Do it.*

Hot anger welled within her. At him and herself. He thought he could touch her? And she would let him?

She pressed her hand against his hard chest, sending a bolt of heat meant to burn and punish.

The corner of his mouth kicked up in a dark smile and he pressed his palm over hers, absorbing what she gave him without reacting at all.

Her jaw slackened. It should have hurt like hell. Made him jump back at the very least, if not fall to the ground.

But his golden eyes flared with desire and his full lips kicked up at the corners.

He liked it.

What the hell?

Malcolm absorbed the heat of her touch, relishing the burn. It wasn't that he liked it, necessarily. But he liked that it made him feel something. And that it came from her.

Sofia's skin was smooth and soft, her hand so tiny beneath his. She made him feel like a great, hulking beast. Which he was. As part wulver, the wolf was inside him. And the things that beast wanted to do to her…

Suitable for one such as him. But another voice in his head suggested that those things ought not be done to one as beautiful and delicate as she. That part of his mind was quiet enough to ignore.

15

He wanted her too bloody much. He'd wanted her for centuries—a gnawing, aching need that only got worse as the years passed.

Finally, after centuries without her, he'd caved. Power could keep him warm for only so long. He'd taken the dagger to help his brother, the one person that Malcolm had managed to maintain a semblance of a relationship with after becoming a warlock. Felix had needed the demon blade to save his mate. Afterward Malcolm had decided to keep it for himself.

So that he could have her.

And she'd come to him as he'd expected. As he'd forced her to.

She jerked her palm free. He almost reached out to snatch it back, but he clenched his fist. She still had him by the balls after all this time, but there was no way in hell he'd let her know it.

"I don't care why you took it. I don't have time to care," she said. Her sultry voice, laced with the hint of Brazilian accent, wrapped around him. Her dark eyes flashed with rage and her normally full lips pressed into a thin line.

She was so lovely. Golden skin and the elegant features of her Brazilian and Portuguese ancestors. Still the most beautiful woman he'd ever seen, and he hadn't been able to forget her.

"That dagger is this year's tribute to the High Witches," she said. "I need it back. *Now.*"

He knew. He'd known when he'd taken it that she needed it to protect her village. In exchange for not destroying her village, the High Witches demanded that she find and bring them a treasure of their choosing.

"Are you late in offering it?" he asked, though he also knew that answer. He'd been keeping an eye on her for centuries. Every year, on October the twenty-eighth, she made the offering. Today was that day.

He'd been waiting for her.

"I am." Fear flashed in her dark eyes. He didn't like it. He especially didn't like that it dampened the desire he could sense in her. "And you're going to come with me to make the offering. To explain why it's late. And to take the hit if necessary."

"Am I?"

"You are." Her voice was hard, its normally husky tone replaced with steel. "Your theft made me break the terms. That's punishable by death. And if one of us has to die for this, it'll be you."

A growl rose in his throat at the idea of the High Witches daring to threaten either of them. "Why would I do that?"

Her hand flashed up and lightning streaked from her palm, hitting him square in the chest. He grunted in pain, smelled singed flesh, and then grabbed her wrist tight enough to make her stop. The little witch had put more into this second strike.

"You can't threaten me. You're quick, but not nearly as powerful as I." He rubbed his thumb over the smooth skin at the base of her slender wrist.

Her features hardened. "I know that all too well."

He didn't want to talk about their past, so he made his offer. "I'll help you, in exchange for a favor."

"What kind of favor?"

"Any sort of my choosing."

Wariness lit her eyes.

"Your alternative is death and the destruction of your village." It'd been so long since he'd negotiated with a woman, since he'd had more contact with one than a quick fuck, that he knew he was rusty. He should feel like a bastard for putting her in this position—for manipulating her like this—but his conscience was long dead.

"Is this why you took the dagger? For this favor?"

"No. But it's a nice side effect."

She scowled. Desire surged through him. He wanted to yank her to him and kiss her, to feel her soft lips. His hands trembled with the need.

"What's your answer?" he asked, his voice gruff. "Death or a favor?"

Once, he'd have vowed that the favor would be better than death. And it would be—that was certain. But as an Oath Breaker, he could vow nothing or fate and magic would conspire to see it broken. He could tell her how delicious the favor he begged of her would be for both of them, but he could not promise.

He'd learned to be noncommittal. To nod to indicate agreement and to suggest that it would all go as planned—but never to promise.

Indecision flashed in her gaze as she bit her full lip. At the sight, his shaft pulsed. Desire coiled low, a deep, familiar want that was specific to her. There was something stronger about this need. Surreal. Anytime he'd seen her over the last four hundred years, he'd felt it. Only this time, he was touching the soft skin of her wrist. He was only inches from her full lips.

He could have her. If…

"You're running out of time. You're already late." He added fuel to her fear with no remorse. He'd make her agree. "I'm stronger than the High Witches, but only as individuals. Together, they are too strong, even for me. If we're too late, any leniency will be gone."

And they'd need that leniency. This was a risk, even for him. His magic—and brute strength—could defeat a few of the High Witches when they combined their strength. But not all. Not when they were together, as they would be when the tribute was presented. They were the most powerful coven in the world, fueled by a dark magic that took its power not only from the aether, as all Mytheans did, but from destruction as well.

"Fine. A favor. Any favor."

"Excellent." He rubbed his thumb against the tender skin of her wrist. "We'll go now. We'll aetherwalk, I presume?" Teleporting via the ephemeral substance that connected earth and the afterworlds was a skill that they both possessed, but as he didn't know where the High Witches lived, she'd have to take them both.

She nodded.

"Then lead the way."

She closed her eyes and the aether pulled at them.

CHAPTER TWO

Sofia opened her eyes at the edge of the dark forest. Enormous, leafless trees reached for the dark sky, their branches angry claws that threatened to sweep her up. She shuddered.

Kitty hissed. She hated this place.

The entrance point to the High Witches' afterworld was freaking creepy. It was always night, the sky black and ominous. A sickly orange moon illuminated the haunted forest ahead of her and reflected off the eyes of black owls who sat in the trees, watching.

"Are we in an afterworld?" Malcolm's rough murmur drifted over her. His accent was the same as she remembered—that of a refined English gentleman. But he wasn't one.

The owls shifted nervously at the sound of Malcolm's voice. As if they sensed his power. She glanced toward him. His dark sweater and trousers blended well with the forest, but it was his golden eyes and almost cruel handsomeness that most suited this place.

No, he wasn't the man she remembered. But she wanted him all the same. The desire thrummed within her like a living thing, unwilling to be stifled by her anger or fear. Not even by the memory of their past. He'd made her feel like her heart had been torn out of her chest, but the worst of her pain was buried by the years.

One by one, the owls began to take off, their wings beating the air, as if they feared remaining in his presence. Magical beings were good at sensing a threat. She was no exception. The way that Malcolm blended so well with this evil place made her heart race. Combined with his height and the muscled power of his body—not to mention the immense magic that radiated from him—she couldn't help but take a step backward.

If he noticed, he said nothing.

"Yes," she said. "The High Witches are too conspicuous to live on earth. They destroyed the souls who lived on this afterworld long ago and took it for themselves."

She'd been raised on the terrifying stories of the High Witches' attack on this afterworld. The nightmarish tales spun by her mother for as long as she could remember kept her fearful and in line. If the High Witches could destroy all the souls who'd come here after death—Sofia had no idea what religion had created this afterworld—then they would have no trouble destroying her village.

"Where are they?" Malcolm asked.

"We're at the edge of the haunted forest. Their stronghold is on the other side. This is the only place I'm allowed to aetherwalk to."

"Why the hell don't they just let you enter through the garden?"

"They like to play with me."

He scowled. There was something odd in his gaze. Concern? Had he not realized how dangerous her role was? What she risked to save her village?

Welcome to my life, jerk.

She turned back to the forest, swallowing hard. Part of the game was that they filled the forest with nightmares. Or perhaps the forest did that itself. She'd never known if this afterworld had been a heaven or a hell, but if she had to put money on it, she'd say hell. Though mortals weren't aware of the fact that the heavens and hells of their religions existed, Mytheans were. Some could even travel to them.

Sofia reached out a hand for Kitty, who had turned into smoke and now hovered at her side. Nothing could touch Kitty in that form. Sofia wished she could do the same.

"We'd better get started." She set off toward the forest, wincing at the eerie sponginess of the ground. Once, it had wept blood. After that, she'd stopped looking down.

Malcolm joined her as she picked her way between the trees. Something slithered in the distance. She drew her wand from the aether and gripped it tight.

"What have you been doing these past centuries?" Malcolm's voice broke the silence.

"Why do you want to know?"

"Pass the time."

"I'm not here to entertain you. That time has passed."

"You were never merely entertainment to me."

"Whatever." She couldn't even look at him. His voice sounded too good. Smooth and dark. And she still liked it. Fates, she hated her weakness. She'd held her anger close for centuries. It had protected her. It would protect her now. She focused on the forest ahead, choosing the path that stayed farther from the trees lest they reach out and grab her.

"I want to know about you because I'm interested."

Hot rage flared within her. "After all these years? You gave up your right to know when you chose magic over me."

"It was necessary," Malcolm said.

Sofia looked at his face then. Really looked, for the first time since she'd seen him last. They didn't really have the time to argue, but she couldn't help herself. So little of the young man she'd known remained. This Malcolm was harsher. Darker. Nearly unrecognizable.

"No it wasn't. You simply wanted the power more than you wanted me." Despite the years that had passed, the words made her throat tighten, and tears threatened. She swallowed hard and forced them away.

"I wanted both."

"Not possible." She turned her attention back to the forest path and began walking again. This was her least favorite part. Tree roots climbed out of the ground, eerily white. They looked almost like bones.

She quickened her pace, trying to ignore him. He was a shadow at her side, so big and present that it was damn near impossible. When a tree root ripped out of the ground and lashed at her, she barely managed to lunge aside. She fell to the dirt on her knees, cursing. This is what she got for letting her guard down.

Malcolm threw out a hand and sent a blast of flame at the root. It turned to ash instantly.

"Why didn't you use your magic?" he asked.

"The High Witches block it. I'm powerless here." She glanced at him. He towered over her, his hand still outstretched and glowing. He looked like a wild god, tall and strong, his dark hair flowing back from the masculine beauty of his face and golden eyes. He was part wulver. That strength and wildness was so clear when she saw him like this. It made her want him, and she hated herself for it.

He lowered his hand to help her to her feet. She ignored it and stood on her own, then set off along the path again. Tree roots stretched up to grab at her, but Malcolm stopped them every time. Normally, she'd be exhausted and dirty by the time she reached the edge of the forest. The High Witches liked to see her bedraggled and miserable from clawing her way through. Each year, a new set of obstacles blocked her path.

But apparently Malcolm's magic wasn't affected by this place. Either because of his strength or because the High Witches didn't know to expect him and therefore had not crafted a block for his magic.

Either way, she tried not to appreciate how much easier it was to make her way through the forest with him at her side.

"Is that it?" Malcolm asked after a while.

She glanced up. The High Witches' enormous stronghold loomed on the horizon, standing guard over the dark moors that surrounded it. It looked like the worst haunted house a mortal could dream up, only ten times as big. Lightning cracked overhead, making the window glass flash like winking eyes.

"Yes." She didn't know why the lightning always boomed and the place smelled of sulfur, but her mother had theorized that it was the dark magic.

They made their way across the moor, her feet occasionally sinking into the boggy ground. Kitty stayed well away from the wet muck in her ghostly form, but Sofia wasn't so lucky. The pervasive cold in the air soaked into her bones. A fine mist hovered unnaturally over the ground, slowly seeping into her shoes and freezing her toes. She'd once gotten frostbite here. It'd taken her almost a full day to recover.

She was shivering by the time they reached the enormous front doors. The black wood was studded with dull metal spikes.

With an ominous creak, they swung open to reveal the vestibule. Her heart began to pound as she stepped into the dark room and let her eyes adjust to the dim light of the flickering candles.

"We wait here to be called," she said.

A yellow light caught her eye and she glanced over to see Malcolm's hand glowing with power. He held it at his side, directed at her feet. Warmth enveloped her toes as the icy water from the moor dried.

It calmed her—the knowledge that his power worked here—but she didn't like it. She couldn't rely on him. Not after the choices he'd made.

She had too much riding on this to be placing any kind of faith in him. She didn't know why her line had been given the task of paying off the High Witches, but they had. Perhaps it was because they were the strongest Bruxas in Bruxa's Eye.

But she didn't feel very strong when standing in the High Witches' stronghold.

"Enter!" The voice boomed through the vestibule. Sofia shuddered. She stepped forward, but Malcolm swept in front of her and pushed open the door. She frowned in confusion, but followed.

The great hall loomed ahead of her, nearly as big as a football field. The ceiling soared high overhead, snow falling to disappear right before it hit the floor. A faint glow emanated from the ceiling, lighting the way but leaving the room dim and threatening. Towering, leafless oaks lined either side of the space, their great trunks surging up through the stone-slab floor.

Even Malcolm was dwarfed by the space, though he didn't look the least bit uncomfortable. His powerful stride ate up the ground as they approached the platform at the far end. Thirteen figures stood on the platform, all dressed in white. Sofia had always thought the color an odd choice.

"You brought someone," the High Witch said. Her sparkling white robes fell from her shoulders, emphasizing her height. She was over six feet tall and slender as a reed. Her eyes were like black marbles in her otherwise pale and perfect face.

Sofia stopped a dozen feet in front of the dais, grateful for Malcolm's looming presence beside her. She hated relying on anyone—especially him—but she needed all the help she could get here.

"Malcolm the warlock." The witch on the far right stepped forward, her brow creased.

There was a murmur from the rest the witches, then they stepped forward, drawing their eerie ivory wands.

"Your reputation precedes you, Malcolm," the High Witch said, her gaze suddenly much more wary.

Sofia had been right to bring him.

Malcolm inclined his head, then held out the Demon Blade. "I believe this is what you want?"

Sofia started to bristle at the way he took over, but then she remembered that she really didn't want to talk to the High Witches at all. If she could just disappear now, that would be perfect.

"It's late." The High Witch's voice cracked across the room, sharp as thunder.

Sofia couldn't stop herself from staring as the High Witch rubbed her wand with her thumb. Outright fear replaced her apprehension.

"There are penalties when one is late. Punishment!" Her wand hand struck out, sending a jolt of bright blue lightning at Sofia.

One second Sofia was staring at the lightning streaking toward them, and the next, Malcolm was in front of her, his body lit by the electric glow. His back arched and his limbs stiffened, but he made no sound.

An enraged shriek tore through the room. The High Witch waved her arm and the rest of the witches lifted their wands, directing them at Malcolm. Twelve more bolts of lightning shot toward him, lifting him off the ground. He roared in pain, his bellow echoing off the stone walls. One bolt hadn't been enough for someone as powerful as he, but thirteen could break him.

"Stop!" Sofia raced forward. "Stop it!"

The High Witch's head swung toward her, her black eyes blazed. "You dare to give orders?" She jerked her wand toward Sofia, sending a bolt of lightning her way.

White hot pain enveloped Sofia, stiffening bone and tearing muscle. She shrieked, held aloft by the lightning, unable to collapse. It went on for an eternity, ripping her apart until she felt like a shell.

Finally, she dropped. She gasped, trying to force her thoughts away from the pain. Her skin was so hot that the snowflakes that fell from the ceiling evaporated when they hit her skin.

What had just happened? She'd brought Malcolm here to take the hit for her lateness. He was the reason, after all. But she hadn't expected him to throw himself in front of the danger. For her.

She couldn't wrap her mind around it. Not that she had time to.

Once she could move her muscles, she struggled to her knees. Her entire body ached. She glanced over at Malcolm, who was on his knees beside her. His great chest heaved with breath, and his head was bowed. Disheveled dark hair shielded his face.

After a moment, he shook himself and rose to his feet. She had a distinct feeling that he wasn't used to being overpowered.

Kitty pressed her shadowy form against Sofia's side. Warmth and power flowed through her from her familiar, just enough that she could stumble to her feet.

"You're even stronger than we thought," the High Witch said to Malcolm. "Tales of your power are well known of course, but to survive thirteen lightning whips? My, my. It seems that selling your loyalty *does* result in great power."

He sneered at her but didn't speak. He was probably biting his tongue pretty hard right now. Though he could take a few of them, all the High Witches combined could overpower him. Power such as theirs was exceedingly rare, however, and it was likely he'd never come across a Mythean stronger than himself.

"I assume you'll be more cooperative now?" the High Witch asked.

Malcolm growled.

The High Witch narrowed her eyes. "See to it that you are. Sofia, we still need to decide on a suitable punishment for your tardiness. Now that you have a partner of such extraordinary power…"

Shock hit Sofia like a bat to the face. That agonizing pain hadn't been the punishment? And what did they mean, partner? "Malcolm isn't my partner."

The High Witch's brow rose. "No? He threw himself in front of a bolt of lightning for you."

"A momentary lapse in good judgment." Malcolm's voice was so cold that it chilled her lightning-heated skin. It also made her believe him.

"Perhaps." The High Witch's gaze met Sofia's. "Either way, you're the first person she's ever brought here. And that changes things."

Sofia held her gaze, wondering if she'd get zapped again. "Changes things?"

"Indeed. Enjoy the dungeon while we discuss." The High Witch waved her ivory wand and Sofia felt pressure envelop her. She gasped, her air cut off, and fought to break free. The world around her faded to black and she came crashing to the ground a moment later.

She scrambled to her feet and gazed around wildly. Hundreds of skulls grinned back at her, lit by a cold glow that came from the ceiling. Her heart threatened to jump out of her chest. Every wall of the small room was covered in skulls, ivory and yellow and all featuring gaping black eye sockets.

She was alone.

Kitty hissed.

"What the fuck?" This had never happened before. She raised her wand and held it out toward one of the walls, searching for a hidden door, but her wand's magic was blocked. She could see no exits.

And where the hell was Malcolm?

She made her way around the walls, pressing on the skulls to see if any would give way and reveal a secret door. The feel of them under her fingers made her shudder, as if their souls were still trapped inside.

The air changed suddenly, tingling with magic, and she whirled around.

A hulking golden wolf loomed in the corner. It was huge and wild, all muscles and teeth and so bright a gold that it seemed to glow. Unnatural. Not a real wolf. One sent by the High Witches?

Sofia stumbled back. Without her magic, it'd be just her against the wolf and she didn't have the strength—or the teeth or claws—necessary to protect herself.

Fear strangled her, stealing her breath, as the wolf approached, its stride powerful. Kitty leapt in front of her, back arched and hissing like mad, determined to protect her.

"No! Kitty!"

Kitty was fierce, but too small to fight the wolf, no matter her enhanced familiar strength and speed.

Sofia was about to reach out and grab Kitty when the wolf stopped, looming over Kitty. He leaned down and sniffed Kitty's head.

Sofia jerked back.

What the hell?

The wolf was snuffling at Kitty—like he was getting to know her—and Kitty had flattened out her back and stopped hissing. She was even nuzzling him back.

When Kitty suddenly turned into smoke, Sofia realized that the wolf was partially transparent. Not a real wolf, but a ghost or an apparition. It explained its unnatural color. In her panic, she hadn't noticed. Had Kitty changed to be more like the wolf?

Fear still vibrated along her nerve endings, but confusion was quickly replacing it. A crazy thought jumped into her head. But no, this couldn't be Malcolm. Wulvers turned into wolves. She'd never heard of golden apparitions.

The wolf sat down, front legs stretched out so that it was low enough that Kitty could sniff his neck and head. Purring, Kitty put her ghostly front paws on the wolf's big shoulder and began to knead. Like a weird cat massage. Sofia glanced at the wolf's face.

It looked… happy?

This was too weird. Menace still thrummed in the air, but it wasn't the wolf, she now realized. It was just the place. The wolf was something different.

What the hell was going on?

Suddenly, the wolf gave Kitty one big lick—which made her hiss in annoyance—then stood and approached Sofia. She tensed, but wasn't as terrified as she had been before Kitty had decided the wolf wasn't a threat.

The wolf sniffed her, then rubbed his head against her hip. When the big animal pressed its side against her front, an image blasted into her mind.

Malcolm, leaning back against a wall of skulls. He was in a room that looked identical to hers. It was an eerie sight—such a vital, handsome man surrounded by grinning death.

The vision faded when a voice interrupted her thoughts.

"Sofia? What took so long?"

Sofia jerked. Malcolm's voice was in her head. And there was a feeling of connection. As if they were touching.

"Malcolm?" she asked.

"Yes. Are you all right? Why did it take my wolf so long to reach you?"

"Your wolf?" She'd been right. It was him. But how?

"Part of my soul. The wulver side. I'm locked in this skull dungeon, but I sent it to you."

Of course. He wasn't a normal, full-blood wulver.

"Are you all right?" he demanded.

"Fine, besides being trapped in here. How are we speaking like this?"

"My wolf connects us. If he stops touching you, the connection breaks."

"All right. Do you have any idea how to get out of here? Can you aetherwalk?"

"I can't. I already tried. The cell dampens my other magic as well."

"But not the wolf?"

"It's not magic in the way they think of it. It's just my soul. They didn't block me from moving, so my wolf is free to move as well. But we're trapped here until they let us out."

Sofia nodded and began to pace, her mind racing. This was bad. In all the history of her line, she'd never heard of anything like this happening. Were they destroying her village even now?

No. No, they couldn't be. They'd give her another chance. She was good at hunting tributes. She could bring them the best magical antiquities, most powerful amulets, and rarest potions. They'd want to keep that gravy train going.

But they'd reap so much power by destroying her village.

"They aren't destroying your village." Malcolm's voice broke through her reverie.

"How do you know? How did you even know that's what I was thinking? You can't read my mind, right?"

"No. But you got silent all of a sudden, and of course you're worried about your village."

"You can't be sure." She clung to the feel of him in her mind, trying not to find comfort in his presence.

But fates, she was glad she wasn't alone. Had he sent his wolf to her to check that she was safe? To comfort her?

Hope fluttered in her chest. Stupid hope that he still cared for her, even though she was done with him. She had to be done with him. She couldn't take the pain again. And it didn't even make sense that he'd care about how she felt. He'd chosen magic over her centuries ago, and now he'd gotten her into this mess.

"You're such a bastard," she said. "This is all your—"

Sofia's words were strangled when she felt the familiar tightness squeezing her whole body. The High Witches were calling them back.

A second later, they stood in the creepy great hall. The space loomed even larger after their confinement in the dungeon.

The High Witches still stood in a line, watching her.

"We've thought of suitable recompense for your lateness," the High Witch said. Her voice was colder than the snowflakes that still fell from the ceiling. "The Salem Coven is in possession of a Grimoire. Their Grimoire. The most valuable of its kind. It possesses secrets that even we don't know. We want it. You'll bring it to us."

Sofia's stomach dropped. The Salem Coven? She'd never met them, but tales of their viciousness and power were legendary. They'd had nothing to do with the silly witch trials that were so famous amongst mortals—that ridiculousness had been all about mortal greed and evil. The innocents who'd lost their lives in the trials were as far from the Salem Coven as bunnies were from tigers.

And like tigers, the Salem Coven had a reputation for devouring their opponents. "For next year's tribute?"

"Within the week. It shouldn't be so hard for the two of you. True, it's guarded heavily. And the Salem Coven is nearly as powerful as we are. But you might manage the task." Her grin was malicious as her gaze swept between them.

Oh, hell.

"I owe you nothing," Malcolm said. "And I've little interest in tangling with the Salem Coven. Like your own coven, their numbers are great enough to be an issue."

"True. You could abandon Sofia to her attempts. Perhaps you will. To us, it doesn't matter. We'd like the Grimoire. But we'd also like to destroy Sofia's village and reap all that delicious power." The High Witch turned to her companions, her eyes bright. "Think of it, brethren. The burning. The screaming. Buildings collapsing and lives being sucked away. All that destruction, all that power."

Sofia shuddered. The High Witch's desire was all too evident. The picture she painted too real.

"So you see, Malcolm," the High Witch said. "We win either way."

Sofia swallowed hard. That was the crux of it. There was no escape. She either did it, or the witches would destroy her and everything she loved. Their dark magic was fueled by destruction. Not only did they draw power from the aether like normal Mytheans, they reaped great power from the dark magical energy given off by mass destruction. As the only all-Mythean village in South America, the destruction of her village and its inhabitants would provide immense magical energy.

"Is that all?" Malcolm asked, his tone bored.

"A week." The High Witch waved her hands in a shooing motion. "Now go. Back to where you came from!"

The aether pulled at Sofia, and she had no choice but to let it take her. When she opened her eyes, she and Kitty stood on the main street in Bruxa's eye. Sultry heat enveloped her.

Home. And it was still standing, safe and sound, lit by a nearly full moon. Even better, Malcolm wasn't here. He must have been sent back to Scotland.

Good. She ignored the strange sense of loss, as if there were an empty place inside of her now. Being with him again had been too complex. Anger, desire, longing—it was so hard to sort through the feelings that crashed through her.

She took a moment to absorb the essence of the place she loved, trying to ground herself. To get away from the chaos Malcolm wreaked on her mind.

The smell of rain on the horizon competed with the earthy tones of the jungle. The ramshackle wooden buildings of Bruxa's Eye crouched at the edge of the Amazon River. The screeching and cawing of jungle animals was a welcome sound, one that was replaced by the distant shouts of a crowd.

Of course. It was Saturday night and the fight ring was the place to be. The match must be in full swing and Mytheans loved a good fight.

Bruxa's Eye was one of the few all-Mythean towns in the world. Creatures of all species could walk freely without fear of being discovered by mortals because that lowly species had no idea the town was there—or that its strange inhabitants existed outside of their imaginations.

Fear and a sense of failure crawled up her spine.

They counted on her. She protected them from the High Witches, paying off their version of a mythical mob. If people needed something, they came to her. If there were problems, they came to her. It'd been that way with her mother and grandmother as well, and the women before them. Over two thousand of years of protecting Bruxa's Eye.

And it crushed her beneath the weight of duty and expectation. It was exhausting—she was always on the hunt for new tributes or going to pay the High Witches off.

If she couldn't get the Grimoire and pay off the High Witches, she'd fail these people—her friends, family, and everyone she held dear.

CHAPTER THREE

After a great force shoved Malcolm into the aether, he opened his eyes to see that he stood in his library, the soaring walls of books as familiar as his own face. Heart pounding, his gaze flicked around the room, searching for Sofia.

She was nowhere to be seen.

Did the High Witches still have her? Fear sent an icy chill across his skin.

But no, the High Witch had gestured to both of them when she'd sent them home.

He aetherwalked immediately to Bruxa's Eye. His heart pounded as he looked up and down the quiet, moonlit street. The buildings were ramshackle—like a Wild West town in the middle of a jungle—and the boardwalk under his feet kept him out of the muddy street.

The roar of a crowd sounded at the end of a street, but he caught a slight hint of her distinct, floral scent coming from the other direction. He headed away from the crowd and saw her seconds later, standing at the end of the street.

As he approached, she drew her wand and transformed herself into an old Crone, a black cloak draping her shoulders. Kitty was black as pitch against the fabric.

"Don't bother trying to hide," he said.

"I'm not hiding from you, idiot." She nodded to the street behind him. "There are people coming."

He spun around to see two men approaching. Their gait was unsteady and they were arguing good-naturedly. Drunk. A shifter and a vampire, from the look of them. He'd been so distracted by his need to find her that he hadn't even heard them coming.

Disgraceful.

They stopped abruptly a dozen feet from Sofia. The shifter's green eyes widened and he bowed low. "*Honored one.*" A sign of respect.

The vampire bowed low as well and they made their way past.

Of course. He'd forgotten, because he'd never seen her in her Crone form.

Like many witches, Bruxas believed in the Maiden, the Mother, and the Crone. The Crone was the most powerful. The Protectors of Bruxa's Eye always appeared as the Crone when in public.

"Don't you hate hiding yourself like this?" he asked.

"Of course. It's tiring and I can't have a normal life." Her voice was bitter. "But it's tradition. The threat to our village is real, and I'm the first line of defense. People expect this. I'm strongest in this form. As the Protector, it's my duty to present my strongest front."

The words sounded memorized. She'd inherited this role from her mother. No doubt it'd been drilled into her. But he too knew something about the dictates of family expectations. They'd been half the reason he'd given her up.

He'd never known anyone like Sofia. She was the loveliest woman he'd ever met—small and curvy with golden skin. He hated that she covered that up. But she was fierce, and she was committed to protecting her village. Was willing to do anything to save it. He'd have to use that to his advantage.

He grasped her arm and aetherwalked them back to his library. He used his magic to remove her enchantment so that she looked like herself again and wore her normal clothing.

She jerked out of his grasp.

She glanced down at herself and scowled. "Bastard."

Kitty hissed. Her fat little familiar glared at him out of its one good eye. The other was squinty, just as he remembered it. He'd always liked Kitty and Kitty had liked him. Until he'd chosen becoming a warlock over a life with Sofia.

As he'd expected seeing her in his home warmed a cold part of his soul. This room was better with her in it. Brighter, somehow. The firelight from his ever-burning hearth gleamed off her dark hair. He'd always loved her hair—the way it hung in shining curls down her back. He'd always loved everything about her.

"Why the hell did you bring me back here?"

"I want you here." What he'd done was fucked up—he knew it was—but he'd wanted to see her again. He was sick of being alone and trying to forget her. Seeing his brother with his new mate had revived memories of Sofia. Had revived his unslakable desire for her. "I wanted you to come to me. So I took what you needed."

"You manipulative ass!" Rage flared hot in Sofia's belly as she watched Malcolm shrug carelessly.

"It worked," he said. His gaze burned with something unidentifiable.

"Why are you screwing with my life like this? Am I just a pawn to you? Haven't you done enough to me?" She felt like she'd explode with all the conflicting thoughts and feelings ricocheting through her.

He strode toward her, all power and grace, and trapped her against the bookshelf. His arms braced against the shelves behind her as he leaned over her. She felt caged by his sudden nearness. Though he didn't touch her, his heat burned. His thick biceps framed her face and his head dipped over hers. Golden eyes blazed.

"Because I want you." His voice was rougher than she'd ever heard it. "I've wanted you for centuries and I'm sick of denying it."

The words sent a streak of heat through her. Desire pushed through her, furious, hot and insistent. Her skin heated and her sex ached. It happened so fast her head spun. She was an idiot and he was a heavy-handed bastard, but she wanted him. "You're a bastard. And a warlock."

"Doesn't mean I don't want you."

"I gave up being a warlock to be with you. And you threw me away. Do you have any idea how much it hurt to make a sacrifice for our love, but then you didn't do the same thing? Or how much it hurt to realize how little you valued our love?" Just the thought made her chest ache. "No. Of course not. Because you've never even considered sacrificing what you want. How do you think I'd ever be with you again?"

"I'll make it up to you."

Rage flared in her chest, burning out some of the pain. "Even if you did, you can't have anything real. Your curse will destroy it."

He lowered his head to her ear. His voice and warm breath made her shiver despite her ire. "I'm good at getting around the curse."

"Not possible. You remember Laira."

That *wouldn't* be her. Fate was too cruel and too strong.

"That won't be a problem. Love killed Laira," he said.

She flinched. She knew he didn't love her, but it hurt to hear it so bluntly. "So that means you just want to fuck me and then go on your way? Because that's the only thing fate won't destroy."

"I absolutely want to fuck you."

"No." She forced the word out. "You broke my heart. You got me into this situation."

"I wasn't expecting the High Witches to be so pissed off. It was only a few hours late."

"Fat lot of good that does me, now that I'm on their bad side."

"Can you blame me for trying?" The words were rough at her ear. "You're the most beautiful woman I've ever seen. I've wanted you from the first moment I saw you. I'm tired of waiting. Any man in my position would have done the same to have one such as you."

"After everything you've done, what makes you think I would *ever* sleep with you?"

"Because I've missed you. I've spent centuries dreaming of the things I'd do to you. Planning out every touch. Kiss. Lick. I'd make you shiver and shake and lose your mind."

Fates help her, his words were too appealing. Despite everything he'd done to her, a big part of her still wanted him.

But he was behaving like an utter bastard now—putting her in this position for his own gain. And even if she totally lost her mind and fell for him, this could only end in massive heartbreak—or worse, death.

It was crazy and stupid and probably due to the fact that she hadn't gotten laid in about a decade. If the Crone didn't scare the men off, the fact that they thought of her as some sort of holy figure did. Though the worst of the pain of their breakup was gone, she still hated him.

She pushed at his chest, hard enough that he shifted back and gave her enough space to sneak away.

"I'm done with you. I'll fix this myself," she said as she made her way to the door. She had a week. She could do this.

Right?

No. Not really. She was fucked.

"I'll consider helping you. You need my help."

Sofia stopped in her tracks, turned and glowered at him. He was right, damn it. She *did* need his help. She was stuck. Because of him.

Was this all part of his plan? She shivered. She felt like a fly trapped in his web.

He approached her, reminding her of a panther stalking its prey. She backed up, but the desk stopped her. The big chair nudged her hip. It suddenly became very apparent how in over her head she was.

He'd orchestrated all of this. Maybe not the task in Salem—but stealing the dagger, getting her here, and inciting the wrath of the High Witches. "You're a heavy-handed bastard, you know that?"

He shrugged and she caught a whiff of his scent. That same enticing spice. And he was close enough now that she could feel his heat. She hated it, but her mind kept jumping back to the past. To all the good times they'd had. Practicing magic, watching the sunrise, talking late at night while studying the stars. How much she'd loved his kisses. His touch.

He'd hurt her—but before that, there'd been so much good.

Standing so near him right now only reminded her of the fact. He might be a colder, darker version of his old self—no doubt twisted by the loneliness enforced upon warlocks—but he still made her burn.

There was no amount of anger in the world that could stop her from wanting him. And the hurt had faded just enough that her desire could take over. She clenched a fist to keep from reaching out to touch his broad chest and forced her mind back to the task. "So, how are you going to help me?"

"I didn't say I'd help you. Just that I'd consider it."

Oh, the arrogance. Hot rage flared in her chest. She wanted to hit him.

"But first, I want my payment."

"Wh-what?"

"You." His golden eyes blazed with heat. Part of him might be cold, but there was another part of him that wasn't. His wolf's soul, perhaps. Whatever it was, it burned. His gaze

43

seemed to glow, his body vibrating with tension. He didn't reach out to touch her, but she could tell he wanted to.

She'd never been wanted like this before. So much so that she could *see* it. In the heat of his eyes, the way his breath came harder, and his shoulders tensed. "What do you mean, me?"

It was a stupid question, but she needed time to get her wits together. Out of the corner of her eye, she saw Kitty leave the room. Whenever there was the possibility of her Bruxa having sex, Kitty left. If Sofia needed her, she'd feel it and return.

"You know what I mean." His voice rumbled as he reached up and cupped the back of her neck, pulling her to him until her body pressed against his.

His heat and hardness seared her, his erection a brand that ignited fires so intense she hadn't felt them in nearly four hundred years. Since him. They'd never gone past kissing, but he clearly meant to remedy that.

Malcolm loomed over her, his body blocking out the firelight. She shivered. His golden gaze captured hers as he lowered his head. She strained up to meet him, quivering against his strength. Her lips hovered close to his, sending sparks of anticipation down her spine.

His big hand pressed against the small of her back. The sense of being captured overwhelmed her, snapping her back to her senses.

He'd trapped her.

She shoved against his chest, breaking free. The desk pressed against her ass, ensnaring her, but she'd pushed him back a couple feet and gained some breathing room. "No way in hell."

"I've been in hell. There's a way."

"I'm not sleeping with you."

"Why not? It'd be good. I always thought you'd be a good lay."

"A good lay?" Fury boiled in her chest. "You'd better believe it, but you're sure as hell not going to find out."

"Without my help, you won't save your village. The High Witches and the Salem Coven are too strong."

"I have friends who can help me."

He shrugged and she wanted to hit him. He inspired her to violence as much as he inspired her to lust.

"You have friends," he said. "But none powerful enough. You have the strongest magic in your village. They need you to protect them, not to drag them off to fight a war."

Her heart threatened to fall to her feet. He was right. Bruxa's Eye was full of powerful Mytheans. As a group, they were immensely powerful. But she couldn't ask them to wage war on the Salem Coven—and that's what it would take, if she only had their help. Their strength was in their numbers.

No, she needed a single person, at most two—someone whose magic rivaled hers—to help her sneak in and steal the Salem Coven's Grimoire. Stealth and strong magic were the only way to win this.

Malcolm was the only way to win this. The High Witches had seen to it. *He* had seen to it.

Rage dampened the desire he'd stoked, though she hated herself because she couldn't get rid of it fully. Even though she knew it was a bad idea—she could write a novel about all the things that could go wrong between them—it was impossible to keep herself from wanting him.

45

Linsey Hall

He looked as if he'd been made for her. She couldn't keep her eyes from tracing over the powerful expanse of his shoulders and down his arms to where his thin sweater was pushed up to his elbows. His forearms were corded with muscles, his fists clenched as if to stop himself from grabbing her. Her gaze darted back to his face.

He looked at her as if she were a feast and he a starving man. Like she was the first light he'd seen after a lifetime of darkness. The slightest flush rode on his sharp cheekbones and his golden eyes gleamed with heat.

He wanted it all. No question. And there was no way in hell she could give it to him.

"A kiss," she said. Because she wanted it too, despite their past.

"That's hardly worth risking my life for." But his gaze strayed hungrily to her lips.

"With me, it is. Take it or leave it, because a kiss is all you're getting."

"For now," he growled, then pulled her close, his hand pressed hard against her back and the other cupping her neck. His lips barely touched hers, feathering lightly.

Her heart pounded so loud she swore he could hear it. Chills raced over her skin as she waited, the dichotomy of his rough hands and gentle mouth making her head swim.

"I've waited a bloody long time for this," he rasped.

His mouth captured hers, hot and hard. He groaned and pulled her closer, until the entirety of her body was pressed against his.

Though they'd kissed in the past, it'd been nothing like this. He kissed her like he was famished, but with such finesse

46

that pleasure streaked through her. His lips were warm and skilled. A master's.

How had she lived so long without this?

His tongue traced over her lips, demanding entrance. She tried to hold onto her resistance. It was the only thing that protected her. She could lose herself to him.

His teeth pulled at her bottom lip, a little nip of pain that made an ache bloom low in her belly. When the tip of his tongue demanded again, she parted her lips with a whimper. His tongue swept across hers, hot and agile, as his hand held her head steady for the assault.

He'd trapped her in a web of pleasure and strength. He was so skilled with his mouth that if he asked in the right way, she'd give him anything.

"Bloody hell, you taste so good," he rumbled against her lips. "Wanted this forever."

Malcolm took her mouth again, hot and hard, and gripped her hips with both hands. Never letting go of her lips, he lifted her onto the desk as if she weighed nothing. She gasped when he used a deft hand to part her legs and moved one of his own big thighs between them.

When Sofia opened her mouth to protest, Malcolm took the opportunity to taste her more deeply. He couldn't believe she was here with him. Kissing him. He'd waited so bloody long for this. Fantasized about it hundreds of times.

And now she was here. In his arms. His head buzzed with the pleasure of feeling her beneath his hands. When her body stiffened and she tried to move away from him, he gripped her hips and pulled her until her sex pressed against his thigh. He was too tall to pull her against his cock in this position, though perhaps it was for the best. She was wary and he didn't want to scare her away.

He gripped her hips and set up a rhythm, making her ride his thigh. She cried out and shuddered, her fingers curling into his shirt.

He had to make this good for her, make her lose her mind. It was the only way she wouldn't tell him to stop. And he couldn't let her stop this. He wanted it too bloody badly. Had wanted it for centuries.

He wanted to feel her lose herself against him. They'd shared nothing but chaste kisses when they'd been younger. Their love had been sweet. Pure.

There was nothing pure about him now. Nor about what he wanted to do to her.

His cock throbbed unbearably and he ached to sink inside of her heat. She burned his thigh, a hint of the heat he would feel if he took her. He groaned. To know her wet heat and feel her clench around him? Heaven.

To make her come around his cock? Perfection.

He could at least make her come. To know the sounds she made. To know her face as pleasure overtook her.

With a last nip at her lip, he moved his mouth to her neck and tasted her skin. Smooth and silky. A hint of salt. He laved her, unable to get enough of her taste.

Her hips were lush beneath his hands as he worked her against his thigh. How he wished there were no clothes between them, that he could feel her silky flesh against him. See her.

"Malcolm!" she gasped, tugging at his shirt and leaning her head away to give him better access. She whimpered as he bit the crook of her neck and started to move her hips on her own.

Was this what she would be like in bed? Losing her mind and taking her pleasure into her own hands? His hips thrust uncontrollably toward her.

Gods, how he wanted to know her like that. To see her like that. To feel her.

She continued to move against his thigh, her motions becoming less graceful and more desperate. He withdrew his mouth from the smooth skin of her neck and glanced up to see her face twisted into a mask of beautiful desperation. She bit her full lower lip, her brow furrowed as she tried to reach her peak. Low, needy sounds came from her throat. Frustrated sounds.

Wild desire surged through him. Desire to make her come. To help her reach that peak.

He swept a hand over her trousers and called upon the aether, envisioning her trousers disappearing. A second later, her legs gleamed in the firelight, bare.

She jerked. "What? No, you can't—"

He slipped his hand into her white cotton panties and groaned at the feel of her silky flesh. Wet heat met his fingertips.

"Yes," she moaned, dropping her head back. Her legs parted.

His gaze was riveted to her white cotton panties. The way his big hand disappeared down the front was obscene. Nearly uncontrollable pleasure surged through him. He wanted to tear the white cotton off with his teeth and plunge inside of her, feel her close tightly around him.

He shuddered and pulled himself back, focusing on the incredible feeling of her pussy beneath his fingertips. So wet and slick, opening for him like the loveliest flower. His mouth watered to taste her, to plunge deep or flick over her clitoris. Anything. Just to have his lips and tongue on her. To taste her.

But later. He'd waited so long for this, he wanted to savor every moment.

Her hips jerked when he found her little clitoris. She cried out when he began to rub in small circles. Her arms came up to wrap around his neck. Trusting him.

She probably shouldn't trust him. He should stop this.

But there was no way in hell he would. He wanted her too badly. Needed to feel her orgasm too badly. To know what it was to enter her, if only with his fingers.

With a growl, he slipped his fingers down, seeking her entrance. She was slick and ready, her skin silk. Slowly, savoringly, he slipped a finger inside her heat, groaning at the feeling of her clenching around him.

"Malcolm!" Sofia shifted to give him better access, moving her hips on his hand, seeking more.

Gods, how he wanted to see her. To gaze upon her dark curls and the pink flesh between her thighs. She rode his hand, whimpering in his ear.

"You want more?" he asked.

"Yes. Now, Malcolm." She bit the side of his neck. Pleasure tore through him, making his cock jerk and his muscles clench.

"Greedy." He withdrew his finger. She moaned and bit him again. He almost came in his trousers. Bloody hell, he liked how she gave direction.

Unable to help himself, he slipped his hand from her panties and slipped his fingers into his mouth. His eyes nearly rolled back in his head as he sucked on them. He couldn't get enough of her taste.

He worked his hand beneath the white cotton and pushed two fingers inside of her, his hips thrusting as he felt her wet heat close around him. She moaned against his ear as he began to thrust, being sure to press forward against the sensitive pad of flesh within her.

Need roared through him as she began to move her hips, fucking herself on his fingers.

"Malcolm. Malcolm." Her anguished voice sounded at his ear, her breathing hard. She was desperate to come, her body nearly vibrating with need. It ignited his own.

As much as he wanted to drag this out, to feel her moving against him forever, he wanted to feel her orgasm more. His thumb found her clitoris and began to make small circles, increasing the speed and pressure as she begged him for more.

When she cried out and her pussy began to clench around his thrusting fingers, he imagined that it was his cock within her. He tried to draw it out, to make it last. Her thighs trembled violently as her muscles grasped him.

But when she ground herself down against his hand, demanding him deeper, he broke.

He had to fuck her. To feel her around him. Tear off her panties and flip her over and thrust into her tight sheath. He'd make her his. He'd make her know who was gripping her hips and pounding into her. She'd come around him, a dozen times. Until she knew she belonged to him.

The tremors of her orgasm faded and he removed his hand, going to tear off her panties and make his fantasy a reality. Need tore through him, violent and demanding. He had to have her.

He had her panties gripped in his fists when he glanced up to see her barely supporting herself on the desk. Her muscles were lax from pleasure, her eyelashes resting against her cheeks and her dark curls falling around her shoulders.

Malcolm dropped his hands and stepped back, his chest heaving. He had to get control of himself. She looked exhausted. She'd just been tortured by the High Witches.

Now wasn't the time for what he wanted. When he finally had her, he wanted her enthusiastic, not exhausted.

But fates, his cock ached. Malcolm spun away. Stalked to the hearth. When the golden flame didn't calm him, he went to the whisky on the far shelf and poured himself three healthy fingers.

He swigged the whisky, trying to calm his racing heart and raging cock. His hand shook slightly as he squeezed the bridge of his nose and tried to get the intoxicating sight of Sofia out of his mind.

CHAPTER FOUR

Consciousness came slowly to Sofia. Her body still pulsed, aftershocks of pleasure streaking outward from her pussy.

The hard desk beneath her was the first thing she registered. Then the cold air on her thighs.

Holy shit. She wasn't wearing pants. She called her wand from the aether and waved it over her legs. Jeans appeared.

Bastard!

She turned to see Malcolm leaning against a bookshelf, a glass of whisky in his hand. His golden gaze met hers, his face impassive.

Reality crashed back.

Holy shit. She'd let him take her pants off and now he watched her like he didn't give a shit. Of course he didn't give a shit. He never really had.

But she did. Her heart pounded and her breath came short. She felt like she couldn't get enough air through the panic that welled in her chest. The hurt.

She still cared way too much. She'd never been any good at casual sex. She wouldn't have let him do those things to her if she didn't still care for him.

Of course she still cared. The way her heart felt like it was tearing in two confirmed that.

Rage and pain lit a fire in her chest that threatened to consume her. She looked at the blazing hearth and realized one very important thing.

She couldn't stay here. She couldn't be around him, not when she still felt this way and he so clearly did not.

And it didn't even matter if he cared. He was a fucking warlock! He could love her to the ends of the earth and fate would conspire to tear them apart. *He'd* chosen that for them.

Even if no one in her village was strong enough to help her get the Grimoire, she could find someone. It wasn't as hopeless as he said. She could definitely get the book.

"You know what, Malcolm? Forget it. I don't need your help. Thanks for the orgasm, but I'm out." She just had to find Kitty and scram.

Malcolm surged away from the bookshelves he'd been leaning against, his glare ominous. "The hell you are."

"This was a mistake. It was supposed to be just a kiss and it turned into a hell of a lot more." *Like me with no pants.*

"You wanted it."

She growled. Cocky bastard. "Fuck. You. You're not the most powerful person I know. I can get help elsewhere."

She turned and stalked to the door. Kitty appeared in the doorway a second later and trotted over to her. Once Kitty had leaned up against her side, Sofia closed her eyes and focused on her home.

Within a second, she felt the familiar tug of the aether.

Home, here I come.

Then it stopped. Like a wall had shot up.

Her eyes flared open and darted to Malcolm. "What the hell are you doing?"

"Blocking the aether. You're not leaving."

"What the hell do you mean, I'm not leaving?"

"Exactly what it sounds like." He strode toward her, his gaze intense and his dark hair falling over his brow. So damned handsome.

And she hated him.

Fates, what had she gotten herself into?

"You're staying with me. At least until this is all over." His voice was rough, possessive.

Fuck that shit! She drew her wand from the aether and flung her arm out toward him, sending a lightning bolt into his chest.

He stumbled backward, then growled and surged forward, grasping her wrist and lowering it.

So freaking strong! His magic and his body. She didn't stand a chance against him.

Malcolm pulled her toward him, looming over her. Her heart threatened to break her ribs.

"You can't just kidnap me!"

"I think I have."

She struggled to break free, but he held her firm. "Fuck you, Malcolm. You don't even seem to give a shit!" Her breath was heaving and she knew she had crazy eyes. She didn't care. He freaking deserved it.

"Don't give a shit? Of course I care. Of course I want you."

She almost growled at him. "Kidnapping isn't a great way to woo a girl."

He shrugged one big shoulder. "Maybe. But it's the best weapon in my arsenal, so I'll use it."

"Bastard. So suppose I stay here, trapped in your creepy castle—" It actually wasn't that creepy, but she was pissed. "—what happens to my village? You help me save it?"

He nodded. "For a price."

"What? You were just trying to convince me that I needed your help."

"And you thought I'd offer it for free? I'm a mercenary, Sofia. I have been for nearly four hundred years. Of course my help isn't free."

She seethed, grinding her teeth until she thought they might crack. Bastard. Every awful thing he did now made her realize how stupid she'd been to ever be hurt by him. He deserved her rage, not her tears.

"You need my help," he said. "And you're trapped here, by the way."

"I could fight you." She gripped her wand tight.

"You'd lose. Right now, I'm your best bet. Agree to another favor, and I'll help you save your village."

"Favor? Another kiss?"

"No."

"More?" Her mind raced. She hated the idea. And loved it, just a little bit. The anger only stoked her desire. She was sick.

"Maybe. You liked the first favor."

"Bastard!"

He shrugged.

"Let go of my arm." Her whole body vibrated with anger. She couldn't stand next to him for another second.

He dropped his hand. She stalked to the other side of the room and turned her back to him, gazing out one of the big windows. Her reflection stared back. The color in her cheeks was high, her gaze bright. Kitty pressed herself against Sofia's calf, her presence warm and comforting.

What the hell was she going to do?

She tried to aetherwalk one more time, straining to send herself home.

Nothing.

She'd never known anyone to be able to block another from aetherwalking. It was possible, of course, but took great power.

Which Malcolm had. There was no disputing that he was strong. And ruthless. He was willing to help—for a price.

But in return… Could she grant the favor? Something physical, she was sure.

The years had left Malcolm cold, selfish, and damaged. One minute he looked at her like he couldn't get enough of her, the next, his gaze was arctic. Calculating. What had his life been like, that he'd turned into this?

Dark and lonely, no doubt. Power couldn't keep one warm. He'd had centuries to learn that.

Sofia squeezed her wand tight. She wouldn't feel bad for him. He'd *chosen* this life. She'd tried to offer him the opposite. Love. Partnership.

He'd chosen power and become a cold, broken beast.

But he'd thrown himself in front of the High Witch's lightning for her. That had been…unexpected. He would protect her, which meant that even if he'd kidnapped her, at least he didn't intend to harm her.

And he lit her on fire. When he'd been kissing her, he'd wanted her to feel pleasure. No question. He'd liked making her feel good and he'd been immensely skilled. Everything she'd liked, he'd noticed and done more of it.

Maybe it was an ego thing?

Perhaps—and there was no doubt he had a huge ego— but it hadn't felt like that. No one had ever made her come that hard before. Or had made her come without expecting the same in return.

Why?

She drew a blank, then shivered at the idea of staying with him, at the thought of whatever his next favor might be.

Not that she had much choice in whether or not to stay with him. If she fought him with everything she had, he might let her go. A fragment of the old Malcolm had to be inside of him.

But could she risk it?

His help *would* be invaluable. And though his demand for a favor pissed her the hell off, it intrigued her as well.

A boulder sat on her chest, but the situation was clear. She turned to Malcolm. "Fine. I'll stay without fighting. I'll pay your favor. But in return, you will do everything you can to help me save my village. *Everything*."

His gaze lit with satisfaction as he nodded. He didn't vow it or promise to stand by his end of the deal as a normal person might, but that was for the best. A warlock couldn't. Fate would intervene if he did and then it'd all be pointless.

She'd have to trust him. The idea chilled her skin. But it was the best she had right now. "Do you know anyone in Salem we can go to for help?"

"No. First, I think you need to consider moving your village."

She blinked. "Move it? I thought you were going to help me."

"I am. Saving your people is your priority, correct? This ensures the High Witches can never get them. Moving your village might be best. Disbanding, even better."

"So you think you can't get the book?"

"I can get the bloody book. But more than that, I want you do be done with paying tributes to the High Witches. Since I can't break that curse or deal or whatever it is you have worked out with them, removing the reason for your labors seems like the best option."

"No! Never. It's the only all-Mythean town in South America. And Central America. Mytheans need it! The ones who can pass for human could go elsewhere, maybe, but it would destroy their livelihoods. But the ones who can't pass? They'd be screwed. There aren't enough all-Mythean settlements. There's no way we can move. The magic that hides the village is too ancient and too great to recreate. The village would be completely destroyed, my people scattered. Many of them have been there for generations. They helped build the town and they would die before leaving." Tremors shook her as she considered his words. Kitty pressed up against her leg, purring like a motor boat.

"Shhh, calm yourself. Everything is all right." Malcolm's voice was soothing. He stepped toward her and she immediately stepped backward. He pulled to a stop.

Why was he suddenly being so kind? His voice had completely changed. Did he still care for her a bit? Or was he working another angle? Trying to lure her with the promise of help and kindness?

"We'll find the information we need to get the Grimoire," Malcolm said. "That shan't be a problem."

She nodded, forcing away her speculation. Salem was like Edinburgh and Cartagena. There was a huge Mythean population living secretly amongst mortals. They'd be able to find info about the Salem Coven and where they lived and worked. They just had to be clever about it.

"It's too late to go now," he said. "Nearly two and you're tired. We'll go in the morning."

She frowned. She itched to get started, but he was right. She was almost shaking from exhaustion—mostly from the High Witch's lightning but also from what he'd done to her.

"Fine. We leave in eight hours. Where do I sleep?" She gave him a hard look. "Not with you."

"Take your pick of the rooms above."

She nodded and turned from him, desperate to find some quiet and space for herself. His gaze burned into her back as she left, sending unwelcome heat across her skin.

"We sure know how to get into it, huh, Kitty?" she asked as she made her way down the hall. Her mind kept racing with everything that was at stake. Not just her village, but she'd be spending more time with Malcolm.

She'd never anticipated that. She didn't even know how to handle it.

She'd just have to do her best to ignore him. She had a village to save. Her home. She could do this. She *had* to do this.

Kitty led the way up the sweeping staircase. The wide wooden steps gleamed beneath her feet. Malcolm either employed an army of house elves or he used magic to keep the place clean.

Given the isolation he seemed to bask in, she'd guess the latter.

Sofia reached the top and debated whether to turn left or right. Both hallways were identical, from what she could see. Wide corridors, the walls of each were plastered with priceless art. At least she assumed it was priceless. Art wasn't really her thing. Maybe it would have been if she'd had time to get a hobby, but taking care of Bruxa's Eye occupied all her time.

She shrugged and turned left, choosing the first door. It opened to reveal an opulent sitting room. Green brocade upholstered mahogany settees and chairs.

A door on the left wall of the room stood opened.

A bedroom? She entered and crossed the soft rug. Kitty stopped and dug her claws in, scratching. No doubt it was a priceless antique.

"Good work, Kitty."

Kitty purred and Sofia grinned. Malcolm could afford to fix it. Hell, a wave of his hand and a shot of magic could spiff it right up.

As she'd thought, the door led to a beautifully appointed bedroom. An enormous canopied bed occupied the space, its green silk drapes hung in elegant folds. The fire in the hearth burst to life as soon as she crossed the threshold.

She frowned. What magic could already be here? The fire was enchanted to light, but were there other spells? A spying one, perhaps?

She raised her wand and spun in a slow circle about the room, removing any spell that might have been placed upon it. The fire died. The room felt different, as well. She didn't know what spell he'd put on the place, but she'd broken it.

Good enough for her. A huge yawn stole over her. Kitty mimicked it.

A second later, she fell into the bed. She barely got the covers up over her head before she passed out.

Malcolm watched Sofia walk out of the room, her little black familiar on her heels. At the door, Kitty turned to glare at him out of her good eye, then flicked her tail and stalked out.

He frowned, then downed the last of his whisky, trying to ease the tightness in his chest. His wolf was restless, as if it sensed something of great value was near but out of reach.

No matter how hard he tried, he couldn't get the image of Sofia out of his mind. Images of her from tonight were acceptable. That was about sex. But he kept seeing her as he remembered her, from their first meeting.

So beautiful. Smart and determined, she'd been so quick-witted she made his head spin. He'd first seen her sitting in Corrier's study where they'd had their lessons. Corrier hadn't arrived yet. It had been just them amongst the towering bookshelves stuffed with ancient tomes and trinkets.

He'd walked into the study to find her sitting in front of the fire, Kitty at her feet. The feline had assessed him with her one good eye, but Sofia had ignored him, preferring to spend her energy studying the book in her lap.

He hadn't been able to look away from her. She'd made him feel something he didn't understand. His life had been all work and preparation for becoming a warlock. Life was very staid amongst sorcerers and emotions weren't something his sorcerer kin expressed.

Eventually, she'd glanced up at him, spearing him with her sharp gaze. "Do you need something?"

"Your name," he'd said.

"I'd hardly say you *need* that."

"But I do."

She shrugged. "Sofia Viera."

Beautiful. Like her. "What are you?"

She raised a brow. "Don't you know that's rude?"

"Is it?" With her, he lost his mind a bit.

Apparently, he still lost his mind when it came to her. He'd only been back with her for a few hours and he was reeling. This wasn't how he'd expected to feel when he'd forced her to come to him. In fairness, when he'd come up with this plan, he hadn't done much thinking about what would occur after he had her here. He'd just known that he was done being without her. For centuries, he'd thought he was fine the way he was. He had as much power and wealth as any Mythean could want.

It wasn't enough.

Now he had to go up against the Salem Coven—and possibly the High Witches if they failed to get the Grimoire— or he'd lose more than Sofia. As much as his ego hated to admit it, they might need help. Not tomorrow. But if everything went to shit, they'd need someone to call on.

He wouldn't risk Sofia's life like that.

Malcolm set the tumbler on the mantle above the blazing hearth and envisioned his brother's home in Iceland. A second later, he stood on the doorstep. Frigid wind whipped off the glacier, freezing his skin. The Aurora Borealis danced overhead—blues and greens lighting up the night and making the snow sparkle.

He knew why his brother had chosen to live on a godforsaken patch of ice in the middle of nowhere, but the Vatnajokull glacier was not where he'd have chosen. He might be a loner, but this was taking it too far.

Malcolm pounded on the heavy wooden door, eyeing the golden glow of the windows to his left. This place always looked like a bloody Christmas card. Pretty cabin, snow-covered eaves, windows lit with warm light. He'd love to just aetherwalk in, but his brother had a new bride and well... Best not to.

At least they appeared to be here. They'd spent the last several months traveling.

Finally, the door swung open to reveal Aurora, his brother's mate. She wore flannel pajamas that were decorated with pumpkins and black cats.

"Malcolm!" Her golden brows rose.

All of Aurora was golden, from her skin to her hair and eyes. She was a soulceress, one of the most despised species among Mytheans because her kind got their magical power by stealing it from the souls of other Mytheans. Whereas all other Mytheans could draw power from the aether using their immortal soul—and that's what actually fueled the unique magic each species was capable of—Soulceresses could not. They took it from others. It made them immensely powerful and equally despised.

It didn't bother Malcolm because he had unlimited access to the power of the aether, so he just let a smile crack his face.

"Aurora." She and Felix would be a great help to them if he needed to call upon them. Neither were as powerful as he—almost no one was, he wasn't too modest to admit—but there was strength in numbers when all else failed.

"Come on in," she stepped back to let him in. The cabin was cozy and warm, the large living room lit by a crackling fire that gleamed on the honey-colored wooden wall. Aurora's familiar, a sleek black cat named Mouse, watched him from the back of the couch. Her golden eyes were luminous, her posture straight.

He recalled that Mouse liked to play. As an afterthought, he waved his hand near the floor and a rat made of smoke darted across the floor. Mouse leapt off the couch and streaked after it.

"You like familiars," Aurora said.

He shrugged and was saved from answering when his brother entered the room.

Felix was as big as he was, though younger. They shared a father—the man who'd given them the wulver half of their soul. Felix's mother had been a timewalker. Time travel was a powerful strength, but Malcolm would take his own mother's powers any day. The sorcerer half of him had given him the magical ability necessary to become a warlock.

A twinge of regret streaked through him.

Regret? No. Definitely not. He pushed the strange feeling aside and greeted his brother.

"Good to have you visit," Felix said, glancing at the clock. "At two in the morning."

"Sorry about that."

Felix joined Aurora and wrapped an arm around her waist. He leaned down to press a kiss to her head.

A jolt of jealousy shot through Malcolm. He swallowed it down.

That right there—seeing his brother so bloody happy with Aurora—was the reason he'd finally caved and sought out Sofia.

Their happiness shined a light on the great, gaping hole in his life. Maybe he'd always known it was there. Maybe not.

But he knew now and was unable to ignore it any longer.

"You remember the dagger I brought you? The one that returned Aurora's soul to her body?"

Felix nodded, rubbing Aurora's shoulder. Her gaze had grown dark, no doubt recalling the horror of learning that a huge part of her soul had been stolen by an old enemy. Mouse appeared at her side, leaning against her shin. The smoke rat had been abandoned in favor of comforting her mistress.

"I didn't return it. On purpose, but now I could be in a bit of a bind."

"What do you need?" Felix asked.

"I'm going to Salem to retrieve the Salem Coven's Grimoire."

"Oh shit," Aurora said, her eyes bright. "You sure you want to do that?"

"Yes. If I fail, I'll have a problem with the High Witches."

"Double shit," Aurora said.

"Do you want help in Salem?" Felix asked.

"No. Stealth is the only way to get the book and I should be able to get it. But in the unlikely event that we fail, the

High Witches will destroy my friend's village." He didn't like calling Sofia his friend. He wanted to call her something more than that.

Soon.

"Can't they move?" Felix asked.

"I asked. Not possible. I'm going to Salem tomorrow to retrieve the Grimoire. If I don't have it within a week, we're going to need help with the High Witches. A lot of help."

"Not a problem," Felix said.

"I'll get my sister, Esha. And her best friend is Andrasta, Celtic goddess of war. For that matter, Logan and Sylvi might step in as well, as they did when I was in a bind. And we can put the word out at the university. This is right up their alley."

"Thank you." He'd worked at the university for a few decades, though it was easier to come to his brother for help. The Immortal University, as it was called, was located in Edinburgh. It was more of a governmental organization than a learning institution, dedicated to maintaining the order and secrecy of British Mytheans. Sofia had no ties with them— they normally didn't operate outside of Europe—but at Aurora's request, they would.

"I'll leave you then," he said.

"Can't you stay for a drink?" Felix asked.

Malcolm shook his head, though he wanted to nod. While he'd managed to stay in his brother's life, it'd been at the periphery since he'd become a warlock. He'd helped Felix after he'd been captured by a sadistic seer three centuries ago, and again with saving Aurora, but for the most part, Malcolm had had to stay scarce. He loved his brother. Only by keeping himself scarce could he help mitigate the risk.

"I'll let you know how we get on in Salem," Malcolm said. "Thank you."

"Good luck," Aurora said.

Malcolm nodded, then aetherwalked home.

He found Kitty standing at the base of the stairs, staring at him. Glaring, more like. Familiars were notoriously loyal. Kitty might like his wolf, but she didn't trust him.

"Did you miss me?"

Kitty just stared.

"I went for backup."

The cat bobbed its head.

"Good night, Kitty." Malcolm passed by the familiar and climbed the stairs, stopping just briefly at the closed door to the room Sofia had chosen.

He pressed a hand to the door, then shook his head and continued on.

CHAPTER FIVE

Sorcerer's Tor
Entrance to the Sorcerer Afterworld
Dartmoor, England
1606 AD

Cold wind whipped across Sofia's cheeks as she watched Malcolm, who stood a dozen yards away from her. It was colder on Dartmoor than she had expected. Her cloak wasn't suited to this chill weather.

She wasn't suited to this chill weather.

But when Malcolm had told her of his mother's death and that he had to go to Sorcerer's Tor, the sorcerer's sacred space, to make an offering in her name, she couldn't help but ask if he wanted her to accompany him. She'd only known him for a month, but she'd quickly grown to care for him.

Kitty pressed against her leg, huddling under her cloak with her little black head peeping out. Despite her thick fur, she too was used to the heat of the jungle. But sorcerers were a strange group—as least, Malcolm's clan was. They lived in a remote part of southwestern England, just at the edge of Dartmoor.

At the highest part of the moor, on a desolate tor formed from the biggest granite outcropping in England, they said goodbye to their dead. According to Malcolm, there was a crevice in the rock on Sorcerer's Tor that led to their afterworld. Only the dead could enter, but it was here that the living paid their respects when someone passed.

Her heart ached as she watched him. Tall and strong, his black hair and cloak whipping in the wind as he stood with his head bowed. He was so beautiful that she almost couldn't believe he was real. When he'd started courting her, she'd been surprised. He seemed so distant, so cold.

That coldness came from the sorcerer within him, but she sensed there was more than just coldness. She'd fallen for him. Enough that she accompanied him to say goodbye to his dead mother, though he'd never spoken of his family before.

He turned to face her then, a sad smile kicking up at the corner of his mouth. Dusk cast his face in shadow. His stride was powerful as he approached her. He reached for her hand, his grip strong and warm.

"Are you all right?" she asked.

"Fine. Thank you for coming."

She nodded. "Shall we get back?"

He shook his head. "Wait with me a moment. The sun will set. I know how you love sunsets." His big hands gripped her shoulders and turned her gently to face the setting sun.

Sofia smiled. He'd remembered. Even more than sunrises, sunsets symbolized renewal to her.

She sighed when he pulled her back to rest against his chest and wrapped his arms around her. Comfort washed over her. In all her life, she'd never thought she'd find a man like him. She was falling in love.

"See?" His whisper was rough at her ear.

The sun had just flared into a beautiful orange and yellow sunset, fingers of color streaking across the sky and lighting it up.

"You were right. I've never seen anything like it. It's the most beautiful place I've ever been." She turned her head to look up at him.

At his eyes. He looked at her like she were life itself.

"I can't believe what you've come to mean to me," he said. "I didn't know it was possible to feel like this."

She shivered.

"Everything that's happened—my mother's death, meeting you, being here with you—makes me feel like I want to be part of something bigger," he said.

"What do you mean?" Her heart fluttered with hope. She tried to crush it, but failed.

"You, Sofia. I want to be with you." He rubbed her arms and kissed her temple. "Forever."

"Forever?" A smile stretched across her face.

"Forever. I can help you protect your village. Once we're warlocks, we can surely free you of the burden of providing tributes."

The breath whooshed out of her. He wanted to be with her forever, and help free her from the High Witches. Even if they couldn't manage it, to have him share the burden would be incredible. She wouldn't be alone.

Better, she'd be with the man she loved.

She spun around, leaned up on her toes, and kissed him. He groaned and pulled her closer, his mouth slanting over hers and stealing her breath. Stealing her heart. She clutched his cloak tighter, trying to pull him closer to her. To never let him go.

If she lost this, lost him, it would break her.

CHAPTER SIX

Malcolm's Castle
Glencoe, Scotland
Present Day

The bed shook hard enough that Sofia almost bounced out onto the floor. Her eyes flew open.

What the hell?

Sunlight filtered through the sheer drapes at the windows, illuminating the beautiful green room. Everything looked normal, except for the fact that the house was vibrating.

Kitty stood at the base of the bed, hissing. Sofia scrambled out from beneath the fluffy covers and found her footing. Everything continued to vibrate. The chandelier above tinkled as crystal clashed with crystal. Paintings rattled on the walls. It took her a second to remember why this felt familiar, then it hit her.

Malcolm must be accessing the aether in massive quantities.

"Come on, Kitty. Let's go check this out." She hadn't seen the pure white light of harnessed aether energy in centuries. Only warlocks could harness and compress the cold darkness of the aether into pure magical energy.

She made her way out of the bedroom and down the hall, her whole body vibrating slightly. She followed the tremors, holding onto the stairwell, as she made her way down to the first floor. Every painting and artifact on the walls and tables sat calmly. Though the floor vibrated, even the furniture stayed still.

Malcolm must have enchanted everything in the house not to bounce and break. She'd taken the charms off of the bedroom, therefore the bed had shaken her awake. Sofia made her way down the house's second main corridor—the one she hadn't gone down last night—passing many closed doors and a few open ones.

She didn't take time to explore—her gaze was trained on the door at the end of the hall, from which the vibrations were emanating. Of course, just like his office, his workspace was at the end of a hall.

How ominous. It was as if he liked being a scary warlock, or something. Frightening folks away before they could become bothersome.

Sofia didn't hesitate when reaching for the doorknob. The door was made of heavy wood, dark and ornately carved. The iron knob turned easily beneath her hand. She pushed the door open to reveal a dark stairwell. Rough stone steps spiraled down into the basement. There were no lights on the wall or above, but a glow flared up from the beneath, lighting the way.

Kitty followed her, hissing occasionally. The nearly-unrestrained access to the aether had always made her nervous. Warlocks were specially trained to access and control it, but it was still a difficult job. Kitty was right to be wary.

Sofia reached the bottom of the stairwell and found a small antechamber. A door on the opposite wall a dozen feet away glowed around the edges. She moved quietly toward it, twisting the knob slowly and inching open the heavy wooden door.

A huge stone-walled room opened up before her. It was easily the size of the entire castle, if not larger, all built under the stone of the Glencoe Mountains.

In the center, a glowing white light shined. It was a great orb, outlined by a hazy, shimmering glow that floated in the middle of the room, bright as the sun but easier to look at. Malcolm stood between her and the orb, his tall form silhouetted by the bright light. His arms were outstretched toward the aether, both controlling it and drawing power from it.

The power of the aether bathed her in its glow, though she couldn't harness it for her own use the way Malcolm could. She'd have to rely on what her soul could reap, which, while substantial, was nothing like this.

Jealousy streaked through Sofia. She'd wanted this. The unlimited power that could have helped her destroy the High Witches.

But the cost had been too high for her. Faced with the enormous power before her, she couldn't help but think that maybe being an Oath Breaker wouldn't have been so bad. Malcolm could do almost anything he wanted. He could wave his hand and make one of the surrounding mountains rise. He could bring lightning down upon his enemies, striking them dead. He could mimic almost any supernatural talent with his magic—like creating fire. If he wanted, he was strong enough to battle a god.

She shook herself. There was no point in being jealous, because no oaths meant no love. No close family. She couldn't live without that. Worse, she might have had to break her vow to protect her village. She'd had to stand her ground—giving up Malcolm and all the power accessible to a warlock.

It'd been the right choice. The *only* choice. The fact that her life was nearly as cold and lonely as his was beside the point. Protecting her village might take up so much time that she couldn't have a real life, but it was her sacred duty.

Sofia lowered herself to the ground and leaned against the wall. There wasn't a stick of furniture in the empty room, but she was happy to just sit here and bathe in the glow of the aether, letting the warmth and power wash over her. Normally the energy from the aether was dark and cold, but a warlock's power converted it to bright, pure energy.

Kitty climbed onto her lap, purring like a little jet engine. Kitty wasn't as fierce as some familiars—hence her name—but she more than made up for it in love and support. Familiars increased their mistress's connection to the aether, giving them power and strength when needed. Kitty was always quick to donate hers. It was one of the reasons that Sofia was such a powerful Bruxa.

She watched Malcolm as he stood before the aether that pulsed and shimmered, performing some kind of magic she didn't quite understand. Power radiated out from him. She could feel it, like an eerie caress against her skin. Only the strongest Mytheans radiated power.

She'd given up a chance to be one of them so she could have a normal life. One in which she could keep her vows and thereby have family, friends, and a husband. Too bad it hadn't worked out. She should have known that duty would get in the way no matter what. The position of Protector was too important. It took up too much time. Not to mention the fact that she was expected to appear as the Crone whenever she was out and about in Bruxa's Eye.

It was tradition. Most citizens didn't even realize that it was her—Sofia Viera—who protected the village. It was the Protector, appearing in the most powerful form a witch could take. A symbol meant to comfort as well as do the dirty work of keeping the village safe.

She remembered begging her mother to allow her to appear as herself when she'd first begun her transition to Protector. Sofia had just gotten old enough to realize she liked the way boys looked at her. Willingly looking like an old Crone? No way.

Her mother had refused. Tradition was vital. The Crone was a symbol of power. Strength. Everything a protector needed to be. But Sofia had been stubborn. On their next mission to retrieve a tribute, Sofia had taken her own form halfway through. They'd been deep in an Egyptian temple, hunting for an ancient magical necklace worn by the Pharaoh Hatshepsut. Magical booby traps that had been held at bay by the power of her Crone form were no longer silent. They'd sprung to life, charms meant to dismember intruders.

She'd almost lost a leg. Her mother had lost a finger.

But it had been her mother's words that had stuck with her: "Sofia, you *will* die fulfilling your role as Protector, as I will die fulfilling my role and as my mother died before me. It is our fate to serve until our lives are cut short by circumstance. Though other Mytheans may live forever, we will not. Our job is too dangerous. It will kill you. Do not let that moment come early by dropping your guard or the protection that the Crone offers you."

Sofia had never gone without the Crone form in necessary situations ever again.

The downside of it was that she'd never had a chance to have a normal love life. Malcolm had been her only shot. She'd truly thought they'd be together forever. Not only had she loved him, he'd become her best friend. When he'd abandoned her, she'd felt as if her most vital organs had been torn out. She'd thought losing him would be the worst thing that could happen to her. That it would break her into a million pieces.

How wrong she'd been. Naive. She'd become stronger. Tougher.

Especially after she'd returned to the village from Norway and learned that her mother had died on her last mission to recover a tribute. Sofia had been thrust into the position of Protector. That had toughened her up real quick. Eventually, she'd gotten over him.

She'd taken on the form of a Crone every time she was out in the village. True, she often spiced it up with a Halloween witch's hat and broom, but even that was no longer funny. She'd had some relationships, though none had lived up to what she'd had with Malcolm. About two centuries ago, she'd just gotten sick of trying. One-night stands would have been her ideal, but those were impossible in her village since her public image was the Crone and those who knew her without the visage respected her position too much to ever fuck her.

Was that why she'd been so quick to succumb to Malcolm last night? Maybe. She'd prefer to think that she'd been desperate, rather than admit she might still feel something for him. The bastard had kidnapped her.

Power had clearly gone to his head.

She scowled as she watched Malcolm manipulate the aether. As usual, she was in a hell of a bind.

Finally, the aether began to dim. Seconds later, the room was entirely dark. A glow of flame appeared in the middle of the room. Sofia squinted. It hovered over Malcolm's hand, a magical flashlight. She created one in her own hand, unable to resist drawing his attention.

He turned. "Sofia."

"Malcolm. What were you doing?" She rose.

"Crafting a charm that can shield my power from Mytheans who might sense it." He approached her and raised his arm. She saw a wide wristband of beaten metal around his thick wrist. "We'll need it in Salem. It'll be best to keep a low profile."

"All right." She followed him out of the room and up the stairs into the hall. "That's your aether room? I didn't sense any magical shields on it."

While warlocks could draw a moderate amount of extra power from the aether under normal circumstances, if they wanted a huge burst of it, they needed to have a magically reinforced room built to contain a portal to the aether. Normally, the room had to be built into a place that had an excess of magical energy, either from a large population of Mytheans or because the place itself was special.

"Yes. I used to have one at the university. It was excellent. So much magic there, it was easy to contain the aether." He turned to face her. "But I wanted to be on my own. There were too many people at the university. So I practiced. Eventually, I could contain it, so I moved here. There's a bit more magic in Glencoe than elsewhere, so that helps. But now I'm powerful enough to contain the magic myself."

She didn't sense any arrogance in him now, though she wouldn't be surprised if she had. Controlling a portal to the aether on your own took a huge amount of strength. He was even stronger than she'd realized.

She shivered. His strength, combined with the way he looked at her—like he wanted to devour her—was nerve wracking. If he didn't want to let her go once this was over, she'd have a damned hard time getting away.

She'd just better hope he kept helping her. And figure out a way to force his hand if he reneged. Or tried to keep her.

"We need to plan our story for when we're in Salem," she said. "I don't think we can just walk in there and say we want to find the most powerful witches in town."

He nodded. "Let's plan while eating. I'm starving."

She followed him down the hall to a huge kitchen, Kitty at her side. Sweeping counters were topped with tall windows that looked out on the Glencoe Mountains. On the other side of the kitchen, a large hearth burst into flame. It was like something out of a magazine.

Sofia couldn't take her gaze off Malcolm as he walked to the huge, stainless-steel refrigerator and pulled open the door. His slacks were expensive and tailored to fit him perfectly. The sleeves of the black sweater he wore were pushed up to reveal strong forearms and big hands. It hugged his strong shoulders and fit his waist perfectly. He looked like a billionaire on vacation. The wide metal cuff gleamed dully on his wrist.

It had been a good idea on his part. Her level of power wasn't quite enough to cause alarm in most Mytheans. She was on the stronger end of the spectrum—able to cause destruction and come up with some pretty nasty spells—but Malcolm's was the kind that made people run. Especially since, as a warlock, he specialized in destruction.

"Are omelets all right?" He turned to glance at her.

Damn. She wished he weren't so handsome. The dichotomy of his big, muscular body and his elegant features was enough to make her head spin. "Yeah, fine."

He pulled out ingredients and put them on the counter. Grabbed two fine plates from a cabinet below the counter, then waved his hand over the lot. A second later, a steaming omelet sat on each plate.

Neat trick. "Not much for cooking?"

"Cooking for one is a bit of a bore, isn't it?" he asked, then pulled forks out of the drawer in front of him. He picked up the plates and approached her. He nodded to the space behind her. "We'll sit there."

Sofia turned and went to the delicate wooden table in an alcove surrounded by windows. The mountains stretched out before her, their rounded tops glittering with snow.

Malcolm put the plates on the table. Kitty hopped up onto a chair.

He glanced at her. "Hang on."

He walked back to the ingredients, pulled out another plate, and made another omelet. He returned and set it in front of kitty.

"Thanks," Sofia said.

Kitty meowed.

Malcolm shrugged, then turned back to the counter and got down two coffee mugs and a bag of coffee grounds. He filled the cups with water, then waved his hand over them. A second later, they were full of steaming coffee. "Cream or sugar?"

"Neither." She took the cup gratefully and sipped. Not bad. "So, what's our cover in Salem? It's a small, notoriously tight community. They'll notice strangers. Most of Salem is mortal, but I've heard that the Mytheans have their own secret street. Mortals can't see it, but it's hard for even Mytheans to find."

He sat and took a bite of his omelet, met her gaze while he chewed. She tried hers. Also not bad. Kitty was scarfing it down, so she clearly approved. Familiars weren't normal cats, thank fates, so their diet could consist of pretty much anything.

After he swallowed, he said, "What if you're looking for your sister? You've heard recently that you have a half-sister who is a witch with the Salem coven."

She thought about it. "Not bad. It's not out of the realm of possibility, so it could work. You're my, what? Bodyguard?"

"I was thinking—man. I'm your man. You don't go anywhere without me." His gaze was serious. Dark and intense.

Her stomach muscles fluttered. "How about personal assistant?"

He laughed, his gaze lightening. He looked surprised. At his own laughter?

His gaze turned serious then. "I think not. I'm your man."

It was a loaded sentence she didn't want to explore. She also didn't want to argue. They needed to get started. "Fine. Whatever."

She polished off her omelet quickly, swigged the rest of her coffee, then stood. He rose and stepped toward her, his clean, spicy scent sweeping over her. She wanted to breathe him in forever.

Bad idea. And his clean smell only reminded her that she hadn't showered in ages. She hadn't even changed. She'd just gotten out of bed and gone to seek him out.

She definitely had a problem.

"I need a quick shower," she said. "Is there a bathroom attached to the green room?"

"There is."

She left without another word, her nerves twisted into knots over the way he made her feel. Eating with him had reminded her of what they'd once had. True, it had been far more fraught with tension this time, but it had taken her back to quiet meals with him at Corrier's home. They'd fallen for each other during those long nights.

He'd been a different man then. Happier. He'd never been a jokester, but he hadn't been entirely serious and dark.

She'd never failed to get a laugh out of him if she wanted to. As she'd done this morning, in fact. She hadn't meant the personal assistant bit as a joke. Not really.

But she'd liked it when he'd laughed.

Idiot. He didn't deserve her soft thoughts. Nor could she afford them.

Pushing thoughts of him from her mind, she raced up the stairs to the green bedroom and found her way to the bathroom.

Whoa. The castle might be old, but the bathroom certainly wasn't. Marble and wood gleamed. An enormous shower beckoned.

She made quick work of washing up, though in any other circumstance she would have hung out a lot longer. Maybe tried out the huge sunken tub.

A wave of her wand gave her fresh clothes and a warm jacket.

CHAPTER SEVEN

"Holy shit, it's cold here," Sofia said.

A grin cracked Malcolm's face as he glanced at her. Surprised, he almost reached up to touch his own cheek. It was the second today. A record.

They stood in an alley near Salem's main street, having just aetherwalked from his home.

"I suppose you don't get out of the jungle much," he said. She wore a puffy brown jacket that somehow still managed to highlight her curves. He still wasn't used to actually seeing her. After so long apart, it was hard to keep his gaze off her.

Kitty stood at her side, scowling. The familiar didn't like the cold either.

"Not to cold places," she said. "How is it colder here than in Scotland?"

"Gulf stream. But it's not much worse. You're just used to the jungle."

"True." She set off down the alley, her footsteps silent on the cobblestone.

They walked out onto a residential street. Behind them were shops. Being one of America's older cities, Salem was a mix of long-standing houses and shops pressed up against one another.

"Looks like a Halloween bomb exploded here," Sofia said, surveying the street avidly.

Malcolm dragged his gaze from her. Red, orange, and yellow leaves rustled in the trees and floated through the air to land on the brick walkway beneath their feet. The homes on the other side of the street were all New England charm. Clapboard fronts with jack-o-lanterns on the stoops and a mishmash of other Halloween decorations. Two women in witch hats giggled as they walked down the other sidewalk.

"Mortals," Sofia said. "I hear they like it here around Halloween. It's commercial, but the magic beneath it all is what draws them, I think."

"Makes sense. Some mortals are sensitive to it." Though they had no idea that another world existed alongside their own, full of real witches and things that went bump in the night.

"Let's see if we can find the entrance to the Mythean street. Salem Hollow, I think it's called."

They turned and headed up the street. A black wooden building sat on the corner. With a steep roof, an overhanging second floor, and mullioned windows, it looked to be from the seventeenth century.

"Creepy," Sofia said.

"From the witch hunts, no doubt," Malcolm said. Evil lurked around the place. The two giggling mortals who stood in the front yard of the ancient building beneath a brilliant red-leafed tree didn't appear to feel it.

The house was a reminder of Salem's dark history, though the place was entirely different now. The streets were brightly festooned with Halloween garlands and jack-o-lanterns. An emblem of a flying witch was emblazoned on dozens of surfaces—signs, shop windows, cars. It was cheerful in a way that its history was not.

Sofia shook herself. "Come on, let's go find Salem Hollow. Maybe things will feel more normal there."

They made their way down a street lined with stores. Mortals in costumes bustled down the street. Magic shops butted up against t-shirt stores and bars. Wooden folding signs for psychic readings sat on the sidewalk and tour guides hustled for patrons.

"This is… interesting," Malcolm said. It made him itch, being so close to so many mortals. Two screaming children dressed as demons raced down the sidewalk in front of him.

"That's one word for it. It's really very charming," Sofia said. "Let's go in here. This shop has potential. I'd bet dollars to donuts we'll find Mytheans peddling goods to mortals in a few of these places. They can tell us where to find Salem Hollow."

Malcolm ducked through the low doorway behind her. The shop was small, with bundled herbs and flowers hanging from the ceiling and candles and knickknacks on every surface. Books crowded the two tables inside. Wicca, or whatever it was the mortal witches practiced, was obviously the theme of this particular shop.

He sensed no magic within. The proprietress, a blond woman wearing layered skirts and about a dozen scarves, smiled at him. He nodded at her, then caught Sofia's eye. She nodded briefly, and after a moment of browsing, they turned and left.

"All right, that was a bust," Sofia said. "I mean, if I wanted my house to smell nice, that's the place I'd try. But for anything more than that? Nah."

It took them three more shops before they found one that reeked of magic. Black and red candles burned in the window and pentagrams were painted on the glass. He pushed open the heavy door and held it for Sofia, then followed her inside.

The interior was dark and cramped. It screamed black magic—or at least, what mortals thought black magic might be. Crystals and candles decorated the shelves, along with animal bones and vials of brightly colored liquid. Fog drifted along the floor, coming from a black door in the back.

A young, dark-haired demon from an unidentifiable afterworld sat on a stool behind the narrow counter, snapping her gum and reading a book. She glanced up when the door shut, her eyes widening slightly behind black-framed glasses. She looked like something out of the 1950's, with bouffant hair and red lips.

"Can I help you?" she asked. "You're not from around here."

"No, I'm not," Malcolm said. "What's a demon doing selling spells and trinkets to mortals?"

"Gotta make a living. And besides, they'll pay out the nose for this crap. I stay away from the Wicca stuff. Respect their religion and all that—I'm not a monster."

"What do you sell?"

She shrugged. "Folks who frequent my fair establishment aren't interested in mortal witchcraft. They just want to curse their colleagues and make people fall in love with them. So I don't exactly feel guilty about selling them a bullshit spell and a black candle."

"Fair enough," Malcolm said.

"What are you?" Her green gaze darted to Sofia. "She's a witch. What kind, I don't know. But I can't tell with you."

Good. The charm was working. "Sorcerer. We'd like to find Salem Hollow."

"Oh? Why's that? You know we locals like to keep that on the down low. Hard to hide the street from mortals if we have all kinds of strangers coming and going."

"We'll be subtle. My friend here is looking for someone."

"How do you know you'll find them in the Hollow?"

"A hunch."

"Hmm. Well, it'll cost you."

"How much?"

Her gaze ran up and down his form. "Thirty minutes in the back."

"That's quite the offer."

She smiled. Before it could fade from her lips, he slipped the charmed cuff off his wrist and reached out to touch her temple, sending a burst of his magic and will into her mind that broke down her barriers.

He lowered his hand. "Do you know anything about the Salem Coven?"

In a slightly wooden voice, she said, "They live here. Not sure where. No one really knows."

"No?"

"No. They keep to themselves. Not all witches are part of the Salem Coven, though. Only twelve. Maybe thirteen. No one is quite sure. They're secretive."

"Where's Salem Hollow?"

"Off Derby Street. In front of the water. To the right of the old Custom's House, there's a row of shops and bars. Next to the Witch's Brew Cafe, you'll find an alley. There's a gate within—looks like it leads to a basement apartment. It's fairly well hidden. Push the gate with your right hand to enter. Mytheans will walk onto Hollow Lane. Mortals will just walk into a small empty courtyard."

"Thank you. You'll forget us in five minutes." He turned to Sofia and nodded.

She led the way out of the little shop and into the brisk autumn air. The door shut behind them with a clang.

"Why didn't you just do that to start?" she asked as they turned left and headed down to a cross street that would take them to Derby.

"I wanted to find out what kind of demon she was. Some of them are particularly resistant to mind control."

"You can do that? Control minds?"

"It's just another facet of destruction. I break down the barrier that keeps a person from telling me what I want to hear. One who might keep silent because it's in her own best interest can no longer do so."

They made their way down the shop-lined street, past old buildings and under bright-leafed trees. The autumn wind was sharp and the smell of candles burning inside jack-o-lanterns permeated the air.

"What exactly have you been doing the last four hundred years?" Sofia asked as they dodged a group of be-hatted mortals sipping coffee from paper cups.

"You're interested?" His ego hated to admit it, but he was flattered.

"Strangely, I find that I am. But don't worry—it might not even be interest in you. After all, I wanted to be a warlock too. Until the cost became too great." There was bitterness in her voice.

Darkness filled his chest. She'd never forgive him for leaving her. He shook the thought away. But being without her was no longer bearable, so he would make it work. "I've been a mercenary. First for the money. Then to keep myself busy. I only take on work I like now."

"Did you have any standards, or would you do any old thing? Destroy villages, perhaps? Destruction is the specialty of a warlock, after all."

Sharp-tongued. But he liked it. Better than false sweetness bought with his gold or power. "I never destroyed any villages, no. But remember, destruction can be used to break evil magic. Dark spells. Plague. I didn't say no to much, though. It wasn't all good."

"Hmmm." Disappointment.

"I never did anything too terrible," he said. He didn't have much hope of her forgiving him, but he could at least try not to add to her dislike. "Mostly only to people who deserved it." *Mostly.*

"Have you been happy?"

He blinked, unsure of how to respond. Had he been? "I've been all right."

"I imagine the wulver half of your soul wouldn't like the cold life of a warlock."

No, she was right about that. Wulvers valued clan. Family. Love. But he'd been raised by his mother's people—sorcerers who prized magic and power over all else. That part of him had been ignored. Suppressed. "That hasn't been as easy."

"Is it why you've abducted me?"

His step faltered, but he forced himself to keep going, trying to cover it up. He hadn't expected her to figure it out. He almost hadn't figured it out. Was it the wulver part of his soul that had demanded he bring her back to him? Or just his desire? "Perhaps." He needed to change the subject. "What about you?"

"That's Derby Street up there." She pointed to a sign at the corner ahead.

"Not going to answer?"

"No."

"It's fair. I answered your questions."

"Life isn't fair, Malcolm. I know that as well as anyone."

He couldn't argue that point.

They stopped on the corner, looking out at the bay across the street. A glance left revealed that the old Custom's House sat down the road. The tall, elegant building looked to be mid-seventeenth century. Perhaps earlier.

It took them only a few minutes to find the alley between the shops next to the Custom's House. They slipped down the narrow passage. The gate sat at the end as the demon girl had said, a wrought iron affair that was rusted in places.

He put his right hand to it and glanced at Sofia. She nodded.

It swung open easily and they stepped through. A narrow street opened up before them, lined on both sides by shops and bars that looked far older than the mortal ones just outside. Mytheans had been here far longer, after all.

"Like freaking Diagon Alley," Sofia muttered.

"What?"

"Nothing. I think we should find someone that you can *talk* to."

"It's getting dark. The pubs should be filling up. Let's find one. We can ask around."

"All right."

They set off down the street. Brick and wooden buildings rose three stories high on either side, pressed cheek by jowl. Shops and bars sat on the bottom levels and Sofia guessed the apartments were on top. It was the most magical place she'd seen outside of her own village. Like a northern version of her home—Mytheans allowed to use magic in the streets and walk around freely even if they couldn't pass for human. Outside of places like this, Mytheans were supposed to keep a low profile.

Within protected spaces, they went wild. Even more so than in her own village. A trio of fae with lavender skin and gossamer wings walked in front of them. Some sort of demon with large horns and blue skin strode down the other side of the street, his huge shoulders hung with two great swords that crossed over his back.

The chimney of a narrow wooden building to her left belched pink smoke. The brick storefront next to that was painted with ancient runes. A seer worked within, from the look of them. A black cat streaked across the cobblestone road, its fur sparkling like dark diamonds.

Kitty hissed.

"I know, Kitty. What a show-off," Sofia said. "But if you like, I can make you a glittery purple."

Kitty looked up thoughtfully, then shook her little head once and continued on.

Noticeably absent were magic shops, though Sofia wasn't surprised. The Salem Coven wouldn't be the sort to sell their magic. But otherwise, there were restaurants, clothing shops, and weapons retailers. A potions store had the most elaborate front window Sofia had ever seen. Gleaming bottles full of jewel-tone liquid lined the shelves in artful array. Smoke snaked around their bases.

There were no cars. Many Mytheans could aetherwalk, so there was no need. For others, they'd just have to make do, no doubt. Sofia couldn't see anyone successfully driving out of the alley.

"What do you think of this place?" Malcolm stopped before a quiet storefront that sold fantastical furniture. He nodded toward a set of stairs that led down from the street and through an arch.

"The Cauldron Bar." The sign hung above the archway. A little emblem of a witch flying on a broom was etched onto it. Only the witch was flying backward, facing the broom bristles. "The demon at the shop said that not all witches here are part of the Salem Coven. Maybe we can find some others in there who can tell us what we need to know?"

"My thoughts exactly." Malcolm started down the stairs.

Sofia followed, marveling at the breadth of his shoulders. He moved so smoothly for such a big man. Quiet and elegant.

They reached the bottom. Kitty hissed. Sofia squinted down the narrow, stone-paved passage. The brick walls were studded with yellow gas lamps and Malcolm's head brushed the narrow ceiling. At the far end, a wooden door beckoned.

"These witches are freaking creepy," Sofia said.

"Stay behind me." Malcolm started down the alleyway.

Sofia bristled. She could take care of herself, damn it. No one talked to her that way. She was the Protector of Bruxa's Eye.

But then, if there was a hit coming, perhaps she should let him take it.

She should definitely let him take it.

Suddenly, the floor dropped out from under her. She screamed as she fell. Pain streaked through her legs as she crashed to the ground. Kitty's smoky form floated beside her. Heart racing, she looked around. Dim light illuminated a stone-walled room. Dungeon, more like.

She glanced up to see that the ceiling above her was normal. No hole through to the street upstairs. It began to shimmer, then opened up to the street above. Malcolm jumped down into the room, landing gracefully beside her.

He leaned down to help her. "Are you all—"

The door crashed open. Malcolm surged upright and moved to stand between her and the door. She scrambled to her feet, wincing at the pain in her leg. But it was already a bit better. She drew her wand from the aether.

"What 'ave we here?" The burly blue demon that she'd seen walking down the street entered.

Another one loomed in the doorway. This one had smaller horns but bigger muscles and deep red skin. No swords, just wicked looking knives strapped all over his body. They both had to duck to get in. They were at least a foot bigger than Malcolm. "Looks like a witch. Though I've no

95

idea who this bloke is. Or how he triggered the trap. Should've only caught the magic one."

Sofia glanced at the beaten metal that gleamed dully around Malcolm's wrist. No doubt that had stopped him from triggering whatever booby trap she'd just set off and kept the demons from sensing what he was capable of.

"What the hell is this place?" he demanded.

"You was trying to enter the Cauldron," the blue one rumbled. "That's invite only. Everyone knows that. And you're not invited. So now we feed you to the hounds." He lumbered toward them.

Kitty hissed. Sofia flung out her wand hand, sending a jet of flame at them. Nothing happened. Magic fizzled at the tip of her wand.

"Ah, ah. No magic down here."

Fuck.

She wasn't terrible in a fight, but she sure hated getting other people's blood on her.

Malcolm lunged for the biggest demon. He was all lethal grace. At the same time, the golden wolf burst from his chest, a shimmering apparition of snarling fangs and glowing eyes. It lunged for the other demon, going for his throat.

Like in the High Witches' dungeon, his wulver soul wasn't contained by the magic.

She stepped back, eyeing the fight for an opportunity to jump in and help. Kitty danced on nervous paws beside her. Not the best in a fight, that one.

Malcolm grabbed the big red demon by his collar and swung him away from Sofia, toward the other side of the room. The beast lunged out, swiping a huge fist. Malcolm ducked, then delivered a quick uppercut that slammed the demon's head back. He plowed a fist into its gut.

He was so fast, and his wolf so savage that Sofia just leaned back against the wall and watched. They didn't need her help.

His wolf had the blue demon on the ground and was ravaging his throat and chest. Malcolm was grappling with the red demon, a battle of wits and muscle.

The demon landed a punch to his head that had him staggering back, blood trickling from split skin at his temple. Malcolm shook himself, then charged the demon, grabbing his shoulder and spinning him around so that he could reach up and break his neck.

The sound turned Sofia's stomach, but she was grateful to see the demon slump to the ground.

Malcolm looked up at her, fury in his golden gaze. His dark hair fell over his forehead and his chest heaved.

He looked so good it almost made her head spin.

"Are you all right?" he demanded.

"Fine."

He nodded, then glanced at his wolf. It stood guard, its front feet on the blue demon's chest. Blood pooled around the demon's body.

"Check the hall," Malcolm said as he walked to where they'd fallen through the ceiling and pressed his hands against it. "It's blocked. The spell closed it behind us."

Sofia peered out into the dark hall. "Empty."

"Okay. We'll sneak out. We're not getting into the Cauldron." He bent over the fallen red demon and heaved him up over his back in a fireman's carry. "We need to get these bloody bastards out of here."

"Are they dead?" she whispered as she crept out into the hall. The golden wolf dragged the blue demon behind her. Kitty joined in to help, pulling at his shirt with her teeth. Sofia doubted it did much good, but she clearly liked the wolf.

"I don't believe so. They heal quickly. But I need to get them somewhere that doesn't block my magic so I can enchant them into forgetting they saw us."

"We should go left. Leads back to the street, I think."

He nodded and set off, his heavy burden not even bowing his back. She'd forgotten how physically strong he was. But then, wulvers usually were.

The underground passage wound around to the right. Sofia kept her wand out, though she wasn't sure it would work. Her heart pounded in her chest as they crept along. If anyone saw them—Malcolm carrying one and his wolf dragging another—they'd be shit out of luck. She just hoped no one checked the little room and saw the blood on the floor.

They came to a set of stairs and Sofia tried not to heave a sigh of relief as they made their way up. She peeked out to see another alleyway like the one they'd been in before. Empty, thank fates.

She held the door for Malcolm and his wolf as they unceremoniously dumped their baggage on the ground. When the door shut behind her, she could no longer see it.

Malcolm tapped his chest and his wolf approached, stopping briefly to nuzzle Kitty's head, then blended seamlessly into Malcolm's form until he disappeared entirely. Malcolm drew the charmed cuff off his wrist and leaned down to touch the temple of each demon, no doubt destroying their memories of the encounter.

"I'll be right back," he said, then crouched down and grabbed each demon by a wrist. He disappeared.

A moment later, he returned. He slipped the cuff back on and wiped the blood from his forehead. No one would be able to tell he'd just been in a fight.

"Where'd you take them?"

"Siberia. It'll take them a while to get sorted out. We should be gone by then."

"Good." She glanced around at the creepy alley. "Let's get out of here. Find somewhere else."

He nodded and led the way down the alley. Sofia's shoulders relaxed a bit when they reached the main street. It was still vaguely creepy, like all of Salem, but it was far nicer than where they'd just been. Even Kitty seemed less nervous as she stalked at Sofia's side.

Sofia rubbed the back of her neck. Were they being watched? Or was it just creepy Salem? Full dark had fallen while they'd been in the cell, and clouds drifted in front of an orange moon. The leaves rustled on the trees overhead. Dim yellow light from shop windows and gas street lamps gleamed on the cobblestones.

Most of the shops were empty now, as was the street. Everyone had holed up to get out of the cold. If she had to guess, the temperature had dropped at least ten degrees. Miserable.

"Let's find a place that's not quite so hidden," Sofia said. "I don't exactly want to run into any more demon bouncers."

"Agreed." He pointed up the road. "What about there?"

The road curved left and Sofia could see the gleaming windows of a pub. The Spiked Potion. It bustled with people and didn't look to have any hulking bouncers. "All right."

They slipped inside a moment later and she heaved a sigh of relief when warmth from the crackling fire enveloped her. The pub was large with a low ceiling. The gleaming wood bar took up the back left corner, while trestle tables jutted out from the rest of the walls.

The space was about three quarters full. No one sat alone. About half could pass in the mortal world. The other half... not so much. Besides the wings and horns, there was fur, scales, and an assortment of skin tones that fell closer to rainbow than beige or brown.

They approached the bar.

"What'll you have?" the bartender asked, wiping her hands on a towel. Her gaze lingered on Malcolm and Sofia had to stop herself from sneering.

Of course she didn't care if the hot bartender gave Malcolm an *I-would-bone-you-immediately* look. Why would she?

"I'll have a coke," she said. "And tuna water for my familiar."

The bartender nodded and looked at Malcolm.

"Pint of porter, if you have one on tap."

"We do."

She filled their orders and Malcolm paid her, then turned and headed toward a table in the back corner. Sofia grabbed her Coke and the saucer of tuna water and followed.

"You don't drink?" he asked as they sat. They each took a chair in the corner. Kitty sat on a chair of her own, facing out toward the room so that she could watch the going's on.

"I do. But I'm not as big as you. One beer can make me a little lightheaded, and since I don't know what's coming at us tonight..." But Malcolm clearly wouldn't have that problem. It'd probably take a lot more than a few beers to dull his reflexes.

"Of course."

They eyed the patrons. Sofia tried not to focus on how close Malcolm was to her. His arm was only a few inches from her own. If she really focused, she imagined she could feel his heat.

Oh, how she wanted to feel that.

She started and almost smacked herself. What a damned stupid thought. It didn't matter how handsome he was, or how powerful he'd looked when taking care of those demons.

Or how skilled he'd been with his hands last night.

The memory sent a shudder through her that she barely repressed.

No matter how angry she was with him for leaving her and how much she didn't trust him now, she wanted him. Even if it was only for one night. Which was all it could be. He couldn't keep an oath. He couldn't be in any kind of real relationship.

He'd ensured that when he'd become a warlock.

She scowled at him and asked, "Is your plan to just approach the first person who walks in alone?"

He nodded.

"No. Too obvious. I'll make them come to us." She conjured a cigarette—magic that was small enough to not require her wand—then got up and headed to the door as if she were going to have a smoke. Kitty hopped off her seat and followed. "I'll be right back."

She wound her way through the tables and patrons, ignoring a few appreciate glances that were tossed her way. The door swung open easily and she stepped out into the frigid air and lit the cigarette. She didn't particularly like the thing, but if one was going to be hovering in doorways, it was good cover.

Once she'd determined that the coast was clear and she stood near enough to the door that people couldn't see her through the pub's windows, she drew her wand and ran it around the door frame. Satisfied, she stubbed out the cigarette and went back in, Kitty hot on her heels. She dropped the butt in the trash and found her seat next to Malcolm.

"What was that all about? You don't smoke."

"Know me so well, do you?"

"I once did."

True enough. But she ignored it. "I charmed the door. The next individual to walk in alone will be attracted to me. They'll come sit with us. Then you'll ask the questions. It won't look so strange."

"No one would have noticed us approaching a loner. I'd have seen to it."

She didn't know how, probably with some sort of enchantment, but it wouldn't be a problem for him. "My way is easier."

"Perhaps."

"You're such a bastard sometimes, you know that? You steal my dagger, kidnap me, and are generally a jerk. Yet you throw yourself in front of lightning for me. What's with that?"

He glanced at her, his expression closed, then back at the door. It opened and a man walked in. "He's got potential."

"No he doesn't. Someone's behind him. And you're changing the subject."

"Now's not the time."

She scowled. But he was right. She needed to keep her eye on the room. They were outsiders here. Though she'd heard of tourism even in Salem's Hollow—Mytheans loved going places where there were no mortals—she didn't know how well they blended. Tight-knit communities were always wary of outsiders.

"We need to have some kind of lighthearted conversation. So we look normal, not like vultures waiting for our prey."

He huffed a laugh. "Fair visual. Fine. What are your hobbies?"

"Don't have any." No time.

"All right. I suppose you're too busy taking care of Bruxa's Eye."

"Nailed it. Not that you'd know anything about that. Loyalty isn't exactly your thing." She kept her gaze focused on the crowd. If she looked at him, she was afraid he'd see how much that hurt her. The barb had sounded acidic, but it tasted bitter.

"I'd like it to be. With you."

"Don't exactly have that choice, now do you? You're stuck. A warlock. Can you even—"

Her words stopped when a woman walked through the door. Young and pretty, with golden hair and a red dress, she was alone. Her gaze went straight to Sofia and she walked toward them, her stride intent.

"Women, too?" Malcolm asked.

"I'm not a homophobe." Sofia smiled at the woman as she neared.

"May I?" The blonde asked. Her tone was slightly confused, as if she wanted to sit near Sofia, but she wasn't quite sure why. But she didn't even glance at Malcolm. The spell was working.

"I'd be delighted," Sofia said.

Kitty had smartly arranged herself in the seat next to Sofia, so the woman sat next to Malcolm.

"I'm Caroline," Sofia said. "What's your name?"

"Lucy." Her blue eyes were riveted to Sofia.

Out of the corner of her eye, Sofia saw Malcolm slip the cuff off, then reach up and touch the woman's temple. He quickly slipped it back on and glanced around. Sofia did as well, but no one looked at them. He'd been quick enough that they hadn't noticed his power when the cuff was off. It would have felt like electrical tension, or a tickling on the skin, to be near someone as powerful as he for the first time. But they felt nothing, thank fates.

"Lucy, look at me." Malcolm's voice was low and commanding.

She looked his way immediately.

"What are you? fae?" he asked.

She nodded and slipped her hand into her hair, drawing it back. A pointed ear showed.

"What sort?"

"Melusine."

"Water fae?"

"Yes."

Good. They were powerful, but not overly so. Sofia doubted their new friend would be able to break Malcolm's enchantment or remember it if he told her not to.

"Are you meeting anyone here?" Malcolm asked.

"Yes. But I'm early."

"How early?"

"About thirty minutes."

"Do you know anything about the Salem Coven?" Malcolm's voice had dropped so low it was nearly a whisper.

"Some."

"How many are there?"

Lucy's brow crinkled. "Thirteen, I think."

"All right. Good. Are any here right now?"

"No," Lucy said immediately.

"Where do they live?"

"Near the shore. By the park. Halibut point. The land is enchanted so mortals can't see it. Some Mytheans can't either. But when I'm in the water, my vision is better." She shivered. "It's terrifying."

"Are there any patterns to their movement? Do they ever leave the house?"

"No pattern that I've noticed, but I don't go close very often."

"Good. Can you take us there?"

"But I'm meeting my friend tonight. He'll come looking for me."

"Tomorrow, then."

"Yes, I think so. As long as I'm in the water. That's the only way I can find it. And where my vision is best."

"Excellent. We'll meet you at Salem Harbor. We'll be in a boat."

"All right. But we need to do it at night. I can't let them see me." Her eyes went a bit wild with fear.

"Of course, Lucy. Of course. We'll meet you an hour before dusk at the marina. Then you'll take us."

"All right."

"Thank you, Lucy. If you're asked, you thought you recognized us. You were wrong. We're just here on vacation. We'll see you tomorrow."

She nodded and stood, still slightly dazed, but it was only visible if you knew to look.

"That was good," Sofia said.

"It was. Let's go."

She followed him out into the cold night air, Kitty at her heels.

"We'll head back to my house," he said.

"Shouldn't we get a hotel? Scotland is far." The magical energy required to aetherwalk that distance was pretty large. It'd take her nearly a day to recoup and she'd rather have it on hand for spells and the like.

"Distance doesn't matter for me. I'll aetherwalk and take you with me."

Of course. He could recoup whatever he spent directly and immediately from the aether.

"Fine." She didn't want to wander the streets looking for a hotel anyway. She held out a hand.

He ignored it and pulled her into his arms. His warmth suffused her immediately. The strength of his arms was impossible to ignore, as was the hardness of his chest. Her annoyance at his heavy-handedness made it easy to stifle her sigh of pleasure.

Sofia glanced down to see Kitty pressed up against Malcolm's leg. A second later, they stood in his library. The fire was bright and cozy and she broke free of his embrace to rush toward it.

She soaked in the warmth as she rubbed her arms, grateful that the fire was enchanted to burn continuously.

Kitty had sprawled out on the floor and was trying to toast her belly.

"I'll get us something to eat. You can stay there. Get warm."

She glanced over her shoulder to see him leaving the room. He'd bring her food while she waited in front of the fire? That was nice. Was he taking her words to heart?

Or was she crazy for seeing kindness where there was only more machinations?

Idiot. It didn't matter how nice he was about the little things. He'd stolen her dagger. Kidnapped her. When it had counted, he'd left her. He'd chosen power over anything they could ever have together. That choice made it impossible for them to have a future. So what did it matter if he cooked for her and saved her from danger?

He returned ten minutes later with three heavy bowls full of fragrant stew. He handed one to her and put one on the floor for Kitty.

"Thanks." She inhaled. Fates, this was just what she wanted after a long day. She ignored him and went to a big chair that sat to the right of the fire. It enveloped her in heavenly softness and she ate while staring into the fire. Kitty made contented purring and snarfing noises at her feet.

Malcolm took the chair across from her, but she ignored him.

CHAPTER EIGHT

Malcolm watched Sofia eat, entranced by the way the firelight gleamed on her skin and hair. She was so bloody beautiful.

And so pissed off at him.

This wasn't going to be easy.

He realized that he'd forgotten his stew and started eating. He barely tasted it as his gaze continuously returned to Sofia. When she finished, he took her bowl and his own to the kitchen. By the time he got back to the library, she was standing up to leave.

"We should plan what we'll do tomorrow," he said.

"What's there to plan? You'll get us a boat. We'll leave from the nearest port. And we have all day tomorrow to sort that out."

She was right. But he wanted an excuse to spend time with her. Just being near her after so long filled a dark hole in his chest. He knew he was botching this—she was right, kidnapping was no way to woo a woman—but it was the only hand he knew how to play.

He went to the whisky sitting on the far shelf and poured two glasses, then brought one to her.

"I didn't say I wanted that." Her gaze met his as he held it out.

"I thought you might like it."

"I don't."

"You like whisky." She had once, at least. "And it's an excellent vintage. Made by Cadan Trinovante's distillery."

Her brows rose in interest. So she'd heard of the Mythean who owned a distillery and made the best whisky in Scotland.

"Fine." She took it and sipped, her lids lowering in pleasure. "It's not bad."

His gaze was riveted to her. "Not at all."

Being with her again confirmed for him that Sofia was what he wanted. He'd missed her. More than he'd even known.

But all those lost years... And all the things that could never be now that he was a warlock.

His fist tightened on the crystal tumbler. He reigned in his strength before he shattered it and directed his gaze toward the fire.

He couldn't let her go, but he couldn't have her fully, either. The flame flickered before his eyes. It would take only a wave of his hand to extinguish it. Just as it would only take him falling in love with Sofia to end things between them.

Fate would know. It always did. How could it not? It was everything. Past, present, future. It saw all. And he'd seen what had happened to Oliver and Laira. That wouldn't be them.

"When do you plan to let me go?" she asked. "The problem with my village has distracted me from your creepy kidnapping, but I haven't forgotten."

"I don't know." He couldn't let her go. But she was too strong to hold onto forever. Not when all he could do was fuck her. He could give her pleasure, but little else. Without love, she wouldn't stay.

But ignoring his need for her had gotten him nowhere.

It was time to craft a new fate. One in which he managed this situation, his feelings, and kept himself far enough apart from her that he could keep her without fate taking her away. If all he could have was sex and the occasional conversation, he'd take it.

But he'd have to be careful. He was half in love with her as it was. If he fell all the way, it'd be over.

"Why did you trap me with you? Not that I couldn't get away if I really wanted to. But I do need your help. Which I hate."

"Because I want you."

Her gaze blazed as she looked at him. "It doesn't matter if you want me. You made it so that we could never be together. And you got me into this mess. I'm not exactly feeling kindly toward you at the moment. Nor have I for the last four hundred years."

"You'll get over it."

Rage lit in Sofia's chest as she watched Malcolm. It heated her from the inside and made her fingertips tingle to shoot lightning at him. He was such a bastard. He thought he could have whatever the hell he wanted—including her.

"I've had enough." She set her glass on the hearth and walked toward the door.

"We're not done." His voice was a command.

At the desk, she spun around. "What the hell do you mean?"

"Exactly what it sounded like. I'll take my favor now." His golden eyes roved over her hungrily.

"What?"

"The favor you promised in exchange for my help."

"Jesus. It's going to be just like the last one, isn't it? Well, I'm not having any of it." She turned to go, but before she could move a step, he was in front of her, trapping her against the desk.

That damned desk. Out of the corner of her eye, she saw Kitty leave the room.

"I want you." His golden gaze blazed as he loomed over her.

Heat bloomed in her belly and she hated herself. She wanted him. Gods dammit, she was an idiot. But she couldn't help it. Visions of him touching her flashed through her mind. The memory of last night made heat streak through her. Everything tingled.

She forced the thoughts away and demanded, "What, your favor is sex? You're making me have sex with you in exchange for your help?"

He sucked in a harsh breath and clenched his fists, his gaze darkening with desire. "No. I'm making you do this."

His hands were on her shoulders in an instant, spinning her so that she faced the desk and looked into the darkened room beyond. The wood bit into the front of her hips. He pressed hot and hard against her back, a muscular wall that trapped her. His erection pressed into her spine. A brand.

Fear and desire pulsed through her.

She hated it, but the craving was there. Strong. Pulling at her. The memory of last night only fueled it.

He was big, and dangerous, and strong. And she wanted him.

"As much as I want to have sex with you—to be inside you—" his voice roughened at her ear, "I won't make you do anything to me. I'm not that much of a bastard. I just want to touch you."

Just touch her? But why?

His arms came around her, one wrapping around her hip and the other around her shoulders. Her breath caught in her throat.

"And if I don't let you?" Fear continued to push her desire higher. What was wrong with her?

"Then I won't consider helping you." His lips were so close to her neck that she swore he kissed her.

She shuddered hard, knowing he could feel it.

"Yes. Okay." It was almost an easy decision. It was a bad idea and the only way out. And she wanted it even as she trembled with a strange combination of need and distress.

He groaned softly, the sound reverberating against her skin and sending a frisson of pleasure across her nerves. She stared blindly into the dimly lit library, her senses heightened to insane precision.

When he ran his lips gently down her neck, she dug her fingers into the wooden desk, trying to control her spiraling thoughts.

"Bloody hell, you smell good," he rasped. His lips pressed against her neck, then he bit.

She stifled a cry of pleasure.

"Your skin is so soft." He ran his tongue along the tightened tendon at the side of her neck and she shuddered. "I've wanted to touch you for so long. Dreamed of it."

Malcolm squeezed her shoulder and hip, crushing her to him as he bit her earlobe. A small spike of pain, then a large streak of pleasure.

"The things I want to do to you." His voice was almost a growl, the need so clear. He grasped a handful of her hair and tilted her head to speak at her ear. "I want to bend you over this desk and fuck you so thoroughly that you know you're mine. I want to feel your pussy squeeze my cock, know how tight you get when you come."

She whimpered, her mind a haze of confusion. She wanted that too. "No."

He bit her shoulder a bit too hard. "Not yet, maybe. But I'll take what I can get. Gladly." His hands went to the hem of her shirt and he began to tug it upward. "Raise your arms."

She shivered as cool air kissed her stomach, as the heat of his hands brushed her ribcage. "No."

"Raise them."

She did. Because deep down, she wanted to. She wanted to see what he would do if she succumbed to his desire to touch her. Years ago, he'd kissed her. Touched her breasts. But he'd been a different man. A kinder, gentler man.

This man was cold. Hard. He took what he wanted through coercion or force. He'd only do the things he wanted. Would he squeeze her breasts too roughly, pull at her nipples?

She'd had some good encounters and some bad since she'd left him. Where would this one fall?

The shirt came over her head quickly. His big hands were deft at the back clasp of her bra. She reached up to press the scrap of silk to her breast.

"Don't fight me," he rasped, tugging the material free.

She lowered her hands back to the desk, trying to pulverize the wood with her fingertips. She felt his head over hers, bent to take in the view of her breasts.

"So lovely," he said. His big hands came up to clasp her aching flesh. His palms were rough and hard against her. So delicious that she dropped her head back and moaned.

He massaged her breasts, pinching her nipples just hard enough to make her gasp.

"Fuck yes," he groaned as he ground his cock against her back. "You like that."

She bit her lip, not wanting to give him the satisfaction of confirming it.

"I want to lick these nipples. To bite them. To make you come with just my mouth on your breasts."

She whimpered. "Not possible."

"Perhaps." His hand slid lower, down the expanse of her stomach to the waistband of her jeans.

Did he really intend to—

He flicked open the first button, then began to tug the zipper down. She jerked in his arms, trying to break away, but it only pressed her harder against his cock.

He groaned and bucked his hips against her.

"You can fight me. But I warn you, I'll like it," he rasped at her ear.

Her first instinct was to shudder with desire. The second was to stiffen in fear.

His hand stilled on her zipper. His breath rasped. "If I must stop, zap me with your power. But the terms still stand."

Meaning he wouldn't help her with the witches. But also that he wouldn't force her to have sex with him.

He was ruthless.

And he wanted her.

She said nothing, holding her breath and waiting to see what he would do. The zipper hissed as he drew it down. Her heart pounded.

"Gods, I've wanted this. I've fucked my own fist countless times, all while thinking of you. What you would feel like. Smell like. Taste like." He wedged his big hand into her panties. Her jeans pressed him tight against her flesh.

"Fuck, you're wet." One big finger pressed between the lips of her sex, an invasion that made her knees weaken. It just pressed him deeper. His hand on her breast and the one cupping her sex kept her upright.

How far would he take this? What did he mean by *touching*? Everywhere, it seemed, from the way his hips rocked against her back and his fingers left no fold untouched.

"More," he rasped, his voice almost wild with need. He gently pulled his hand free and pushed her pants down to her knees.

She stood frozen, almost entirely naked with him fully clothed behind her. Trapping her.

Her breath began to saw in and out of her lungs.

When his heavy hand came to rest on her upper back, she almost breathed a sigh of relief.

Then he began to push.

115

"What are—"

"Bend over," he said, pressing harder.

"What? But we're not having—"

"Bend over." His voice was hard with need, the pressure of his hand greater than her strength.

She lowered herself to the desk, her heart racing and her pussy throbbing. The wood was cool against her breasts. Her legs were closed, so he couldn't see anything, but—

He used one foot to nudge her knees apart and her heart threatened to beat its way out of her chest. Cool air kissed her sex. Kissed everything.

Her face burned. She should get up. She should call this quits. Any moment he would undo his zipper. Then she'd be trapped against a desk with an immensely powerful warlock who could do whatever he wanted to her.

She'd just started to push herself up off the desk, to fight the pressure of his hand on her back, when he dropped to his knees behind her.

What the hell?

He groaned low in his throat. "Beautiful."

He had to be looking at her. Her cheeks burned.

She trembled uncontrollably as something brushed against her upper thigh. His cheek? She'd never felt so exposed. She strained her senses in the darkness, trying to figure out what he was doing.

She cried out when she felt the press of his lips against her upper thigh. Then higher. And higher still.

When the heat of his tongue swiped across her pussy, she almost passed out from the shock and pleasure.

So bloody sweet.

This was everything he'd waited for. Everything he'd wanted. Malcolm's cock throbbed unbearably, desperate to break free of its confines and plunge into the tight, wet heat of Sofia's pussy.

He licked her slick flesh again, seeking the exotic flavor. Her scent made his head spin. Bloody hell, he'd dreamed of this. He wanted to fuck her, to feel her clench around him, but he wanted this just as much. To learn every inch of her— what made her moan, what made her writhe, what made her come.

He couldn't believe he'd lived without this for so long. That he'd let other men taste her like this, know her like this.

Though her pussy was wet and her desire scented the air, she was tense against his mouth. It wouldn't do. He wanted her to like this as much as he did, even if he'd been a bastard about getting his way.

He ran his palms up her thighs, marveling at the smoothness of her skin. His thumbs parted her flesh and he leaned back slightly, gazing at the lovely pinkness of her.

She was slick and soft and so small he was terrified he'd hurt her. If he ever got to sink his shaft into her, he'd spend ages preparing her. He'd make her come until she was begging for his cock.

The thought made his shaft grow unbearably harder.

Sofia jerked in his hands as if she didn't like him looking at her, but he tightened his grip, entranced by the way his big fingers pressed into her lush flesh.

"Shh," he murmured, then pressed his mouth against her pussy, running his tongue through her folds and exploring every inch of her.

When he found her clit, she jumped. Gods, he'd never get enough of this. He licked, slowly and leisurely—getting to know her. Her moans drifted through the room, making his cock throb. He wanted more of her moans. Louder. More desperate.

Malcolm began to lick more quickly, focusing on the bundle of nerves until she pressed her hips against his face in a steady rhythm. He groaned against her, loving her greediness.

"Malcolm!" she gasped when he sucked on her clit. Her muscles tensed.

She was close.

He pulled back, swiping his tongue against the expanse of her pussy.

"I was—" she cut off her complaint, as if she didn't want to reveal the weakness.

Too late.

He wanted her to come so hard she lost her mind. There'd been men before him, he was sure. She was over four hundred years old. Of course there had been. But he'd erase them. The best way to do that was to hold off her orgasm until she was desperate.

And if he were honest with himself, he wanted to drown in her taste forever.

She was shaking with need by the time he thrust his tongue into her channel. Her taste was strongest here and he lapped it up, unable to stop his hips from thrusting at the air. He gripped her soft ass, learning her curves.

Gods, how he wished it were his cock plunging deep. He wanted her taste on his tongue while her tight little pussy gripped his shaft. He'd plow into her until she screamed, until she begged him to fuck her harder.

He dragged his tongue free and returned to her clit. He waited until she was fucking his face again, her cries growing more desperate, then he dragged his tongue up, savoring the slickness of her soft flesh.

"I want you to come on my face, Sofia," he growled against her. "I want to feel your wetness slide down my chin and know that I did that to you. I want to taste you and feel you and own you."

She moaned and he wished he could see her face. He returned to her clit, laving as he moved one hand to her entrance. Though he'd thought to thrust his fingers into her while sucking her clit, he realized that he had to see some part of him enter her.

He pulled his face back to look. His fingers were so big and rough compared to the smooth slickness of her pussy. His cock throbbed and his breath caught in his throat as he watch two wide fingers press against her, forcing her flesh to give way and disappearing into her channel. The firelight shone golden on her skin, highlighting the deep pink of her labia as his fingers sank deeper.

Her groan came long and loud as her tender flesh adjusted to the invasion. He feared he was too big, that he'd been greedy and started with too many, but she pressed back against him, begging for more. She wouldn't beg with words, but her body would.

Slowly, he thrust his fingers deep, groaning at the feeling of her closing tight around him.

"Malcolm, Malcolm." Her words were senseless, as if she weren't entirely there.

"You're so damned hot. Wet. Perfect," he said as he began to thrust his fingers.

He placed his thumb on her clit and began to rub in tight circles, concentrating on making her come. He was desperate to see her that way.

She keened high in her throat and began to grind her hips into his hand, trying to get him deeper.

Insatiable. It made his cock throb painfully and fantasies roll through his head. He pressed his fingertips down, rubbing hard against the pad of nerves inside of her.

She stiffened and her legs began to tremble. A cry wrenched from her throat and her interior muscles began to clasp on his fingers.

"Fuck, I can see you clenching." The words tore from his throat. It was the hottest thing he'd ever seen, watching her pussy react to the pleasure he gave her. Desperate to taste her again, he moved his thumb and pressed his mouth against her clit, laving and sucking.

She tried to jerk away, as if she were too sensitive, but there was nowhere for her to go. She whimpered, but after a second pressed back against him for more.

When her pussy began clenching again, squeezing him for her pleasure, he couldn't take it anymore. The taste, the feel. The knowledge that it was Sofia.

He couldn't fucking take it anymore. With his free hand, he tore his fly open and grasped his hard cock. He groaned against her and she cried out.

His cock was so hard it hurt. All he could imagine was her heat, her tightness, wrapped around his shaft. He began to stroke, roughly because he'd used all his control on her, on moving his fingers in a way that would get her off.

Gods, how he wanted to pull his fingers free of her sweet heat and rise to his feet. He jerked his cock and licked her clit as the fantasy rolled through him.

He would grasp her full hips in his hands, pressing his fingers into her golden skin. She might try to get away at first, to fight him. But he'd hold her hips tight and calm her fears. He's smooth a hand down her back, rub her sensitive little clit, until she was begging for it.

Then he'd fit the head of his cock to her tight entrance and push, watching her pussy give way and close around him. He'd grip one of her slender shoulders to keep her in place as he drove his thick cock into her pussy. He could imagine her pinkness enveloping his dusky shaft, the way she'd shudder and moan as she accepted him.

If she asked him to go slowly, to give her time to adjust, he'd manage. Somehow. He'd sooth her and take his time, but once she was desperate for it, once she wanted it hard, he'd give it to her. He'd grip her shoulder and her hip and fuck her until her hot little pussy clenched around him and she moved her hips backward, trying to get more of his cock.

Malcolm groaned against her pussy, thrusting his fingers inside her as he imagined her coming around his cock. He'd give her anything she bloody wanted.

"Malcolm!" She was coming again, harder than ever, her cunt gripping him tightly.

He began to fuck his fist, clenching it as tightly as he thought her pussy would, imagining that he was thrusting into her. Making her writhe on his cock and soak him with her juices.

Malcolm roared against her pussy as the orgasm slammed into him. It tore through his entire body, pleasure so intense he felt like he might explode. He shuddered and shook as his cock jerked in his hand, pumping seed onto the floor.

Her muscles still clenched his fingers as his orgasm faded. When her cries and the movement of her hips stopped, he gently pulled his fingers free and gave her pussy one last lick, savoring her taste.

His breath heaved in and out of his lungs as he watched her back rise and fall with her heaving breaths. Her pussy gleamed pink and tender. Gods, he hoped he hadn't been too rough.

He'd die before he hurt her that way. He'd die before he let anything bad happen to her. But it wouldn't. He'd see to it. He'd protect her.

His spend gleamed white on the floor. A possessive part of him wished that it coated her slick flesh, a brand of possession that marked her as his.

His chest tightened.

Shit. This was dangerous. He could actually feel the soft thoughts forming. He'd loved her once.

He couldn't let that happen again. Love was a vow, even if unspoken.

A warlock couldn't afford vows.

Fate would always break them.

He stumbled to his knees, yanking his trousers up. He waved his hand at the floor and a bit of magic removed his spend.

Sofia lay on the desk, her muscles lax as she caught her breath. So beautiful it made him clench his fists.

Fuck, if this wasn't going to be harder than he thought. With a last glance at her, he left the room.

CHAPTER NINE

The door slammed, startling Sofia out of her daze. She glanced up.

Malcolm was gone.

Quivery pleasure that had weakened her muscles turned to rage. He'd *left* her? She scrambled up and tugged on her clothes, fumbling with her shirt and trousers.

He'd just...*walked out.*

Tears pricked her eyes. She blinked them away, trying to focus on the anger. This was the second time she'd ended up on his desk, coming to her senses and realizing that he didn't give a shit about her. He might spend his time making her come, but then he discarded her.

How dare he?

Rage seethed in her chest, a black tar that threatened to boil over and choke her. She stormed out of the room and down the hall, then took the stairs two at a time. At the top, she glanced left and then right, toward the doors at the end. Because fates knew, he'd be at the end of the freaking hall.

The door at the end of the left hall was cracked slightly, so she went that way. When she reached it, she shoved the heavy wood open so hard it slammed against the wall.

Malcolm spun away from the window to face her. He stood in the middle of a richly appointed round room. Another tower, like his library. All dark, gleaming wood and elegant furnishings.

"What are you—"

She drew her wand and threw a blast of lightning at him. He threw up a hand and blocked it.

"You bastard!" she screamed, then threw another bolt. This one made him stumble back. "You treat me like a fucking sex toy and then toss me away and I'm sick of it!"

Surprise flashed in his golden gaze. "What? I don't—"

"Yes. You. Do. Twice now! And four hundred years ago I was obviously nothing to you. Just like I'm nothing now. Just a thing for you to play with. You risked my life and everything that I hold dear just so you can play with me!" Hot tears burned her eyes and she hated it. She threw a blast of frozen air at him, hoping it would freeze his heart like he'd frozen hers. The tears tumbled free.

Something like pain flashed in his eyes and he was in front of her a second later. He grabbed her arms and pulled her toward him.

She thrashed, trying to break free. "Let go of me, you bastard! I hate you!"

"Don't say that." His voice was rough with pain, his gaze rife with it.

She stilled momentarily, shocked.

"What is your problem?" she whispered brokenly. "Why, after all these years, are you doing this to me?"

125

He shuddered. "Because these last centuries without you have been hell. You're the sun of my life. I didn't realize what I was giving up when I became a warlock. You were the brightest and best thing to ever happen to me and I couldn't spend another day without you."

Shock made her breath catch. He'd been such a bastard to her. "But you threw me away."

"I had to."

"Fuck you." She struggled to break free again, but he was too strong.

"Look at me." His voice was harsh, desperate.

She didn't want to, but she did. And fates, he was handsome. Not in a movie-star way—though gods knew he could pass for one—but in a familiar way. The kind of handsome that happens when you've loved someone for years and have memorized all their features until they become vital to you. The kind of handsome that really mattered. It was a view that tore a gaping hole in her heart.

"You threw me away." She wanted to crumble into his arms—for him to make it better even though she knew he never could. He'd broken them. Broken them and thrown them away and there was no coming back from that.

But he pulled her into his embrace and hugged her close. His heat and strength enveloped all of her, knitting together some of her broken parts even though she'd thought he couldn't do that.

"I made a mistake." His agonized whisper sounded against her hair. "I made a mistake. I realized that soon after."

"Why wait till now to come for me?"

"I fought it. Until I saw my brother with his new mate and realized what a great, gaping hole there was in my life. I thought I had everything a Mythean could want. Power, wealth. But I made a mistake. I'm so sorry, Sofia."

She sobbed against his chest. He was saying everything she wanted to hear, but too late. "What good does that do us now?"

"I don't know. I just know I can't live without you anymore."

"You're going to have to," she whispered against his chest. But she clutched his sweater in her hands and didn't move. She couldn't move and didn't want to move. She wanted to freeze like this forever. This was the closest she'd ever get to what she wanted—him—and she didn't want it to end. But it was a dark comfort, tainted by the knowledge of what he'd done to them.

"I can't. But I'm fucking this up. I didn't leave tonight because I think of you as an object. I left because I'm afraid I'm falling in love with you again. I'm afraid I never fell out of love with you."

Her heart felt like it was tearing into a million pieces. She spoke into his chest because she couldn't look up. "You didn't ever love me. If you'd loved me, you wouldn't have become a warlock. You'd have sacrificed that. As I did. Because I loved you." But she didn't love him anymore. She had too much self-respect for that. But for just a minute, she wanted to cling to the idea of what might have been. So she held onto him.

"I think I'm falling for you now," he said. "And the only way we can have anything is if I don't do that. I need to keep my heart separate. That's why I left."

She looked up at him then, shocked to see the pain in his eyes. "So that's what this relationship has in store for me if I choose to pursue it? You'll never love me, and whenever you feel too much, you'll throw me away?" She pulled out of his arms. "I'm sorry, but that's not good enough for me. And if you do fall for me, I'll end up like Laira. Dead. Or you'll end up dead. Or both of us. Because fate will have its way."

This was done. Her moment of weakness must be crushed. She stepped back and walked toward the door.

"Sofia." His voice broke at the end.

She didn't want to, but she turned.

"I'm sorry." His voice was rough, his face so pained it almost looked broken. "I'm sorry for how I've fucked this up. But I'll make it better."

She swallowed hard against the tears. "You can't."

She turned and walked out the door.

"Fuck," Malcolm hissed when the skillet burned his hand. He blew on it, then grabbed a spatula and flipped the pancake.

Black.

A disgusted sigh escaped him. This was a stupid idea. Even if he could manage to make a decent plate of pancakes, it was still a stupid idea.

Sofia had been right last night. He'd fucked up beyond redemption. Giving her up was the hardest thing he'd ever done. He'd never thought of his actions as throwing her away, but she clearly did. When he thought of it from her perspective, she had a point.

And making her pancakes wasn't going to fix that. Though he wanted to make things better, he couldn't fix what was really wrong. He was a warlock. A real relationship was out of the question. After everything he'd done to her…

Just the thought of her tears last night tore a hole in his chest. Gods, he'd been a bastard. When had he turned into this?

And if these pancakes were any indication, he didn't know how to claw his way back to worthiness. Sofia didn't deserve someone like him.

The only problem was, he didn't know how he'd give her up.

"What are you doing?" Sofia's sleep-roughened voice sounded from behind him.

He turned. "Making you burned pancakes."

Her brows rose. "Why?"

"Because I'm trying to not be an asshole."

"This is sort of like giving someone a band aid for an amputation." She walked to a cupboard near the dining nook and pulled down a coffee cup and some coffee. "But if you turn this into something drinkable, I'll consider eating your pancakes."

Jesus, she was going to make him suffer. But he deserved it. And she was right. His pancakes were barely a band aid. He made her coffee, then returned to the pancakes.

"You don't just want to use magic?" she asked as he poured more batter.

He looked at her. "I feel like I ought to do this the real way, even if it takes a little longer."

"Those look terrible, and even if they weren't, it wouldn't make any difference."

"Maybe it will." He was quicker with the spatula this time and the pancakes turned out all right. He plated them and brought them to her, along with maple syrup.

"For me?" she asked.

He nodded, then set them on the table.

She didn't say anything as she sat, but she did eat the pancakes.

It'd still been a stupid idea, but the sight of her eating what he'd made filled one of the many small holes in his heart. He returned to the counter and waved a hand over the ingredients, making a quick plate for himself.

He sat at the table and began to eat.

"How will we get a boat?" Sofia asked. Her eyes looked tired, as if she hadn't slept well, and he wanted to punch himself. He was a bastard. He'd always known it, but now that he was actually seeing the results of it…

He didn't like it.

"I'll go up, see if we can rent one," he said. "If not, I can conjure one. Though that's a bit more complicated. It'd take quite a bit of magic to make something that large and complex and would leave me drained. I'd need to refill my power from my aether room, and that's not convenient."

"All right. When do you want to leave?"

"An hour or two shall be fine."

"I'll go with you." She turned back to her food. He waited for her to mention last night, but when she didn't, his shoulders relaxed. Actions over words. He'd just have to prove to her that he valued her. That he was sorry.

But how he would do that, he had no idea.

Two hours later, he aetherwalked them to the harbor in Salem. The day was clear and bright. Even the boats were decorated for Halloween. These American mortals couldn't get enough of the holiday. It took them an hour, but they found a Mythean captain who was willing to rent out his boat for the night.

When it came time to pay, Sofia just looked at him. He paid the exorbitant fee gladly. He wouldn't get off so lightly as to be able to buy back her affection, but he'd have happily paid for everything anyway. Money was not an issue. It was everything else that was the problem.

"Now what?" Sofia asked. She stood on the dock, bundled in her warm coat with Kitty at her side. "We've got another three hours until we meet Lucy."

"Do you want to check on your village? I can take you there." He knew she wouldn't waste the magical energy herself, but he had more than enough to spare.

"Really?"

"Yes."

"All right." She held out her hand.

Though he wanted to yank her into his arms, he just took it. Once Kitty had pressed herself up against his leg, he focused on an image of the main street of Bruxa's Eye and aetherwalked them there.

He opened his eyes to see Sofia transform herself into her Crone form. She added a pointed witch hat for good measure. Though she looked vastly different, he still recognized her by the color of her eyes and the slant of her cheekbones.

"Let's go. I'll check in with my friend Aleia. She keeps an eye on things when I'm not around."

"Aleia? The seer?" She was the most powerful in the world. Even he'd heard of her.

"One and the same."

She led him down the boardwalk that ran along one side of the street. Kitty trotted happily at her side. The jungle was sweltering this time of day, so he stripped out of his warm jacket. He'd been here several times over the years, wanting to contact Sofia but knowing she'd just turn him away.

It wasn't that dissimilar to Salem Hollow. The buildings were about three stories high and had more of a Wild West jungle feel to them. Dozens of Mytheans made their way along the boardwalk, many of whom wouldn't pass in the mortal world.

Sofia turned into a doorway nook near the apothecary and knocked on the door. He stopped behind her. A moment later, a dark-haired woman with round cheeks opened the door. The stairs behind her led up to what he presumed was her flat.

Her face lit when she saw Sofia, and she pulled her into a hug. "You're back! Damn it, I thought something had happened to you!"

"It did," Sofia said. She hiked a thumb back at him. "This bastard fucked everything up. And kidnapped me."

"Asshole." Aleia glowered at him. "Come on in. But should he stay outside? I can put out a bowl of water for him."

"I won't be separated from her." Malcolm's voice was hard.

Sofia looked back at him. "No, it's fine."

"All right." Aleia stepped back and let them in. They all went to the kitchen.

"I'm only back for a few minutes," Sofia said. "I just wanted to know if anything weird has happened while I've been gone."

"Actually, yes. A witch with immense power visited yesterday. She didn't speak to anyone. She just walked down the main street. By the time she got to the end, she was smiling. Everyone could feel her power. The kind that makes the skin tingle, you know?"

"I know." Sofia's voice was dull. "Shit."

"It was one of the High Witches, wasn't it?" Aleia asked.

Sofia nodded. Malcolm agreed.

"She's casing the joint," Sofia said. "We've got to bring them the Salem Coven's Grimoire or they'll destroy Bruxa's Eye."

"Damn."

"We'll get the book, Sofia."

She nodded. "Of course. Yes, we will." She turned to Aleia. "For now, tell me what else is going on."

Malcolm waited while they caught up on what was going on in town. He'd always known she was responsible for a lot here, but he'd had no idea how much. She kept the place in law and order. The people relied on her.

Finally, she turned to him. "Let's go. It's nearly time to meet Lucy."

Sofia said goodbye to Aleia, then he aetherwalked them back to the interior of the boat they'd rented.

Sofia stepped out of Malcolm's arms, then used her wand to return to her normal appearance. Once she was dressed in her jeans and jacket, she climbed out to the cockpit. She needed some air.

Kitty meowed. She'd stay down below, or so it sounded.

All day, Malcolm had been making an effort not to be an asshole. It would take a hell of a lot more than pancakes and visits to her village—like him renouncing being a warlock, which wasn't possible—to make her forgive him.

But every time he did something thoughtful, her heart thawed just a little. It was still a giant chunk of ice, no question—but today had been a reminder of what he'd been like when they were younger. She'd fallen in love with him because he'd been kind and honorable.

Once those qualities were gone, her love had followed. It didn't matter how handsome he was.

But if he made an effort to be the man she'd once known?

That would be harder to resist, even though she knew it would end in heartbreak.

She scrubbed her hands over her face and muttered, "Get it together."

"Hello?"

Sofia's head jerked up.

Lucy strode down the dock, her blond hair blowing behind her in the wind. A pretty blue headband covered her pointed ears and highlighted her sapphire eyes. There was confusion in her gaze, identical to last night's. No doubt because of Malcolm's spell.

"Hi Lucy. Thanks for coming." She gestured the fae onboard.

"Thanks. I think."

Malcolm came up from the cabin and Lucy's gaze focused on him. Purpose filled her vision. "I'm here to help you find the Salem Coven's house." Confidence filled her voice. "Of course, I'd almost forgotten."

Forgotten? Not quite. Try *been brainwashed*.

"Thank you, Lucy." Malcolm took the keys out of his pocket and went to the helm of the sporty white speedboat. "Shall you swim or ride along?"

"I'll ride until we get close, then I'll get in the water. That will help me see better. The home is hidden from sight, but when I'm in the water, my magic and my senses are so much stronger. I can usually see through most enchantments."

"All right." Malcolm started the boat.

Sofia stepped forward. "I'll drive."

His brows rose.

"I live on the Amazon. Boats are kind of my thing."

"Fair enough." He handed her the keys.

She hadn't really expected him to give her the keys. He'd been so heavy-handed that she'd just assumed he'd tell her no. Then she'd have had to kick his ass.

All right, true enough, it had been a test. A little one. But he'd passed.

She cranked the keys and the engine roared to life.

She guided them carefully out of the marina and through the harbor. Large homes dotted the shore on all sides. As soon as they made it to open water, she cranked the throttle and the boat burst forth, speeding across the water.

Wind immediately bit through Sofia's jacket. She shivered violently, but couldn't stop the grin from stretching across her face. It froze her teeth, but she'd take that in exchange for the awesomeness of going fast on the water. Gods, she loved this.

The boat cut across the small waves, hardly bouncing at all. She headed north around the coast toward Halibut Point, the place Lucy had mentioned last night. The sun was nearly at the horizon. Dusk was falling.

"Tell me when we're getting near!" Sofia yelled over the engine and wind.

"All right!" Lucy kept her gaze locked on shore.

Sofia couldn't help but glance at Malcolm, but she tried to keep it at a minimum.

"You can stop here!" Lucy shouted.

Sofia cranked down on the throttle and they drifted to a stop. Waves rolled them lightly.

"All right, I'm getting in." Lucy stepped up onto the deck and jumped off, clothes and all.

When she surfaced, she'd changed entirely. Her skin was a pale blue and her hair a bright green. Weeds, Sofia realized. Brilliant seaweed.

"Follow me. I'll stay close to the surface. You should be able to see a bit of wake." She set off, darting through the water, setting off a ripple that spread outward.

"Keep an eye on her and direct me," Sofia said.

Malcolm nodded and Sofia started the boat. He held out his arm, leading her, changing it every so often when Lucy shifted direction.

Eventually, Lucy popped out of the water and waved an arm. They slowed to a halt beside her.

"There." She pointed toward shore. "That's the house."

Sofia squinted, but saw nothing. Damn, the Salem Coven was good. It was easy to hide a place or building from mortals. But from Mytheans? Damned hard.

"I see it," Malcolm said.

Sofia scowled, then pulled out her wand. She waved it in the direction of the land, focusing on her vision and clarity. The air shimmered, then a beautiful white house appeared. Two stories, with expansive decks and glittering windows.

Very different than the High Witches'.

"Thanks, Lucy," Sofia said.

"Not a problem. I think." Lucy rubbed her eyes with a pale blue hand.

"Can you drive a boat, Lucy?" Malcolm asked.

"Sure."

"Can you take this one back to the Marina? Leave the keys near the wheel?"

"No problem." She swam to the side of the boat, then heaved herself out. As soon as she was out of the water, her clothes returned. Her hair became blond and her skin pale.

"And you'll forget about us," Malcolm said. "You've never seen us."

She nodded.

Sofia handed her the keys, then turned to Malcolm. "We'll aetherwalk to the grounds outside, don't you think?"

"Yes. Better to do it a bit farther away in case they are able to sense an outsider aetherwalking onto their property. Then we'll walk there."

"Good. Kitty!" she called down into the cabin.

Kitty bounded up the steps and onto the deck, then pressed herself against Sofia's legs. Sofia held out a hand for Malcolm. He took it, then stepped so close that his body almost touched hers.

"I'll take us," he said.

"Okay." She tried to ignore his warmth.

A second later, they stood amongst the scrub brush on the shore to the south of the mansion. Sofia could make it out far in the distance. Juniper scented the air. She nodded at him and set off, heading toward a copse of trees farther from the shoreline. Kitty led the way.

"Let's keep to these," she said. "They'll provide a bit of cover and we can try to break in through a side door."

Malcolm nodded, then kept close beside her as they crept along the edge of the forest. They neared the house. Lights were blazing from most of the windows. Crows sat upon the roof. Dozens of them. Perhaps hundreds.

"Strange," Sofia breathed. She'd never seen anything like the crows. With the dark sea roiling behind the house, it painted an eerie picture.

They reached the edge of the trees, but there was still at least fifty yards between them and the house.

"Do you think those crows will send up an alarm if they see us crossing the grass to the house?" Sofia asked.

"Possibly. I've never seen anything like it. Animals are attracted to witches, but usually not so many of one species."

A door opened at the side of the house.

CHAPTER TEN

Sofia held her breath as she watched the door.

A woman walked out. She had short, messy dark hair and wore jeans and a t-shirt. She dug something out of her pocket. Cigarettes. She raised one to her mouth as she set off across the lawn. She lit it and headed for the water. No familiar followed her, which was strange.

"Will your mind control work on her? We could get information from her. But I've got to assume she's strong."

"It should. I'm stronger than any of them individually."

"So is it a good thing or a bad thing that she just walked out?" Did she smell a trap?

"Can't say. Could be a setup, but they couldn't know we were coming."

"It's so much easier to try to enchant one of them than sneak into the house. Maybe she'll walk far enough from the house that we can aetherwalk right to her. Then you pull your mind control thing."

Sofia watched, her breath held, as the woman strolled along the cliff edge that led down to the water. The nearly full moon lit her way. It was a lovely night for a stroll, though cold.

Perhaps this was legit.

Either way, they had to try.

"She's far enough away now. Let's go."

Sofia reached out and placed a hand on Malcolm's shoulder. Once Kitty had pressed herself up against Malcolm's leg, he took off his cuff and aetherwalked them to a spot right behind the woman.

She spun around, but before she could say anything or attack, he reached out and touched her temple.

Her wide eyes calmed and she stared at them.

"We're your friends," Malcolm said.

"Of course." Her voice was leaden.

"Who are you?" he asked.

"Inara."

"You're one of the Salem Coven?"

"Yes. The youngest."

"What do you know about the spell book?"

"Which one?"

"The most valuable, the one that other witches covet."

"Ah, the Grimoire. Yes, that one is valuable. It's protected, though."

"How so?" Malcolm asked.

"It's within a special room that is a portal to our afterworld. It's only accessible on All Hallows' Eve, when the barrier between the worlds is weakest. It's the best way to protect it. Only a Salem Witch who is a world walker can access our afterworld. Without dying, at least. And only on All Hallows' Eve."

"Tomorrow," Sofia whispered. No wonder the High Witches had told her to get the book now. But they needed a Salem Witch who was also a world walker. That would be hard, unless….

"Can you take us there tomorrow?"

"Yes. I'm one of the three who can walk across worlds. On years when we need the book, one of us goes to the room to retrieve it. It's never been me, though. I've only been part of the coven for fifty years."

"Do you need the book this year? Is anyone going to get it?"

"I don't think so."

"Then tomorrow, you'll get the book and bring it to us here."

"My magic isn't strong enough. I need someone to link me to this world while my soul goes to the afterworld to retrieve the book. Someone whose power equals my own."

Shit.

"We'll go with you," Malcolm said, his voice firm. "I can link your soul to this world. My power is equal to yours. We'll meet you here and you'll take us to the room. I'll help you get the book."

She nodded.

Unease skittered across Sofia's skin on little mice feet. This was too easy, wasn't it? What were the odds that a witch who could help them would walk out of the house right when they needed her to?

"Malcolm, ask her if she often walks outside to smoke. Or did she sense us?"

Malcolm repeated the question.

"I do come outside to smoke often, though I usually just sit on the stoop. But I sensed you in the forest. I walked to draw you close to me. Like wounded prey attracts a predator. I was ready for you. But I don't know why I didn't attack you. I always turn away outsiders. But there's something special about you." Confusion gleamed in her eyes.

How about, we enchanted you?

"I believe her," Sofia said.

"So do I. And my enchantment is working." Malcolm turned his attention back to Inara. "We'll meet you here tomorrow. Is there a certain time the barrier is weakest?"

"Midnight, of course."

"Then we'll meet you in the woods near your house at eleven pm. You won't mention us to anyone. You won't remember us until tomorrow, just before eleven."

Inara nodded. "Until tomorrow."

She turned and walked away.

"Let's get out of here," Sofia said. Though she didn't want to go back to his house, there wasn't an alternative. She was so far from her home and aetherwalking took so much energy that she needed to go with him. Actually....

"I want you to take me back to my village," she said.

"No." His voice was firm.

"Malcolm. Don't be such a heavy-handed asshole."

His brow creased. "Fine. I'll take you there, but you need to come somewhere with me first."

"What? Now?" It was past ten, which wasn't all that late, but she was beat.

"It should be now."

"Where?"

"To get more help. In case we fail tomorrow."

"Don't talk like that."

"It's not likely, but it's possible. We only have one of the coven on our side. There's a chance the High Witches have sent us on a suicide mission. But we can get around that with help."

"But who's more powerful than you? A god?"

"Corrier."

Sofia stepped back, surprised. "You'd take me to Corrier to ask for help? He must hate me. I left. I abandoned the opportunity he gave me." She hadn't even said goodbye that day when Malcolm had chosen becoming a warlock over her. She'd just run.

"You were his favorite pupil." Malcolm grasped her shoulders and she didn't move, desperate to hear what he had to say. "It broke his heart when you left. For a long time, he was angry. But he's softened. He'll help you."

Sofia shuddered at the thought. Her throat had that raw, trembly feeling that comes with the need to cry. She'd always loved Corrier, but she'd blocked out thoughts of him when she'd left the apprenticeship. She'd been horrified when she'd learned what he'd sacrificed to become a warlock. What he wanted her to sacrifice.

But now she had a chance to see him again? And Malcolm said he'd forgiven her?

Not that she had anything to be forgiven for, she reminded herself. But it was so hard to separate the reality of a situation from the longing of a student to make a favored professor proud.

"Okay," she said. "Take me there."

She held out a hand and he took it.

Nerves made goosebumps pop up on her skin as she waited for Kitty to press against Malcolm's legs and for him to transport them. She'd lost more than Malcolm when she'd turned away from becoming a warlock. Though Corrier hadn't been as important to her as Malcolm had, he'd been her most valued mentor. She'd grown to idolize him as she studied under him.

Now she would see him again.

A moment later, Sofia stood in a familiar valley. An enormous cliff rose in front of her, waterfalls pouring down their faces. Cold wind whipped across her cheeks as her boots crunched the snow.

Norway. After leaving, she'd never returned. She turned left, to where she knew Corrier's fortress would be. It grew out of the cliffside—gray stone, one with the mountain behind it.

"It hasn't changed," she said.

"No."

"Do you come back often?" she asked as they walked to the great wooden doors.

"No," Malcolm said. He opened his mouth, then shut it. Finally, he forced the words out. "I have complex feelings regarding Corrier. I wanted to be a warlock, but as a result, I lost you. I've been bitter."

"That's dumb."

"I know." They reached the huge door and he pounded on it.

They waited only a moment before it swung open. A tall woman stood at the threshold, her auburn hair gleaming in the golden light from the large foyer. An apprentice.

"We're here for Corrier," Malcolm said.

"May I ask who you are?" Her Irish accent was lilting.

"Step aside, Moira. I know who they are."

Moira stepped aside to reveal a familiar figure coming down the stairs. Tall and slender, Corrier's white hair stuck out at wild angles. His dark cloak fell back from his shoulders, revealing gray trousers and shirt beneath. The power that radiated off him made Malcolm's skin tingle. Corrier was the most powerful warlock in the world.

"Sofia." His voice was warm. "It's been centuries."

"It has." Warmth was buried beneath the hint of wariness in Sofia's voice.

Corrier looked at Malcolm. "The same goes for you."

His voice had chilled slightly, but Malcolm understood. Unlike Sofia, he'd completed his training. It was understood when a failed apprentice didn't return to see the mentor. There was no reason to. But warlocks didn't often stay away from their mentors for as long as Malcolm had. And three hundred years was a long time.

"I'm sorry, Corrier. But it's good to see you." He meant it. With Sofia now at his side, some of his bitterness had waned.

"Come, let's have a drink. When someone who's been away as long as you shows up, they normally want something. I'd like a drink for that."

They followed him down the hall to his study. It was so familiar. He could recall stolen moments with Sofia in this very hall. He clenched a fist, pushing the memories away.

They only served to confuse him. Make him regret his actions. Regret was weakness. He just had to go forward with the tools he had. He'd find a way to be with Sofia.

"Take a seat," Corrier said once they entered his cluttered study.

The room was large, but the number of bookshelves and tables made it feel much smaller. Leather-bound tomes and magical instruments littered the surfaces. The fire blazed in the hearth, sending a warm glow into the room.

"Tea?" Corrier asked.

They both nodded.

Corrier went to a table laid out with implements for making tea and waved his hand, producing three steaming mugs. He turned to them and held up a bottle of whisky.

"Absolutely," Sofia said.

"Thanks," Malcolm said.

Corrier poured, then brought them their drinks. Three mugs for them, a saucer for the cat. They sat in chairs in front of the fire. Kitty took up a position in front of the hearth. Malcolm's mind could so easily travel back in time to when they'd all sat here the first time. Even after Corrier had come into the room, he hadn't been able to keep his eyes off of Sofia. When he'd seen her commitment and intelligence, he'd been lost.

"What is it that you need? After three hundred years, people don't visit just to say hello." His tone was kind.

"I'm sorry, Corrier. I never thought to visit," Sofia said. "Though I valued what you taught me, the cost was too high."

"I understand." His gaze moved to Malcolm. "Can you say the same?"

Malcolm sighed. "Honestly, I can. The loss of Sofia proved to be too great."

He felt her gaze on him, but didn't look at her. Admitting these things… wasn't easy. But he had to learn to do so if he wanted to win her.

"That is the nature of the warlock. Sacrifice in all things. Such great power comes at a price."

"I now realize how great," Malcolm said.

"Then how can I be of service?" Corrier asked.

"We are potentially—likely—in some trouble," Malcolm said. He explained the problem with the witches. "So you can see, we need help."

Corrier sat back and steepled his fingers under his chin. "Hmm. That is not good. It's not possible to defeat the High Witches. Not when they fight as a group. Will they?"

"Yes," Malcolm said.

"And your best hope is retrieving the Salem Coven's Grimoire, but you'll have to enter their house to do so. If you fail, you will have to disband your village."

"Yes," Sofia said, her eyes dark with pain.

Corrier leaned forward. "Though I do not become involved in the affairs of my apprentices, I can make Sofia stronger. She is the weaker link—" his gaze met hers "—no offense intended my dear, but you didn't finish the training."

"I know. But become a warlock?" There was dread in her voice.

"No. That opportunity has past. But you have the training. You know how to handle immense power. What I can do is link you to Malcolm. When you are in trouble, he can transfer power to you through the aether."

"Won't that weaken him?"

Corrier met his gaze. "Yes, though only if he gave you more than he could afford to lose. But if you were both fighting for your lives and your magical energy ran low, it'd be safer if he could transfer power to you and you could both continue to fight."

"And he wouldn't have to jump in and save me." From the sound of her voice, Sofia liked that idea.

Malcolm sat back. Break up his power and share it with Sofia? He'd sacrificed everything for his power. Once, sharing it would have been out of the question. But it sounded like he'd have control of it. And Sofia needed it. "Yes. We'll do that."

"Hey! I haven't agreed," Sofia said.

"What's to agree to?" Malcolm asked. "You'll be twice as powerful. At least. With no downside, it sounds like."

Her brow creased and her gaze was thoughtful. "There's really no downside for me?"

"No. For Malcolm, yes. But not for you. You'll have to get a small tattoo, and when you're near Malcolm, you'll feel him, but those are minor," Corrier said.

"Feel him?"

Corrier nodded. "If you're within a couple hundred yards of each other, you'll be aware that he is there. But that's all. And it will be useful when you're fighting a battle together."

She nodded. "Okay, I'll do it. And thank you both."

Something loosened in Malcolm's chest. He'd been worried she wouldn't take the offer. But it would make her stronger. Safer. Now that she would be both, he relaxed a bit. It wasn't foolproof, but it was better than nothing. It'd give him more control, too. He hadn't known how Corrier would be able to help them, but he'd been certain they'd be better off if he agreed to assist them somehow.

"All right, then," Corrier said as he rose. "The first step is to link the two of you, the tattoos will be imbued with magic that will connect you and allow you to transfer magical energy to Sofia."

"I'll go first," Sofia said.

"You hold your wand with your right hand?"

"Yes."

"Then you'll get the tattoo on that arm." Corrier retrieved a feather quill from a shelf, then returned to stand in front of the fire.

Sofia rolled up her shirt sleeve. Corrier held out a hand and opened a small portal to the aether. It glowed bright white, an orb about a foot in diameter that floated about four feet off the ground. Corrier extended the feather quill until it touched the light and waited until it glowed.

Once it gleamed with magical energy, he withdrew it and turned to Sofia. She held her arm out, forearm facing up.

"Picture Malcolm in your head."

Sofia nodded and closed her eyes. She winced when Corrier pressed the quill to her skin, but held still as he drew.

When it was over, she sighed in relief and glanced at it. Surprise flashed in her gaze when she saw the tall, cloaked man on her inner arm.

Corrier turned to Malcolm. "The same for you now."

"My shoulder," Malcolm said as he stripped off his sweater.

"All right then. Picture Sofia."

Malcolm closed his eyes and did as Corrier requested. An image didn't form in his mind, though a feeling of her did. Is this what Sofia had felt? He was about to tell Corrier when the man said, "Good, good. That'll do."

Pain sliced through Malcolm's shoulder, a line of raging fire that made him clench his teeth. He held tight to the sense of Sofia. It felt as if her essence were within him, directing Corrier's quill.

Finally, the pain faded. Malcolm opened his eyes to see Corrier stepping back.

"All done." Corrier returned the quill to the shelf. "If Sofia is ever in a situation where she needs more magical power—say to fight a particularly evil witch—envision sending her some of your power. Focus on the tattoo and the link you feel. It should work."

Malcolm nodded, then glanced down at his shoulder. Surprise flashed through him, then a grin tugged at his lips.

CHAPTER ELEVEN

Sofia stared at Malcolm's shoulder, bewildered. His tattoo was... glorious. A winged woman, powerful and beautiful, decorated his skin.

That wasn't her.

Malcolm tugged on his shirt and her trance broke.

"Thank you, Corrier," Malcolm said.

"Of course. You were two of my favorite students." His gaze met Sofia's. "And I understand why you left the apprenticeship. It's not for everyone. The cost can be too high."

She nodded gratefully, her eyes pricking. She really had hated to leave her studies.

They said their goodbyes and Malcolm aetherwalked them back to his library.

She stepped back, then met his gaze. Unable to stop herself, she said, "That tattoo wasn't me."

"It represents how I see you."

Oh. She blinked. Her heart started to pound.

Holy hell, she was in trouble. It was now clear: the good parts of him that she'd once fallen for were still there—they were just covered up by the jerky shell that loneliness had created. And even that shell was cracking.

He'd agreed to share his power with her. She hadn't thought it possible for him to make such a sacrifice.

Fates, how she wanted to be close to him. To pretend that time and choices hadn't torn them apart. But she was so close to falling for him again, and that was so damned dangerous. She couldn't have her heart broken a second time. And he would break it. Unless...

"Give up being a warlock," she said, desperation clear in her voice. "Take it back."

"I can't." He gripped her shoulders, his gaze pained. "It's who I am. And it's not possible, anyway."

Not true, part of her whispered. There had to be a way.

But it was clear in his firm gaze...he wouldn't pursue it. This was why he was the cloaked man in her tattoo, she realized. When Corrier had asked her to picture Malcolm, she'd just received a feeling. He was inaccessible to her. Reserved.

It made her heart ache. But perhaps it was a good thing. As long as she knew he never intended to try, she wouldn't fall for him. Right? That would just be stupid. And she still hadn't forgiven him for what he'd done.

"I'm sorry, Sofia. I can't do that." His gaze met hers, devouring. "But I can make this work between us."

She shook her head, her heart sinking. "You really can't."

After seeing what had happened to Laira... There was no guarantee that the same wouldn't happen to her— if they fell back in love with one another, *something* would tear them apart. One of them might die or become imprisoned or they'd grow to hate each other.

"Let me try." His gaze was so intense, his desire so strong, that she could almost feel it. "Just stay the night with me. We'll only sleep. But I want to be near you. Now. Forever."

It was such a bad idea, but she couldn't help herself. *For now* couldn't be so bad, could it? Forever was out of the questions. But just one night?

"No sex." It was too dangerous. It'd make her fall for him even faster. "Just sleeping. And just tonight."

A heart-stopping grin took over his face and he swept her up in his arms. She gasped, then clung to him, her heart pounding. A second later, they stood in his bedroom. They'd aetherwalked.

"I couldn't wait," he said.

"Hang on." She drew her wand from the aether and turned her day clothes into sleep shorts and a shirt.

"Gods, you look so good," he said.

"Don't get any ideas," she said, though an enormous part of her wanted him to throw her on the bed. It *wouldn't* happen though.

She watched him strip down to his boxer briefs and stifled a sigh. Fates, he was big. All broad shoulders and planes of muscle. She'd never seen a man as well built and beautiful as he.

His golden gaze met hers. "In bed."

She climbed in and turned away from him. The bed dipped, then his big arm wrapped around her and pulled her into his embrace. The most intense feeling of belonging swept over her. She hadn't felt this in four hundred years.

Not since him.

It took her ages to fall asleep with his hard form pressed to hers, but every second was the most delicious torture.

The next evening, crows gathered on the roof of the Salem Coven's mansion, their forms highlighted by the full moon. Malcolm kept an eye on them from where he and Sofia stood near the trees. All Hallow's Eve had turned into a cold, clear night. The sound of waves crashing on the shore competed with the cawing of the crows.

"She's almost late." Sofia rubbed her arms and bounced on her feet. A dull metal band that matched his own flashed on her wrist.

This afternoon, after he'd given her some of his magical energy, he'd made her a band identical to his own. He'd given both bracelets enhanced dampening charms that would make it so that the other witches couldn't sense them. They didn't provide invisibility—so if they were seen, they were screwed, but at least the Salem Coven wouldn't sense others in their home.

Sofia shivered hard.

He wrapped an arm around her to warm her. She stiffened, then slowly relaxed. Pleasure spread through him. He could make this work. He just had to convince her. Eventually, she'd see they could manage this.

You can't escape fate. He shook away the thought, grateful when the mansion's side door opened. Inara stepped out, clothed once again in jeans and a t-shirt. She approached.

Malcolm tensed, waiting to see if his enchantment would hold. When he saw her dark gaze, slightly confused but determined, he relaxed. She still had no familiar, which was odd for a witch, but she appeared to be under his spell.

"Are you ready?" Inara asked.

He nodded. "Are your coven members occupied? Not looking out the window?"

"They should be."

"Good. Remember, we must not be seen by your coven."

"Understood."

"Lead the way."

They followed her across the lawn, their steps quick and silent on the damp grass. The crows rustled, but they didn't take flight or set up any greater racket. Up close, the mansion was unsettling. White paint peeled off the house siding and snakes slithered in the bushes. Not all witches were creepy—the ones at the university were downright charming if he recalled—but many were exactly as mortals envisioned them. It was mortal belief that had created them, after all, so it made sense.

Inara opened the side door. It creaked loudly. They followed her into a small antechamber. Black and white tiles covered the floor and ornate black wallpaper peeled from the walls. A chandelier burning real candles gleamed above.

"We go down the hall to the main stairs, then into the basement," Inara whispered. "Keep behind me. This wing is used less, but if you hear anyone, duck silently into a room."

They set off after her, Kitty in her smoke form, drifting along beside them. Sofia gripped her wand.

Portraits of witches watched them from walls hung with deep purple silk. Electric lights from another century lit their way.

Malcolm's ears strained. He focused all his wulver senses on the house. If they were caught, it was over. They'd have the fight of their lives to escape and there was no way they'd get the book.

They passed half a dozen closed doors and two open ones, which revealed nothing more than dusty sitting rooms with empty hearths.

A noise sounded ahead. He grabbed Inara and Sofia's arm to alert them and jerked his head toward an open door. They slipped inside and pulled the door closed. Heart thudding in his ears, he listened to footsteps approach.

Two sets.

Closer.

The doorknob turned.

He tensed.

"Wait, I forgot the book," a woman said from the hall.

The doorknob turned back and footsteps receded down the hall.

Once the sound disappeared, Inara nodded and they crept out of the room, making their way more quickly down the hall.

At the end of the passage, a great foyer spread before them. The ceiling soared two stories above, a wrap-around balcony marking the second floor. A sweeping staircase with a blood red carpet was framed by mahogany bannisters.

Inara led them around the stairs to the back wall and pushed open a gleaming wooden door. A narrow staircase led down into the darkness. Inara raised her wand. It glowed at the tip. Light spilled down the passage, revealing stone stairs that looked centuries older than the house.

They followed Inara down, Sofia also using her wand for light. The stairwell opened into a dark, narrow hall. They followed it to the end, ignoring the closed doors on either side.

Inara paused at the end of the hall, then laid her hand against the door and recited an incantation in a language Malcolm didn't recognize. The hair on the back of his neck stood up as he watched her hand begin to glow. Once it was fully immersed in orange light, she pushed.

The door disappeared.

She walked through. Malcolm grabbed Sofia's arm before she could follow. The door opened onto blackness. No floor or walls were visible. Just Inara, standing several feet away, her wand illuminating her form but nothing else. The light seemed to be sucked into the darkness, leaving nothing but black.

"It's fine. Just the nature of the room. The portal to our afterworld makes this room look strange."

Malcolm studied her. His skin tingled in warning, but she looked sincere.

"Wait here," he said to Sofia. "If something goes wrong, just leave."

"We'll see," Sofia said.

Muscles tense, he stepped into the room. Once inside, he could see that there actually was a bit of light. It emanated from a great stone archway that led through the wall to his right. It illuminated the large stone blocks that made up the floor and the ceiling. In the middle of the room sat a basin on a pedestal.

"See? It's fine," Inara said.

Malcolm turned to Sofia. She was already stepping inside the room, ignoring his orders as usual.

"Now what?" Malcolm asked.

"We pay the toll to have access to the portal," Inara said. She approached the basin in the middle of the room. Her wand transformed into an athame. She dragged the ceremonial blade across one palm and let the red drops spill into the bowl, then glanced at him.

He stepped forward and held out his hand. She sliced his palm. Pain flared briefly as the blood dripped into the basin. After a moment, she pushed his palm away, then pushed on his arm so he turned to face the archway. White light pulsed within.

Inara went to stand before the arch. He approached and she handed him her athame. "I will separate my soul from my body and retrieve the book. If I begin to collapse from lack of power, you must stab me with my athame. Only someone of equal power to me can wield my athame. It will call my soul back to my body."

"How likely is that?"

"I don't know. I've never crossed here before. But you must do it or I will die."

He nodded. Sofia had joined him. Inara turned back to the arch and closed her eyes. Malcolm could feel the energy change in the air as she grew deadly still.

Suddenly, a white light separated from her body and drifted toward the arch. It took the form of Inara. A small, ghostly cat walked at the soul's side. Her familiar.

The pair disappeared into the archway. Malcolm waited, his breath held. The house around them creaked, the archway buzzed with power. His skin tingled with awareness and anticipation.

After what felt like hours, Inara returned, her ghostly form drifting through the archway. A large leather book was clasped in her hands. She held it out to him and he took it.

As her soul rejoined her body, he transformed the book into a small coin and slipped it into his pocket. Easier to carry and quick to change back.

A noise sounded from the stairwell. Inara jumped and whirled toward the door. Her gaze was no longer dreamy and confused as it had been.

His enchantment had worn off? That made no sense. He hadn't removed it.

"You need to leave!" Inara hissed.

Footsteps sounded down the stairs. What the hell was going on?

"You have the book you wanted. Go now!"

Malcolm glanced between her, Sofia, and the door.

"What the hell, Malcolm!" Sofia said. "She's not enchanted."

"I helped you for my own reasons, now go!" Inara whispered. The enchantment had clearly never worked, but Inara had helped them anyway. Or had it been help?

The footsteps sounded closer. Malcolm grabbed Sofia's hand. Kitty pressed up against his leg. It was safer to get out of here than stay and fight a dozen witches on their home turf. He closed his eyes, envisioned his home, and began to aetherwalk.

He hit a wall. The aether was blocked. His eyes flared open.

"A trap?" he asked.

Inara shook her head. "The others have blocked the aether, I think. You can no longer aether—"

The door melted away and witches surged into the room. Malcolm tore off his cuff and threw a blast of flame at the door. The witches stumbled back. Several stayed down, but the rest surged forward.

Sofia threw her cuff to the ground and flung out her wand, throwing bolts of lightning at the two witches in the front. Their bodies lit with an unholy glow and they shrieked. Sofia kept the current strong until they collapsed, then transferred her lightning to the next two.

Malcolm continued to throw fireballs, but more witches surged into the room. Too many. They raised their wands in unison and screamed, "Inable!"

A powerful force froze him like ice, his arm still flung out. From the corner of his vision, he could see Sofia and Kitty in the same state.

The witches who had fallen to the ground slowly found their feet. Their faces gleamed with anger. The group, eleven in all, faced them. The coven's clothes were singed and their eyes were bright with rage.

Malcolm fought his magical binding but couldn't budge.

They were screwed.

"Inara! What is this?" The strongest witch demanded. Her power radiated out from her, making Malcolm's skin prickle. She was dressed entirely in black, a gloomy figure with pale skin and midnight hair.

"What?" Inara stumbled back, shaking her head. Confusion flashed across her features.

An act. It was clear now.

"I felt the disturbance in this room. Why are you here? With outsiders?"

"I have no idea," Inara said. "They must have enchanted me."

"Ridiculous. You can't be enchanted." The witch in black pointed her wand at Inara. Chains extended from the wand and wrapped around Inara, binding her until she fell onto her side.

The dark witch turned to Malcolm. "You're strong. I don't know what you are, but you must be strong if you thought you could get in and out of here alive. Either that or stupid."

Malcolm opened his mouth to respond, but he couldn't. Even his mouth was frozen.

"No need to talk," the witch said. "You'll just lie. Or try to enchant me. We can get what we want from your minds easily enough." She glanced behind her at the ten witches who stood at her back. They stared at him, all with dark eyes and tilted heads. It was eerie as hell. "A mind sweeper spell, I think."

The witches all raised their wands toward them. His head suddenly began to ache, pain growing until he thought he would collapse. Only their spell held him upright. He fought to protect his thoughts, but it was powerful magic. He put all his energy toward blocking the thought of retrieving the Grimoire, hoping that Sofia was doing the same. If they were going to make it out of here, they wanted to do it with the Grimoire.

The witches' brows all rose in unison. Inara gasped from where she lay on her side. She was part of this spell? Or did she hear his thoughts because she was part of the coven?

"My, my. That *is* interesting," the dark witch said. "What a fascinating history. And you thought to steal our Grimoire? For the High Witches? But did you succeed? I can't see that in your memory." Her gaze ran over his form and then over Sofia's. "The book is large. It couldn't be concealed in your jacket. If you have it, I don't know what you've done with it. But we shall find it."

She tapped her wand on her hand and stared at them. "Our High Priestess, Malifey, is out for All Hallows' Eve. When she returns, we'll revisit the question. For now, you'll go to the dungeon."

CHAPTER TWELVE

The aether pulled at Sofia and blackness stole her vision. She tumbled to the ground, then scrambled up.

The dungeon was a small, stone-walled room, similar to the room they'd just been in. Kitty appeared next to her. Malcolm stood in the corner. Inara was lying on the ground, still wrapped in the chain.

"What the bloody hell was that?" Malcolm asked. "You weren't enchanted, were you? Did you set us up?"

Inara scowled at him as she struggled to sit. "What do you think, moron? I'm chained up here, aren't I?"

Malcolm growled, then said, "Fair point."

"Why did you help us?" Sofia asked. "If that's indeed what you did."

"I had my reasons. I'm done with this coven."

"Why?"

"You saw those crazy bitches. But there's no way in hell I'm going into detail here. We need to get out."

"We?" Malcolm asked.

"Do you want to know what we learned in your girlfriend's mind? Because it'll be news to her and I'm sure she wants to know it. And you're not going to find out unless I get out of here with you."

"What the hell are you talking about?" Sofia asked.

"You're in a situation that's bigger than you are. There's more to it than even Sofia knows. But I'm not telling you unless I get out of here."

"You mean there's something in my mind I don't know?" The idea freaked her the hell out.

"No. But you're a bit famous. Not big time famous, but your situation is well known amongst witches. The High Witches are pulling quite a racket with you."

Fates. Of course her life was more fucked up than she'd realized. She went to Inara and knelt down. It took a while, but she finally got the chain unwrapped. Malcolm was checking the walls.

"How do we get out of here?" She had spent too much time in dungeons lately. It was starting to piss her off.

Inara stood and rubbed her arms where the chain had cut into her skin. "We don't. There's no way out of here."

Sofia glanced around. No doors. No windows.

She turned to Malcolm, her heart in her throat. The eleven witches in the Salem Coven had overpowered them once. They could do so again. Easily.

"There's no way out from within," Malcolm said.

"Nor without," Inara said. "We can only escape if we're freed by the coven."

"Or if the building is destroyed." Malcolm pounded on a wall. "Or even just a wall. Or the ceiling."

"How the hell do you plan to do that if we're locked in here?" Inara demanded. "Our magic is blocked. We've got nothing."

"Not quite," Malcolm said. "Are any of these walls exterior walls?"

Inara's brow crinkled, but she looked around, then pointed. "That one, I believe."

"Good." He leaned back against the wall.

Though Sofia suspected what was coming next, it still surprised her to see his golden wolf burst from his chest. The animal gleamed in the dim light.

"Holy shit," Inara breathed.

To Sofia's knowledge, there were only two Mytheans in the world like Malcolm: himself and his brother. Half-blood wulvers were exceedingly rare. Inara would have never seen such a thing.

The wolf walked to the wall and disappeared through it.

Sofia waited, her breath held. She had no idea what he was doing, but didn't want to disturb him. Separating part of your soul from your body was always a dangerous business.

After a while, the wolf returned. It melded back into Malcolm's chest and he stood upright. He walked toward the wall that was opposite the exterior wall.

"Come here," he said. "It's safer."

Sofia and Kitty went to stand by him. Inara came as well.

"If we get you out of here, you'll answer our questions...agreed?" Malcolm asked.

"Deal," Inara said. "But I don't know how the hell you think we're getting out of here."

"You'll see. Soon."

Not a moment later, the stone wall opposite them burst outward, flinging rocks and mortar. Malcolm lunged at Sofia and pushed her against the wall, covering her body with his own.

When the rubble settled, Sofia pushed him off her and looked toward the destroyed wall. A group of people stood, silhouetted in dust. Two women held their hands outstretched as if they'd just thrown a burst of magical energy at the wall. One was tall and pale with dark hair, the other short and golden all over. Two black familiars stood at their sides.

They looked like total bad asses, here to rescue them. Sofia grinned.

"I haven't caused this much damage in quite a while," the golden one said. Her eyes gleamed delightedly. "Being on the right side of the law can be quite boring."

The men behind them surged forward, putting themselves between the women and the unknown. The huge, dark-haired one looked a bit like Malcolm. His brother Felix. Malcolm had told her of him, though she'd never met him. The other had honey-colored hair and blocked the taller woman.

"We'd better get on our way," Felix said. "This hasn't exactly been a subtle escape attempt."

Malcolm grabbed her hand and they raced for the huge hole in the wall. He nodded back at Inara. "Grab her. She's coming with us."

Felix grabbed Inara by the arm and followed them.

Sofia stepped out of the room and into a giant pit in the ground.

"Dungeon's in the basement, as all good dungeons are," the golden woman said with a grin. "So we had to blow a hole in the ground."

Sofia nodded, then frowned. Weakness tugged at her. A tingly sense of the power of her immortal soul being sucked away.

These women were soulceresses. No wonder they could blow the wall away.

"We'll aetherwalk to my place," Malcolm said.

She glanced at him, then reached for his hand. Pride shown in his eyes and he gripped her hand.

An enraged shriek rent the air. Sofia's gaze shot toward the dungeon.

Malcolm lunged in front of her, protecting her. She had to peer around his side. The Salem Coven stood within, all twelve of them. An unfamiliar witch, the High Priestess, Sofia assumed, stood in the middle. She raised her wand and threw a bolt of magical energy so strong that Sofia was lifted into the air and thrown out of the pit.

She crashed to the ground, then scrambled to her feet. She was on the front lawn. Chaos reigned. Dust filled the air. Bodies and great stone blocks from the dungeon were scattered all around. Sofia looked around frantically for Malcolm and Kitty. Kitty stood atop an enormous pile of rubble, scratching at it.

Dread settled in Sofia's stomach. Malcolm was under there, she could feel it. Because he'd thrown himself in front of her.

The moon lit a nightmarish scene as twelve of the thirteen members of the Salem Coven climbed out of the pit that their rescuers had blown into the ground.

Shit. Twelve of them versus... She looked around frantically for her backup. The dark-haired soulceress and the blond man were climbing to their feet. Inara raced up to her side. The golden soulceress and Felix were nowhere to be seen.

Four against twelve.

No contest.

She flung out her wand, sending a great jet of flame toward the witches climbing out of the pit. They fell back, shrieking, but would rise again soon enough.

Sofia turned her wand toward the mansion and sent a jet of flame through the night. It blew apart the left side of the porch, sending flames licking up the side of the house.

"Holy shit, yes," Inara breathed, then drew her wand and threw another jet of flame at the house.

"Light it up!" Sofia yelled. A distraction. A coven's home was valuable. Grimoires and potions, wealth and history, all were within.

The coven wouldn't know whether to fight them or save their home.

Out of the corner of her eye, she saw the dark-haired soulceress pull the golden one from a pile of rubble. Their men charged from the dust, heading for the witches. A silver apparition of a wolf ran alongside Felix and the blond man carried a gleaming sword. As they clashed with the witches, the soulceresses appeared at Sofia's side.

"Can you destroy the house?" Sofia asked as she sent another blast of flame at the second story.

"Not a problem," the golden soulceress said.

Sofia spun and raced toward the pile of rubble that covered Malcolm. Kitty still scratched at the stone that was piled as high as Sofia's head. The witches must have blown out the entire dungeon, and Malcolm had caught the brunt of it.

With a flick of her wand, she began to move the stones. Kitty jumped free. After a moment, she caught sight of Malcolm's shirt. She raced to him and dropped to her knees.

His torso was crushed, seeping blood.

Fear shot through her, tearing a gasp from her throat. He lived, but barely. Only because he was an immortal. It wasn't grievous magic or a beheading, so he would be okay. He had to be.

She moved the rest of the rocks from his legs, then glanced at the battle. The soulceresses controlled a giant tornado that was tearing the house apart while Inara and the men held off the witches.

"Time to go!" she screamed as she grasped Malcolm's shoulders and aetherwalked them away.

A second later, they appeared in the foyer of his home. Malcolm lay on the floor, ashen. His breath was shallow and harsh, straining through lungs that barely worked. Fear streaked through her, sending her heart racing.

Oh fates, he lay here because he'd thrown himself in front of her. How many times would he do that?

She couldn't lose him. She couldn't.

Kitty watched Malcolm pensively as Sofia laid her hands on his chest and sent a burst of healing energy through him. She wasn't technically a healer, but she'd learned how to magically mend bone and muscle from her mother. He would heal more slowly, but he *would* heal.

He had to.

He drew a deeper breath and she sagged in relief.

A second later, two figures appeared in the hall. Then three more. Their saviors and Inara.

Felix fell to his knees beside Malcolm. "Is he all right?"

"I think." Her voice trembled.

Felix ran big hands over Malcolm's chest and neck. He sagged. "He'll be all right. He just needs to recover." His gaze met hers. "You're very powerful."

"Yes. More so because of Malcolm." The power he'd given her had definitely enhanced her healing abilities. "We should get him somewhere comfortable." She didn't know when he'd wake, but she didn't want it to be on the floor.

Felix nodded and picked his brother up, then aetherwalked away. Sofia followed, assuming he went to the bedroom. When she arrived, she saw him put Malcolm on the bed.

"Bad luck that he landed under all that rubble," Felix said. "But he'll be fine. He's strong."

Sofia went to his side and laid her hand on his brow. Her heart ached to see him here like this.

"You're Sofia?" Felix's silver eyes studied her. Whereas Malcolm was all elegant strength, he looked like a lumberjack.

"You know about me?"

"Only a bit. Malcolm spoke of you once, when he thought I couldn't really hear him. "

"Really?"

"He did. But it's been over three hundred years and he hasn't mentioned you again."

"No. I suppose not."

Felix sighed, pinched the bridge of his nose. "Malcolm was raised differently than I. With sorcerers instead of wulvers. They worshiped magic and power. *Really* worshiped it." He spoke quickly, as if he wanted to get the words out before Malcolm woke.

"Since he was a child, he has trained to be a warlock. It was like brainwashing. There was no other way for him. In the history of his people, no one had ever deviated. He couldn't conceive of a world in which he didn't pursue that path. As the years passed and he grew into a man, he broke free of the chains of his people's expectations. But too late."

"I know all of this."

"He told you?"

"Not in as much detail, but from what I've heard of his people and seen, it's fairly obvious. But why did he tell you if he didn't tell me? I know he wants my forgiveness. Or at least for me to get over the past and stay with him. He's apologized, but never explained his perspective."

"He didn't tell me. Not really. Once, when I was injured and out of my mind with pain, he talked and talked. I think he thought he was distracting me, but he was actually trying to distract himself from worrying about me. But over the years, I put two and two together. I understand what he is—what it means to be a warlock. That they're Oath Breakers. That was enough to make me able to guess what happened between you."

"Why do you care?"

"I have Aurora now." His silver eyes darkened. "I know what it's like to have lost the one you love. If I lost her again...." His jaw clenched. "I couldn't handle it. I think that you are that person for Malcolm."

"If I am, why didn't he explain this to me? Try harder to make me understand instead of just breaking my heart all those years ago?"

"Would it have mattered? You'd hate him either way. Rightfully so."

"Yes." Her fists clenched unconsciously. She felt for him, being torn between duty and desire, but everyone faced that at some point.

"Exactly. And Malcolm is a man of action, not words. He committed the crime against you. Why try to fix it with words when it's not possible? He'd apologize but not explain."

Sofia reached for Malcolm's hand and squeezed it. She didn't know what to think. What did it matter if he was a man of action when his actions had hurt her?

Except that he was trying to be better now. And from the way her heart pounded and her thoughts clung to Malcolm, she was probably falling back in love with him.

Falling in love with an Oath Breaker. As soon as this was over, she'd have to run from him. They couldn't have anything real. Fate would see to it. She could *die* because of this. Laira had.

"He came to me for help, you know," Felix said.

"Tonight?"

"Yes, but earlier too. He knew this might be dangerous. That you were at risk. In the event that anything went south, he wanted back-up."

Sofia's shoulders sagged. Malcolm had done that and hadn't told her?

Actions over words.

"Why don't you get a few hours of sleep," Felix said. "We'll stay here."

Fates, that sounded good. Exhaustion dragged at her. She just wanted to close her eyes and not think about any of this.

"Inara has something she has to tell me. Something the witches knew."

"It can wait a few hours, can't it? We'll see to it that she stays here."

The lure of sleep was so strong that she nodded. She also didn't think she could handle any more bad news right now. "Thanks. I really appreciate it."

Felix nodded and left the room.

She was so lucky to have these people—although she didn't even know most of them by name—willing to help her. Her gaze was drawn to Malcolm, lying still on the bed.

Although their past had torn out her heart and he was at fault for their current predicament, she felt almost a little lucky to have him too. He had done everything in his power to protect her. He was lying to her because he'd tried to protect her. His theft of the dagger had gotten her into this mess, but if they could get out of it, she could almost forgive him for it.

She knew it was a bad idea, but she climbed into bed next to him and curled up on top of the comforter. She reached out a hand and laid it on his shoulder. His warmth comforted her.

Gods, she didn't want any more reasons to care for him. She had too many as it was. On top of her memories, she now could accept that he'd essentially been brainwashed into becoming a warlock. Not to mention his constant attempts to save her life. He'd made terrible choices in the past— unforgivable choices, no matter his upbringing—but she was falling for him.

She couldn't help it.

And it would be the end of her.

Warmth suffused one side of Malcolm's body. Sofia's scent overwhelmed him. His eyes snapped open. Bright morning sun filtered through the mullioned windows. He glanced right.

She lay curled up against his side, her dark hair gleaming in the light. She wore all her clothes—even her jacket. Dust covered it.

The sight brought back a memory of the night before. The witches charging into the dungeon after Felix had busted through the wall. They'd thrown a blast of magic at them and then…

Nothing.

He remembered nothing after that.

No doubt he'd been knocked out. Sofia had saved him? His brother?

The questions were driven from his mind when she shifted, wrapping an arm around his waist.

Satisfaction and comfort enveloped him. *This* is what he'd wanted all these years. Not just her body or her wit or her strength, but her constant companionship. When he'd first met her, he'd known without a doubt that he'd found his mate, a concept that had only been whispered about amongst his people.

It'd been an entirely foreign notion for a boy raised by sorcerers. Not all sorcerers were like his clan, but he hadn't realized that until he'd been far older. No one in his village had had a mate. It was impossible. They worshipped power to the point that becoming a warlock was the ultimate goal. The *only* goal.

Most of the adults had been warlocks—unable to love another without fate tearing it from their grasp. That extended to children as well. Children were conceived and raised out of necessity, not love. The desire to pass on their line was strong amongst his people, as it was amongst Mytheans and mortals alike.

He remembered being on a trip to the village with his friend Corbin as a boy. A street performer had been singing a ballad about love, a word he'd never even heard. Girls had been gazing at the singer, their eyes gleaming. He and Corbin had watched, completely perplexed. They'd only figured out the meaning of the word through context in the song. It'd barely made sense to him.

Not until he'd met Sofia.

And then he'd fucked things up.

He shook the thought away. He would win her back. He *had* to.

Sofia shifted.

He glanced at her. Her eyes flew open, confused.

He pulled her toward him and kissed her hard, then pulled away and leaned his forehead against hers. "Bloody hell, I was afraid I'd lost you."

She scrambled up until she sat next to him.

"You're all right." There was relief in her voice. She reached out to touch his chest, then drew her hand away.

"What happened?" he asked.

The story she told of the Salem Coven made his brows rise. When she finished, he asked, "Everyone is here?"

"I think so. Felix said they would stay. Inara has to tell us what the Salem Coven knows about me." Worry flashed across her features. She climbed out of bed.

He rose and his gaze followed her across the room. Kitty jumped off the chair by the fire and followed her.

"I'm going to shower," she said. "Then let's all meet in the kitchen."

"Sofia," he said as she went through the door. She turned to look at him. "Thank you for saving me."

Her brow creased. "Of course." She turned and left.

Malcolm scrubbed a hand across the back of his neck. Bloody hell, winning her was going to be hard. She was so skittish. He sighed, then headed to the shower.

Fifteen minutes later, he headed down to the kitchen. His brother and Aurora were at the stove making bacon, from the smell of it. Esha and Warren were pouring coffee, her dark head bent near his blond one. Inara stood at the island, scooping scrambled eggs onto plates.

Felix turned and asked, "Feeling better?"

Malcolm nodded. "Thank you for coming to get us. All of you."

Esha lowered her cup from her mouth. "Not a problem. I enjoyed it. Nothing like a little battle."

"Aye. I don't get out often enough," Warren said.

Sofia walked into the kitchen, Kitty trailing her.

Aurora turned from the stove, her golden hair gleaming. "Morning. I'm Aurora." She pointed at her sleek black familiar who sat at her side, gnawing on a piece of bacon. "That's Mouse."

"I'm Esha." She pointed at the big, scruffy tomcat who gazed longingly at Mouse. "That's Chairman Meow."

"Warren." He nodded at Sofia.

"Nice to meet you," Sofia said. "Thanks for getting us out of there."

"No problem," Aurora said, then glanced at the stove. "Bacon's done. Let's eat."

They all collected plates and sat at the kitchen table.

"My enchantment never worked, so why did you help us?" Malcolm asked Inara before he took a bite of food. It didn't make any sense.

"I had my reasons."

"You're going to have to expound upon that," he said.

She sighed and put her fork down. "Or what?"

"You won't like the consequences." Her knowledge might threaten Sofia. He'd stop at nothing to eliminate that threat.

She glared at him. "Fine. I hate the Salem Coven. I joined when I was young. Two years ago, I fell in love. He ran afoul of the coven. A month later, he was dead. I could never prove anything because they kept it quiet, but I know it was my coven mates. I know it. I can read auras. It's one of my gifts. I read guilt in theirs. When you came and wanted to steal the book, I thought *why not?* Neither of you have evil auras, and I wanted vengeance."

"You aren't worried about what we'll do with the book?"

"No."

Her expression was a bit strange, but before Malcolm could ask why, Sofia spoke. "What does the coven know about me? Why were they so interested?"

"Ah." Inara's gaze dropped, as if she didn't know how to phrase her next comment. "Well, you see, your position is fairly well known amongst the most powerful covens."

"What do you mean?"

"The High Witches have a really sweet deal worked out with you and your line of Bruxas. You bring the tributes or they destroy your village. Did you ever wonder how that came about?"

"Not often, no. It's always been part of my life. And my mother's and grandmother's before me."

"Well, it's an unusual situation. Most Mythean groups don't do things like that—at least not on earth and not anymore. Going to another group of Mytheans—or in your case, a village—and threatening war and destruction is frowned upon. Like, really frowned upon. Organizations like the university in Edinburgh or the Grand Council of Witches or the Weres' Consortium usually lay the smack-down on that kind of large-scale potential warfare. If it were allowed, there's no way we could stay secret from mortals. Not if everyone were off fighting big old battles."

"I know," Sofia said. "But I just assumed my situation was older—established before the rule of law."

"It's not—not really. Witches are one of the oldest groups of Mytheans. Mortals have believed in witchcraft for millennia, after all. We've had our rules in place for that long. A situation like yours is forbidden. Except in certain circumstances."

"Circumstances?"

"You're really powerful for Bruxa. Your whole matrilineal line is enormously powerful. Mythologically speaking, you shouldn't be that strong. Bruxas are moderately strong witches, but nothing like you or your ancestors."

"Our strength has something do to with this problem, doesn't it?"

"Yeah. Your ancestors made a deal with the High Witches thousands of years ago. In exchange for extra magical ability, their descendants and the village of Bruxa's Eye would be forced into the situation you currently find yourself in."

The breath whooshed out of Sofia's lungs. Her color was ashen. "What?"

"Yeah. Your ancestors basically betrayed you before you were born. For the High Witches, it's pretty much the best deal ever. That's why my coven knew about your history. When we were reading your mind and realized who you were, it was easy to put two and two together."

"How can she get out of this?" Malcolm demanded.

"It doesn't matter," Sofia said, her voice trembling. "It's my responsibility. I have to do it."

"No, you don't." Rage boiled in Malcolm's chest.

"She does," Inara said. "I don't exactly know the nature of it, but she's supposed to die if she abandons her post. She's tied to it somehow. At least, that's the rumor."

Malcolm scrubbed a hand over his face. This was bloody awful news.

"I wouldn't abandon my post. Or my village," Sofia said. "And it's okay. We got the book."

Relief loosened the knot in Malcolm's chest. He reached into his pocket and withdrew the coin, then laid it on the table. With a wave of his hand, he transformed it back into its original shape. The tome sat, heavy and bound in leather. Power radiated from it.

"Holy shit—that's impressive," Esha breathed.

"It's our ticket out of this," Sofia said.

It burst into flames.

CHAPTER THIRTEEN

Sofia jumped back. "What the hell?"

Flames devoured the book. Within seconds, it turned to ash.

Her heart began to pound and chills ran over her body. She lunged over the desk and grabbed Inara by the collar. "What the hell happened?"

"I don't know," Inara choked. She shook Sofia's arm.

Shaking, Sofia let go and sat back.

Malcolm looked ready to commit murder. "Explain," he growled.

"I really have no idea what happened."

"That Grimoire is clearly enchanted," Malcolm said. "Why? So it couldn't leave the coven's possession?"

"Makes sense," Inara said. "But I'd really never heard of that before. No one ever talked about what would happen if it left, but that's because everyone assumed it wouldn't be stolen."

Sofia's heart sank.

"It makes sense," Aurora said. "It's an uncommon spell, but the Salem Coven is capable of uncommon magic."

Sofia felt like the ground had fallen out from beneath her feet. "They're going to destroy my home." Her voice sounded dead, even to her ears. "There are no third chances."

She was so screwed. Like, an all-time level of screwed. She'd failed. She'd *really* failed. "We need to evacuate the village. Get everyone out before they come. How many days do we have left?"

"Three."

She pinched the bridge of her nose. "Damn it. Convincing everyone is going to be nearly impossible. They'll want to fight."

"Can't they?" Warren asked.

"Sure," Sofia said. "But we can't win. The High Witches are too strong. They destroyed the population of an entire afterworld to build their home." The memory of the desolate afterworld made her shiver. "The stories my mother told..." As a teenager, all she'd wanted to do was fight. To break free of these chains. "We can't win against them. Not if they could kill everyone in a whole afterworld. They destroyed *souls*. How is our village supposed to stand up to that? And my ancestor apparently put us in this position." Tears pricked her eyes. Damn it. She'd always thought that her line had volunteered to protect the village. That was how the story was told. But to learn that her own family had sold her up the river?

"The village is fated to be destroyed, is what you mean?" Aurora asked.

"Basically. It wouldn't be a normal fight. We don't stand a chance," she said.

"Then we evacuate," Malcolm said, his voice clipped. "Once everyone is convinced, it'll take no time for them to leave. Many can aetherwalk and those who can't shall go with the other. The village shall be clear in minutes. And we have three days."

Sofia wanted to sink under the table and curl up in a ball.

Instead, she placed her palm on Kitty's back for a bit of strength, then stood. "I'm going to go home. Talk to the leaders of the village factions, convince them to leave." She looked at everyone. "Thanks for your help. Really."

They nodded.

"I can come help at your village if you need me," Inara said. "I mean, I don't really have any responsibilities now that I've ditched my coven."

"Thanks," Sofia said. "Yeah. That'd be good." She spun and left the room, walking blindly toward the hall.

She'd barely made it out the door before Malcolm caught up with her. He pulled her into his arms. She shuddered as his warmth closed around her.

"We can mend this," he said against her hair.

"Really? Because it seems hopeless."

"Yes. I'll do anything to fix this." His voice grew rough. "I swear, Sofia, I had no idea this would happen when I kept your dagger."

Fates, how could he have? He was selfish, but not that selfish. She knew she should be angry with him, and she had a feeling that would come, but right now, she was so overwhelmed by what was coming at her that she didn't have time for anger.

She sucked in a shuddering breath. Instead, she would focus on what she could do to fix this.

The first thing would be to take what strength and comfort she could from Malcolm. Shore up her defenses for what was to come. And there was a lot of strength that she could take. He'd shared that with her. He might have gotten her into this awful mess, but he had permanently diminished his own magical power to share it with her.

And she was going to use it. She'd have to.

Malcolm pinched the bridge of his nose and squeezed his eyes shut. This was not going as planned. He, Sofia, and Inara had come to her village after breakfast and arranged a meeting with the faction leaders. Though Sofia was the Protector and the strongest Mythean in town, from what he could see, each group of immortals in Bruxa's Eye had a representative. There were no central leaders. Just Sofia and half a dozen Mytheans of a variety of species who made up the village council.

It had taken a few hours to round them all up, but they now sat in a small tavern at the edge of town. It was dimly lit, with a bar along one wall and tables and chairs along the other. The locals had cleared out and the council members now sat in chairs that had been pulled around to face the bar.

Sofia stood in front of it in her Crone form, explaining what had happened with the High Witches. She omitted any mention of Malcolm, for which he was grateful. He wouldn't have any trouble taking on the assortment of Weres, fae, vampires, and other immortal beings, but if he was going to have a shot at convincing Sofia to spend the rest of her life with him, having her village hate him would be bad.

"So you see why we have to abandon the village?" Sofia said. Kitty sat on a barstool next to her and her hand hadn't left the familiar's back the entire time she'd been speaking.

A hulking Were rose to his feet. Nearly seven feet tall and built like a bull, his face was beat in like a prize fighter's.

Malcolm started to step forward, but the Were bowed deeply, then spoke, his voice like gravel, "Honored One, you have carried this burden for centuries. It is time we picked up the mantle. We will fight these witches and break the curse upon our village forever."

A small woman with sleek black hair stood, then bowed deep. When she spoke, her fangs flashed. "I agree with Hamish. You've carried this burden long enough. The vampires will join the Weres in fighting the High Witches. When they come here, we will be ready. If we kill them all, the curse will be broken. You'll be free."

"It's not an option," Sofia's voice was sharp. "I appreciate the sentiment, but we cannot win this."

A tall, slender woman with sparkling wings folded at her back stood and bowed deeply. "I am sorry, Honored One, but I do not agree. I believe that we can beat them if we are all united. Particularly if we can bring the fight to their door. I can call upon other fae who do not live in Bruxa's Eye who owe me favors."

"It's not possible," Sofia said. "I'm the only one who can access the High Witches' afterworld. I can bring someone with me, but I'm only strong enough to bring one—maybe two—at a time. I couldn't bring enough of us to wage a fair fight. And there is no fair fight. They got that afterworld by destroying all the souls there. They're more powerful than all of us combined. We must depart. For all our lives."

Disagreements rose in the air, each faction leader voicing their support for battle.

Sofia turned from them to face Malcolm, Inara, and Aleia, who stood at his side. "They won't believe me," she hissed. "They want to stay too badly. This is their home. We need to convince them."

"How?" Aleia asked. "If they're disagreeing with you—which I've never seen—there's no one left to convince them. There's no one higher than you."

Sofia scrubbed a hand over her face and sighed. "What if we could contact my ancestors in the afterworld? They could confess to what they've done and if we could have all the previous Protectors speak to the wisdom of leaving, perhaps the leaders would listen."

"But how?" Aleia asked. "Calling forth one ancestor is hard enough. You want to try for all of them? There are six!"

"I'm stronger now." Her gaze connected with Malcolm's. "With Malcolm's help, and possibly Inara's, we can call them forth."

"It's worth a try," Aleia said.

Sofia turned back to the crowd. When her gaze fell upon them, they quieted. "Tomorrow at dawn, we'll meet in the sacred circle. I'll call my ancestors forth and they'll speak to the wisdom of abandoning Bruxa's Eye." She paused. The pain in her eyes was so clear that it made his heart ache. "I don't want to abandon Bruxa's Eye either. It's my home. But a battle that we cannot win and the inevitable slaughter that will follow is worse."

The leaders shifted silently, then rose and bowed.

"Of course, Honored One," the vampire murmured, her head bowed.

The rest echoed her sentiment.

"Good. Until dawn," Sofia said.

The leaders filed out. Sofia collapsed against a barstool. "Fates, that sucked. And tomorrow is going to suck worse."

"Why wait until dawn?" Malcolm asked.

"It's easiest to contact an afterworld at dusk or dawn, when the barrier between night and day is weakest." Sofia glanced toward the window. "And the sun has already set tonight."

Malcolm waited while she made arrangements with Aleia and Inara to meet before dawn.

Sofia felt Malcolm's gaze on her like a brand as she said goodbye to Inara and Aleia. Her own home didn't have a second bedroom for Inara, who would be spending the night with Aleia in her two-bedroom apartment over the apothecary.

She turned to leave, her gaze flashing over Malcolm.

Would he follow?

He caught up to her at the door and pushed it open. No one was on the street, so she transformed back to her normal self, sighing in relief as she re-entered her old skin.

Of course he would follow. He seemed determined to stay in her life these days. To the point that his actions had put her whole village at risk. Anger seethed in her chest as she stomped down the boardwalk toward her home.

"I'll do everything in my power to see to it that your friends are safe," Malcolm said.

"It's too late now. You've done your damage."

He grabbed her arm and gently pulled her to a stop, then swung her toward him. "I know that. I apologize." His voice was graver than she'd ever heard it. "I would never have kept the dagger had I realized these would be the consequences."

She believed him. He *was* sorry. And he wouldn't have done it. She was pissed he'd done it, but also mature enough that she could forgive him.

But it was so hard to forgive him for becoming a warlock in the first place.

She looked up at him, struck by how handsome he was in the moonlight. His hair was ink black and his golden eyes were so gorgeous. Her gaze strayed to his mouth. Why did he have to be so godsdamned beautiful? And so good in bed?

Or on a desk, rather.

The memory made her shiver.

She wanted him and it pissed her off. It was stupid.

"You should go," she said as she turned and walked down the boardwalk.

"Not bloody likely. I'm staying to help."

The words made her feel a little better, which only pissed her off more. She stomped faster. "Why?"

"Because I want to. I want to make this right. And I want you. I've wanted you for centuries."

His words made her heart race and her skin prickle. She tried to ignore it as she stopped at her door and pushed it open. She stepped into the small foyer and turned, intending to block him.

"Go, Malcolm. If you want to help so badly, meet us at the temple tomorrow." She started to shut the door in his face, her heart and body aching to let him in.

He stepped forward and clasped her waist, lifting her and kicking the door closed behind him. His strength made desire flash through her, followed quickly by anger.

"You bastard!" she tried to shove him, but he didn't budge. He loomed over her, making her heart race. "All you do is butt into my life. You forced your way in by taking the dagger and now you're forcing your way into my home. I'm sick of it!"

He grasped her wrists in his big hands and forced them down, then pulled her to him. "I can't help myself. I want you too bloody badly."

The way he growled the words sent a shiver through her. He was so strong, so beautiful. His scent and strength were intoxicating, making her dizzy with want.

She hated that she wanted him, hated that he was here.

Most of all, she hated that she could very well die as a result of this mess.

And it wasn't really his fault. It was her ancestors' fault. She'd been set up for this for hundreds of years.

And now she might die without knowing what it would be like to be with Malcolm? It wasn't fucking fair. Her life wasn't fair. She'd given it all up to help save her village and now she wouldn't even accomplish that.

And this man who drew her like a moth to flame was here for the taking. He wanted her. She wanted him. So what if she got burned, if she were going to die anyway?

Anger and desire pulsed through her, fueling her. She grabbed his shirt and swung him toward the little living room.

"You want me?" she asked as she pushed him backward toward the couch.

He let her, desire darkening his gaze. "Forever."

The words just pissed her off more. "Impossible. But this isn't." She shoved him onto the couch, then straddled him.

His hands came up to grip her hips.

"Yes," he breathed as she crushed her mouth to his.

His lips were delicious beneath her own, lush and firm. She sank her hands into his hair and slipped her tongue into his mouth. She wanted to taste more of him. All of him.

She was so mad and needy that she kissed him roughly, angrily. All her rage over her circumstances came out in her kiss, in her motions. She ground herself against him, moaning into his mouth when she felt his hard cock between her thighs.

"Bloody hell, Sofia," he rasped as he gripped the back of her head with one big hand. His other palm pressed against her lower back, forcing her closer to him.

She reached up and grabbed his hand at her head, then forced it down to the couch. "No, damn it. I'm in charge. You're always in charge. It's my turn now."

He growled at her, his golden gaze glinting in the dim light that shined through the window, but when she pressed her mouth back to his, he put all his anger into his kiss, thrusting his tongue into her mouth and bucking his hips so that his cock pressed against her clitoris.

She shuddered and moved to get closer to that amazing feeling. Her head spun with desire. All she could smell was him, all she could feel was him.

With a shiver, she broke the kiss and scooted back. Her hands trembled as they tugged at his shirt. He sat up and ripped it over his head, revealing the broad expanse of muscle that made her mouth water.

"Gods, you look good," she said as she ran her hands over his broad pecs and the ridges of his abs. His shoulders were so big that she didn't know where to start.

When her gaze caught on the new tattoo on his shoulder, a pang hit her heart. She almost growled. She had no time for soft feelings.

All she had time for was this. Fucking him.

Her hands and gaze went straight to the fly of his pants, to the cock that pressed angrily against the rough material. It was so big that it made the breath catch in her throat.

With trembling hands, she undid the button of his fly and dragged the zipper down. He groaned, low and guttural, as it parted to reveal black cotton forced upward by his cock.

She gripped it, shocked by its size, and rubbed. Dampness at the tip made her pussy clench. He wanted her. As much as she wanted him.

She glanced up to see it reflected in his gaze. He watched her avidly. His hands went to her shirt and began to pull it up. She pushed them away.

"No. I'm in charge," she said.

"Sofia," he growled in warning. Then her shirt disappeared. Her bra followed.

"Bastard," she hissed.

"Bloody hell, you're lovely," he whispered.

She glanced at his face, seeing awe in his eyes. It only pissed her off more. If he hadn't become a warlock, she'd be the recipient of that look every night. Instead, all she had was this. One night.

She looked back at his cock, too angry to look at him. How could this rage and desire coexist so easily within her? It couldn't be healthy, but she didn't care.

Her gaze was rapt as she drew the fabric down. His shaft, long and thick, emerged. It was so beautiful it made her mouth water. Veins laced the sides and the head was graceful and gleaming.

Her first thought was that he would never fit. Her second was that she was determined to try. She gripped his cock, savoring his guttural groan and the way it jerked in her hands.

So smooth. So hard. She pumped her fist, her mouth watering as she watched the dusky head disappear and reemerged from her hand.

CHAPTER FOURTEEN

Malcolm groaned as Sofia's hand worked his cock. Gods, how he'd dreamed of this. He watched as her small, delicate hand moved up and down. A bead of fluid gleamed at the tip. With her thumb, she swiped at it, spreading it over the head of his cock.

His hips jerked, driving his shaft upwards. He wanted to bury it inside of her so badly that he shook. To feel her accept him as he plowed deep…

But bloody hell, she was so much smaller than he was. He glanced up to see her biting her lip, her gaze avid on her hand. Her pretty breasts trembled as her arm moved.

When she reached for her fly, his heart threatened to pound out of his chest.

He'd know her tonight. "Do you have protection?" he rasped. Mytheans didn't carry disease, but pregnancy was a concern. As much as the though of her carrying his child made his heart swell, now was not the time.

She nodded. "A spell."

He pulled her head down and kissed her. She moaned and parted her lips.

Once she was panting, she scrambled off his lap and toed off her boots, tugging her jeans and underwear off at the same time. Her dark curls drew his gaze and worry struck him again. He remembered how tight she'd been around his fingers.

In a second, she was back atop him. She gripped his shaft in her hand, rising up on her knees. Her gaze gleamed with desire and anger.

He gripped her arms. "Wait."

"No." Her eyes flashed.

"I want to make sure you're ready for me."

"I am."

"No, you're angry and want to fuck," he growled. "But you're small. The first time I sink inside you, I want it to be like sliding home. I want you desperate for it."

She struggled, trying to tear out of his grip. "I just want to fuck you, Malcolm."

"You'll get to. Eventually."

"Fuck you," she hissed as she tore out of his arms and got to her feet. She turned to leave.

No way in hell was he letting her get away. He gripped her arms and pulled her back until she sat on his lap, her legs straddling his own. His cock settled into the cleft of her lush arse.

Her head tipped back on his shoulder and she moaned. "Yes. Gods, yes, Malcolm."

"Good girl."

She growled at him, but the sound turned to a moan when his fingers found her pussy. She parted so easily, welcoming. His cock throbbed against her as his fingers dipped into her wetness.

A groan rose in his throat as he remembered how pink and beautiful she'd been, how delicious she'd tasted. He imagined swiping his tongue over her clitoris as his fingertips made circles around the tight bud.

She shuddered, her breasts trembling. The sight of her spread out over him, her legs forced far apart as his big, rough hand disappeared between her legs made him thrust his hips unconsciously, seeking her tight warmth. His cock, lubricated with his own wetness, slid between her lush cheeks.

Just the feel of it, the thought of it, of one day fucking her there, made him almost lose his seed. He wanted to know every part of her. Her body. Her mind.

But for now, he had this. The feel of her splayed over him, trembling as he sank a finger into her tight sheath. She was so hot and wet.

She moaned and writhed, torturing his shaft and his mind.

"More," she begged, moving her hips.

He gave her what she wanted, pressing deep into her tight, hot channel.

Gods, how he wanted to see her come, to feel her tighten around him and her body shake. He rubbed her clitoris with his thumb, thrusting his fingers within her, relishing the way her body drew him deep.

The way she felt made his head swim. He dragged his gaze from her body, unable to take the stimulus, and bit the side of her neck.

She moaned, tilting her head, and he bit her again, lower.

"Gods, yes," she said, shuddering.

He ran his hand down the length of her body, cupping her full breast as his fingers worked her cunt. She was hot and wet, her slickness easing the way for his thrusting fingers.

"Please, Malcolm," she moaned. Her thighs trembled and her back arched. "Fuck me."

His cock grew even harder at the thought of lowering her onto his shaft and feeling her take him deep.

But he wanted her to beg him with her body, to feel her clench around his fingers and gasp in his ear. He wanted her so desperate that his cock filled a gnawing need inside of her. And fates, how he loved her orgasm. If he were inside of her, he'd be so distracted that he wouldn't be able to savor the shivers and moans that came with her pleasure.

"I'm going to make you mine," he growled into her ear.

She shuddered. "Gods, yes."

He curled his fingers forward to press against that sensitive spot inside of her and circled his thumb faster. The feel of his fingers sinking into her pussy made him want to bury his face in her and drink her down.

When her muscles tensed and her thighs began to shake, he steadied his rhythm. Her sheath clenched and she cried out.

"Please, Malcolm. I need you inside of me." Her voice was desperate at his ear.

He withdrew his fingers and gripped her hips, raising her up over his shaft. She was so small beneath his big hands, and he prayed to the gods that she could take him.

When he felt her hand gripping his shaft and positioning him, he lowered her, throwing his head back and groaning at the feel of her sex kissing the tip of his cock.

"Please, Malcolm," she begged, trying to force herself down upon his shaft.

He gritted his teeth and lowered her slowly, hissing in a breath as her pussy accepted him. She was tight and hot and so delicious that he wanted to thrust deep and fast to feel her close around him.

Instead, he lowered her slowly, fighting the urge out of fear of hurting her.

He heard a slick sound and realized that she was touching her clitoris. The mere idea made his balls draw up tight and his orgasm threaten to overwhelm him.

"Fuck yes," he rasped. "Take your pleasure."

"More, Malcolm," she moaned.

He lowered her farther, almost half way, resisting his desperate need to thrust hard.

"Gods, you're big." She writhed on him, trying to take more of him. "You won't hurt me."

"Make yourself come and I'll fuck you as hard as you want."

He heard her hand speed up. Seconds later, her back arched and a cry escaped her throat. Her thighs shook and her pussy began to clench around him, a delicious silken grip that stole his control.

He surged home, burying himself to the hilt and savoring her cry of pleasure. She was coming on his cock now, her body shaking and one hand gripping his hair. Pain tugged at his head, but he liked it.

He replaced her hand with his own, wanting control of her pleasure, and began to thrust, bouncing her on his shaft. She writhed and trembled as he made her come again. Her skin was slick on his, delicious.

The feel of her pussy, of knowing that he gave her that orgasm, made pleasure streak through him. He shuddered as she gripped his cock.

Sofia was dying from pleasure. Malcolm's cock speared her and his hand was magic on her clit. She couldn't control her trembling or the orgasms that wracked her body, sending pleasure through every one of her nerves.

Malcolm's huge body was hot and hard beneath hers. His plunging cock stole her breath and forced a continuous orgasm to explode through her. She was trapped within a vortex of sensation.

His hand pressed against her upper chest, fingers lightly encircling her throat, as if owning her. The rage that she'd felt all night tried to flare at the thought, but it was forced away by another surge of pleasure as his cock plunged deep.

His motions picked up speed, his cock thrusting harder. He growled and his fingertips left her clitoris. He gripped her hips as he thrust, his motion losing all grace. He was like a powerful animal and she was trapped in his grasp, helpless to the feelings that overwhelmed her.

He stiffened beneath her, gripping her hips as he roared, his orgasm triggering her own. She shuddered as the pleasure wracked her, a kaleidoscope of sensation, as his cock plunged deep and hard.

She rode the wave, finally collapsing on top of him, woozy from pleasure and exhaustion. Malcolm's breath came harsh in her ear, his chest heaving beneath her.

"That was amazing." His voice was rough, hoarse.

It had been. And it terrified her. She scrambled to get away from him, but he stood, lifting her into his arms.

Oh shit. Her heart couldn't take any tender post-sex cuddling. She was too close to falling for him already.

"Where's your bedroom?" he asked.

"Upstairs. But I think you should take the couch."

He'd started carrying her to the stairs before she even finished her sentence. "I'm not letting you out of my sight."

It was almost frightening to be carried upstairs by a man. She wasn't worried about falling—he was so big she had no reason to fear that. It was the intimacy that would come if they slept in the same bed.

She'd slept in bed with him last night because she'd been worried about him and couldn't bear the thought of being parted from him. But now he was conscious. It would be too intimate. The last time she'd slept in bed with a man had been nearly a century ago. Henry had been her attempt at having a real relationship. A boyfriend.

But it hadn't worked, because she'd kept comparing him to Malcolm. Since then, she'd kept it to one-night stands when the loneliness got to be too much.

Malcolm found the bedroom without any problem and set her on the bed. It was wide enough for two, but barely, especially considering his size. He flicked on a lamp to reveal her familiar quilt, bedside table, dresser, and lamp. The butter yellow walls gave the room a cozy feel that was at odds with her emotions. She couldn't keep her eyes off of Malcolm's huge, beautiful body. His skin gleamed in the low light.

"I really think you ought to sleep downstairs," she said.

"I don't think so." He climbed over and sat on the other side of the bed, then pulled her into his arms so her back nestled against his front.

Warmth and comfort suffused her. If only she could have this forever.

She shook the thought away.

Impossible.

"I want you to come live with me," Malcolm said.

Her head snapped back as she tried to look at him. "What?"

"It was a mistake to give you up." His voice was gruff. "I own the action and won't make excuses, but I regret it. I made the wrong choice."

Her heart thundered. "When did you decide this?"

"Honestly, probably a long time ago. Though I ignored it. There was no other option. But after you left the apprenticeship, my world was darker than it'd ever been."

"But you wanted the power." She glanced up. It looked like he was about to argue, but he closed his mouth. He wouldn't blame it on his upbringing, she realized. Though that really was the reason he'd chosen magic over her.

The reason didn't matter now, not when they couldn't be together, but it helped her understand.

After a moment, he said, "Yes, I wanted power. But I was mistaken. I returned to my sorcerer clan after the apprenticeship, but it no longer made sense the way it once had. The way they live... No love, no real affection. They'd be better off as loners, but Mytheans are always stronger as a group. So they built some strange bond based on the worship of power. But to do what? It's all well and good to have immense capability, but after a while, what do you use it for? What's the point?"

"I never thought I'd hear you speak this way."

He shrugged. "Time. Life. They change a man. I built my fortune and reputation with power, but it's been empty for a long time."

She bit her lip, then asked, "Did you leave the sorcerers? You live alone now."

"I did. I went to my father's people. Wulvers. Being a half blood is probably why I didn't fall completely in line with the sorcerers."

"Did you like it there?" Though it was a bad idea to grow too close, she found that she was ravenous for information about him.

"It was all right. I got to meet my brother, Felix. And to know my father a bit before he died. But even that didn't suit me. I was searching, I think, for what I felt with you. I never found it."

Sofia's hands twisted in the comforter.

"When this is all over, I want you to live with me," he said again.

She tried to crush the stupid desire that welled in her at the idea. "What about my village?"

It was a dumb question. They couldn't be together, so it didn't matter. She would be with them no matter what—at least the ones who chose to relocate with her.

"We can live with them if you prefer," Malcolm said. "Establish a new settlement somewhere. The curse shall no longer apply since it's not Bruxa's Eye. I'll help you build it."

Aching want was crushed by dark disappointment. "Build it? You're a warlock. Your specialty is destruction. And we can't be together. You know that. You've heard the stories. You *knew* Laira. You saw what happened to her. Fate will find a way to tear us apart. I can't take that. Not to mention, the way fate does its work, it could be terrible."

"I can make it work. I can keep fate off our backs."

"How? By not loving me?" she asked. Her throat tightened at the thought. She blinked quickly, trying to hold back tears.

"Yes. It's the way it has to be."

He didn't love her. She knew that. He might have once, but he no longer did. Not loving was safest. It had to be that way.

But why did it hurt so badly?

"If we're careful, we can make this work." He rubbed his hand gently over her arm as if he couldn't get enough of touching her.

"By careful, you mean you'll never love me. Never make promises. Never really be with me."

"It has to be that way."

He was right. It did have to be that way. But she couldn't accept so little. He'd hurt her once before and she couldn't let it happen again. She'd be so close to what she wanted, only to have it slowly eat away at her heart until it was devoured entirely.

She pulled out of his grasp and curled up on her side, away from him. The slight soreness between her legs only reminded her of what they'd had. "It's not enough for me, Malcolm. It wasn't then, and it isn't now."

He lay beside her and pulled her to him. Sofia stiffened.

"Just for tonight," he said.

Slowly, she relaxed.

Just for tonight. Because tomorrow they would be through.

CHAPTER FIFTEEN

Mud squished beneath Malcolm's boots as he made his way through the jungle alongside Sofia. It was still thirty minutes before dawn and Sofia lit the way with her wand. Kitty went ahead, jumping from tree root to tree root to stay out of the mud. His wulver night vision sufficed to get him through the forest, but he kept glancing at Sofia, who was lit by the light of her wand. She was once again in the guise of a Crone, but he could see her beneath it.

Lying next to her last night had been a revelation. Truthfully, the last few days had been a revelation.

He wanted her more than he wanted the power. He wanted her more than he wanted anything. But he'd done wrong by her. Guilt clawed at him for his role in her village's dire straits.

He was to blame for this. No question—he'd have to do everything in his power to see that these people stayed safe.

And Sofia… If he wanted any chance at convincing her to stay with him, he was going to have to find a way to shed his Oath Breaker curse. Which meant getting rid of his warlock powers.

He clenched a fist. The idea of giving up his power made him sick. But even worse was the idea that there might not be a way.

"We're almost there," Sofia said.

The jungle was alive around them, giant trees on all sides and night animals rustling and filling the air with screeches and growls. The path opened up to a clearing that was bordered on all sides by enormous jungle trees. In the middle, thirteen tall, flat stones rose toward the air. The six faction leaders who made up the council each stood in front of a stone, waiting. All were positioned on one side of the circle.

He'd thought stone circles were primarily found in the British Isles. "Who built these?"

"Our ancestors," Sofia said. "A long time ago. This isn't the only stone circle in Brazil, but it's the only one built by Mytheans. It's a place where we can come to contact the dead. To be closer to those we've lost."

He followed her into the circle. Aleia and Inara stood near the middle. Sofia greeted the council members who'd taken up their positions in front of the stones, then turned to Aleia and Inara.

"I'm going to open a portal to our afterworld, then I'll call my ancestors forth. Inara, since you're a world walker, perhaps you can assist me."

"I can use my magic to amplify your call," Inara said. "Just tell me the names of those we're calling."

Sofia repeated the names of her ancestors, then turned to Malcolm. "Could you do the same?"

He nodded.

"All right." She glanced toward the east, where the sky was beginning to turn brilliant pink and orange, the colors bleeding across the sky. "We can begin."

She turned to face the other side of the circle, toward the seven stones that had no one standing in front of them. Kitty sat at her right and Inara stood at her left. Aleia drifted back to stand in front of a stone.

Malcolm could feel the gazes of the observing council members at his back, and though he didn't usually like putting his back to other powerful Mytheans, there was no helping it now. He'd committed himself to doing whatever Sofia needed from him. He stepped up to stand next to Kitty.

Sofia swept her black cloak away from her shoulders and raised her wand. She murmured quiet words under her breath, so whisper-soft that he couldn't make them out. Her wand moved in a square pattern, the tip alight.

As the sun broke over the trees, a glowing space—like a doorway with no door—opened on the other side of the circle. Magic trembled in the air, quieting the jungle animals until all he could hear was the breeze.

Sofia raised her voice, calling the names of her ancestors. Malcolm and Inara joined her, repeating the names she'd told them just moments ago.

"Laís, Karajá, Nauquá, Panenoá, Aparai, Oriva," The strange, ancient names echoed through the jungle.

The empty, glowing doorway pulsed, its light going from bright yellow to pure white. Malcolm's skin prickled from the power that radiated outward.

The pulsing glow ceased, halting on pure white. A figure approached the door, cloaked in black and appearing as a Crone. She shimmered slightly. She was a soul given form, not an actual body. She stepped through the door and out into the jungle.

"Mother," Sofia said, joy in her voice.

"Daughter. How I've missed you." Sofia's mother's voice was warm, loving.

Another figure stepped through the door and took up her position next to Sofia's mother. She also wore a dark cloak and the Crone's visage.

"Grandmother" Sofia said. Her voice was still joyful, though more respectful. As Malcolm recalled, Sofia had never met her grandmother.

"Child," the grandmother's voice was also warm.

Four other figures stepped out of the portal, one by one. All appeared as black-cloaked Crones. Sofia greeted each of them and was greeted in turn.

The last Crone to step out—Oriva, she'd been called—spoke in a voice heavy with power. "Why have you called us forth?"

"I've learned something troubling," Sofia said. Quickly, she explained their situation with the High Witches. "And I understand that you originally made the deal with the High Witches that bound us to this. In exchange for magical power for our line, you tied your progeny to the High Witches, forcing us to provide tributes or be responsible for the destruction of our village."

The souls that stood next to her gasped, their heads whipping toward her in shock. They hadn't known. He'd suspected as much.

Oriva's brows rose. Her gaze was a sharp black that sent a chill down Malcolm's spine. Her voice was like ice. "You do not enjoy the gift of power?"

"Yes," Sofia said. "But not at the expense of my village."

"That is not your decision to make. You are too young to understand. Or perhaps you are too stupid."

Malcolm stepped forward, but Sofia's hissed warning stopped him.

"Either way," Sofia said. "The High Witches are going to destroy our village."

Oriva nodded her head. "Yes. I am not surprised. They thrive on destruction."

"You knew that and still made the deal?" Sofia asked.

"Yes." Her voice cracked like a whip. "I've never been terribly concerned with my progeny. It suited me, therefore I did it."

Bloody hell, and he'd thought his sorcerer clan was bad.

Sofia's mouth twisted in disgust, but she spoke evenly. "The council members are resisting abandoning the village. But we cannot fight the High Witches and win. They're too powerful. And because you made this deal with them, fate is on their side."

"I fail to see how you expect me to solve your problem."

"Agree that we can't win and convince the council that we should abandon the village."

The other souls were rustling agitatedly now, as if they didn't like what Oriva was saying, or possibly the position in which she'd placed Sofia and the village. Malcolm didn't blame them. They'd been caught in the same trap Sofia was, spending their entire lives in the role of Protector.

"Why?" Oriva asked, her voice emotionless. "It is not the place that is cursed. It is the people. A place is nothing without the people who live within it. The High Witches thrive on the destruction of lives more so than they do on the destruction of property. All the descendants of the original villagers are cursed."

Sofia stepped back, shock on her face. There were gasps from behind them.

"How? That's not possible," Sofia said.

"Of course it is. It would take time, but the High Witches are talented and strong. You can all run, scatter to the far ends of the earth, but the High Witches will still find you."

"But—why? Gods, that's awful. How could you do that?" Sofia's voice shook.

She shrugged. "It was not difficult. Thousands of years ago, my father died. He'd founded the village. As his progeny, I became its leader. When the High Witches approached me, offering me immense power in exchange for lives other than my own, it was easy to agree." There was no remorse in her voice.

"But the people of the village were your family. Your friends!"

"As long as I paid the tributes, no one I knew personally needed to die." Oriva's eyes were cold. "It's been over two thousand years and they are only now coming to collect. The current citizens of Bruxa's Eye might be descendants of some of my friends, but they aren't my actual friends. And some of the people who live here aren't even descendants. Their fate is no concern of mine."

"There's has to be something we can do!" Sofia said.

"Fight them and hope to win." Oriva shrugged. "Though that will be nearly impossible."

Sofia's shoulders sagged.

The five other souls who stood next to Oriva erupted into shouts. They converged on her.

Sofia waved her wand and the souls and portal disappeared. She turned to the others, her eyes dark. "I'm so sorry."

"Fates, your ancestor was a piece of work," Inara said.

"That's the truth of it," the big Were said. "But we wanted to fight the High Witches, and we will fight them."

Sofia tried to force her body to stop trembling. "More than half of the village are descendants of the original cursed villagers. Perhaps even more. The others could flee, but…"

"Then everyone would die," Amira, the vampire, said. "I will stay, though my family has only been here for eight hundred years. Our strength is in our numbers. Our combined powers. I won't turn my back on my friends."

Gratitude welled in Sofia. Should she encourage them to leave? To save themselves? But if she did, she'd be consigning the rest of her village to death.

Kitty pressed against her leg and she focused on her warmth, drawing strength and comfort from her familiar.

"We'll need as much help as we can get," Sofia met the gazes of the council members, who'd all come to stand before her. "Talk to your factions. Let those who are not of the original descendants make their own choice about whether or not to fight. But if they will stay, ask them to get what help they can. Friends and family who live in other places. The High Witches will converge upon the village with magic the likes of which we cannot imagine. We'll need numbers to fight them."

"I can talk to the transients," Aleia said.

"Good." Sofia nodded. Bruxa's Eye drew dozens of visitors every day, many of them repeats. Often, the population of the village was at least doubled by their numbers. "I will do what I can to find help from elsewhere. We still have two days before the High Witches expect us to return with the Grimoire. When we don't appear with it, they'll attack. Do what you can to add to our numbers and we will meet again tomorrow morning."

The council members nodded and said their goodbyes, then left the circle. When it was just her, Inara, Aleia, and Malcolm, Sofia almost collapsed. Despair stole her strength.

Unable to help herself, she glanced at Malcolm. He stood so tall, a pillar of strength in the middle of the stone circle. Early morning sun gleamed on his dark hair. Pain stabbed her, a blade to the heart. Gods, she almost loved him. Yet his actions had led her here.

How the hell was she supposed to reconcile that?

Did it matter, considering what they were facing?

They couldn't win this. If, for some insane reason they did, it wouldn't be without enormous loss of life.

Just the thought of it forced steel back into her spine. She didn't have time to collapse. She had to keep going. There had to be a way—build their numbers strong enough, attack the High Witches on their home turf, do *something*.

Malcolm came to stand by her side, his gaze fierce. "We can fix this."

"Can we?" She had no idea how.

"My brother will help. We can go to the university and request more assistance. They have a vested interest in not letting the High Witches destroy an entire village, even if that village isn't in their territory."

She nodded. She'd been thinking of going to them. There was no central organization like the university in South America. Her village was the closest thing to a large, organized group of Mytheans in the entire continent. Salem served the same purpose in the north, but they had no friends there. Not after they'd destroyed the Salem Coven's home.

"We'll go to your brother," she said, feeling not a whit bad about using him for his contacts. He owed her. "His wife has contacts with the university, right? And powerful friends."

"Yes. We can go now."

Sofia nodded, then turned to Inara. "Will you stay for the battle?"

"Yeah. You helped me get back at the Salem Coven, I'll help you with this. But if it looks like I'm about to get offed, I'm aetherwalking away."

"Fair enough. Thank you." Sofia held out her hand to Malcolm. "Lead the way to your brother's place."

His big hand grasped hers and she shivered, unable to help the streak of pleasure that ran over her skin. A second later, they stood in the snow. Bright sun gleamed on the icy whiteness, nearly blinding her. A charming cottage—like something out of a fairy tale—stood before her.

Kitty turned herself into smoke to avoid the cold. Sofia used her wand to remove her Crone's visage and to replace the cloak with all-weather gear. Malcolm seemed not to notice the cold, though he wore only a t-shirt and dark jeans with leather boots.

They knocked on the wooden door, which swung open seconds later to reveal Aurora, wearing pajamas covered in wine bottles. Heat wafted out of the house, along with the delicious smell of bacon and eggs. How could something as normal as breakfast be happening when she was about to lose everything she loved? Maybe even her life?

"Ah, fuck," Aurora said. "If you're here, it means things have gone to hell, doesn't it?"

Sofia nodded, her throat tight but her back stiff.

Aurora stepped back. "Come on in."

They stepped into the warmth just as Felix walked in from the back room wearing loose sweatpants and a t-shirt. Mouse was draped over his broad shoulders, yellow eyes watching them thoughtfully. Felix carried a fluffy cat toy in his right hand.

"This can't be good," Felix said.

"It's not." Malcolm scrubbed a hand over his face.

"Why don't we take a seat and you can tell us what you need?" Felix asked.

They sat. Mouse jumped down and went to greet Kitty, who'd chosen to sit by the fire. They sniffed each other, then sat down companionably to enjoy the warmth.

Sofia took a deep breath and began to speak. It didn't take long to spell out exactly how dire her situation was.

"We're happy to come," Aurora said. "And we can get some help from the university. My sister of course, and her friend Andrasta, I'm sure. She's a Celtic demigod and her man is the Celtic God of War. Camulos, I think he's called. Logan and Sylvi will help as well, I'd bet. I used to think the university was full of assholes and egos, but most of them aren't that bad and they're happy to jump into a worthy battle."

"Thank you." Sofia took a deep breath. Maybe they could win this. Maybe even without too much death. They had immense numbers on their side, and powerful allies. She had to cling to hope.

"We can go there now," Aurora said. "I have a flat on campus. We can use it as a base."

Sofia nodded gratefully. "Thank you. Really."

"It's not a problem. I understand what it is to be in a bind. Let us change, and we'll go." Aurora and Felix left to change.

Malcolm came to sit next to her. He rubbed her back and a small bit of tension dissipated. She hated that he could make her feel better. He'd left her. He'd stolen her dagger and gotten her into this mess. But she still melted when he was near.

It was annoying as hell. She had huge things to worry about. Obstacles that were likely insurmountable.

But then, wasn't that a good reason to take comfort where she could find it?

She shook the thought away. A moment later, Felix and Aurora returned, dressed in jeans and coats.

"Get a move on, Mouse, we're headed back to the university," Aurora said.

Mouse glanced at her, then rose, stretched, and sauntered toward Aurora like a tiny jaguar. The little familiar had as much feline grace as her larger brethren, but Sofia would take roly-poly, squinty-eyed Kitty any day. She smiled at Kitty as she made her way toward her.

"Malcolm, you remember where Aurora's flat is, aye?" Felix asked.

"Yes. I'll take Sofia." Malcolm wrapped his big arms around Sofia and transported both her and Kitty to the base of a tall stone tower. Rolling green hills and giant, gnarled oaks surrounded it. In the distance, Sofia could make out huge, ornate stone buildings. The air had the bite of autumn, with winter coming.

The Immortal University. They were outside of Edinburgh, Scotland. It didn't look like she'd expected. It was greener. But then, she'd never thought much about Scotland or the university. Though the university was vital to British Mytheans, she'd never had a reason to come.

Until now, when she hoped to find as many powerful Mytheans as she could who were willing to fight a deadly battle with her.

This wasn't going to be easy.

Aurora and Felix appeared next to them, Mouse at Aurora's side.

"Come on," Aurora said and led them to the door at the base of the tower.

They made their way up the spiral staircase to a landing at the top. Aurora ran her hands over the door frame.

Removing a charm. So that's why they hadn't aetherwalked straight inside. They'd have gotten zapped, or worse.

"Flat, sweet flat," Aurora said as she led the way in.

Sofia's brows rose when she entered. The flat was one large, round room with a section walled off for the bedroom. The main room had a small kitchen that faced the living room. The space was full of electronics. Televisions, computers, blenders, fans, flashlights. Half of them were assembled, some were vomiting their circuit boards and wires into the room.

"I had a bit of a thing for electronics when I first got out of the pokey," Aurora said.

Pokey? Did she mean prison?

"Anyway," Aurora said, "I'm mostly over that now. I've figured out how it all works. Lost its allure. She nudged an old rotary phone with her foot. "I really need to clean this up. But, another time. First, we need to find you some help."

"I'd like to bring my friend Aleia here, if you don't mind. She's a seer and I think we could use all the advice we could get."

"Good plan," Aurora said. "You do that, I'm going to try to find some folks. I'll be back soon. Hopefully with some fighters."

CHAPTER SIXTEEN

Malcolm pounded on the great wooden door of Corrier's house. He'd left Sofia at Aurora's flat on the university campus. He'd return to help her recruit assistance, but first, he had something to do. This would hopefully only take a few minutes and then he'd be able to return to Sofia with news that would bury their troubles.

Cold wind whipped down the valley, making this part of Norway seem more desolate than he remembered it.

Or maybe, it was his situation.

His heart raced as he waited for the door to open. Now that he'd committed to this plan, nerves and anticipation thrummed beneath his skin.

What if there wasn't a way to forfeit his warlock's power and stop being an Oath Breaker?

The thought sent a chill over his skin.

That was *not* an option. He'd find a way around this. Once the battle was over and he had no use for his immense power, he'd forfeit it. There would be a way. There had to be.

Finally, the door swung open to reveal the same woman who had opened it on his earlier visit with Sofia. Her green eyes widened at the sight of him.

"You return so soon," she said.

"Indeed. Corrier?"

She nodded and stepped back into the hall. The sense of familiarity washed over him again at being in Corrier's home. He'd spent so long here. Met Sofia. Made stupid decisions.

"Malcolm." Corrier's warm voice carried down the stairs. His cloak flowed behind him as he walked, presenting an impressive figure. "Is there something I can do for you?"

Malcolm nodded. "Could we speak in your study?"

"Of course." Corrier led the way, his steps quick.

Malcolm accepted the glass of whisky Corrier handed him, but ignored it. "I need to no longer be an Oath Breaker."

Corrier's eyes widened and the glass halted halfway to his lips. He lowered it. "That's not possible. Warlocks are Oath Breakers. That's the curse. There's no way around it."

"Then I need to no longer be a warlock." It didn't phase him a bit to throw away his power. Not like it once would have. Now, with Sofia on the line, he'd give it up in a second.

"Ah. It's Sofia, isn't it?"

Malcolm nodded sharply.

"I wondered when I saw you here last. In fact, I wondered when you were an apprentice. I wasn't surprised when she opted out." His gaze searched Malcolm's. "In fact, I was a bit surprised when you decided to break your vow to Sofia to become a warlock. But then, there's your family."

Darkness settled over Malcolm at the mention of his family. He hadn't seen them in centuries, not since he'd really understood the pain of losing Sofia. After that, it'd been easy to separate himself from them. But not before. Not when it would have made a difference.

"I made a mistake," Malcolm said. "A terrible one. Now I need out. No longer a warlock, no longer an Oath Breaker."

Corrier's face fell. At the sight, a cold sweat broke out on Malcolm's skin.

"A warlock's magic always comes at a price. It's a power that is not inherent like that of a witch or a sorcerer. It's greater, but at greater cost. As you know, the strongest spells take something from the warlock. Becoming a warlock took sacrifice and abandoning the path would also require sacrifice. But there's only one way out." Corrier's voice was grave. "The greatest sacrifice."

Death.

"Death," Corrier said.

It was a blow to hear, nearly sucking the wind from him.

"But not just any death. A death in sacrifice. Else you'll be a warlock and an Oath Breaker in the afterlife as well."

Malcolm just stopped himself from crushing the crystal. "Then there's no way I can be with her?"

"No. Not short of death, and then, only if she goes to the same afterworld as you. Her beliefs would have to match yours. You knew this when you signed up, yet you did it anyway."

Malcolm dragged a hand down his face.

This was real. And there was no escape.

"Don't try to be with her," Corrier said. His tone was sharp, as if Malcolm were still his pupil. "It will end badly. You remember what happened to Laira. And to those who came before her."

Malcolm's jaw clenched.

"And Sofia is in danger now, is she not? Her village under a curse by the High Witches?"

Malcolm nodded. "They'll attack in three days."

Corrier gripped his arm hard, fingers digging in. "You must not fall in love with her. Make no commitments. She's already in danger. Fate will take this opportunity to tear you apart. Our world is dangerous. There are many opportunities for a cursed union such as yours to fail, but this is just asking for it."

A cursed union.

Sofia sat on the plush red couch in Aurora's flat, Kitty at her side. Malcolm had gone to do some kind of errand and she'd been too distracted to ask. He hadn't seemed like he wanted to share. As soon as he'd left, she'd felt the tattoo connection between them break. She'd grown used to it and really only felt it when he arrived in her vicinity or left, but it was still odd.

She bounced her knee as she waited for responses to their requests for help. Most were made by phone, though in some cases, allies needed to be tracked down via aetherwalking. They already had Esha and Warren's promises of help, now she awaited assistance from Aurora's other colleagues.

Gods, how she prayed that the council members were having luck convincing their factions. There were so many Weres, vamps, and fae in the world, but they weren't all a united front. They couldn't count on the entirety of the Were or fae population to come to their aid, but those Mytheans who lived in her village often had friends and family in other places who would step in to save those they loved.

And fates, it was so necessary now. Every Mythean in her village had a target painted on her head. A target drawn by her own ancestor. Her own *blood*.

It made rage sizzle in her chest, fighting the despair that tried to drag her under. It would not win. They had a lot on their side.

Aleia was in Aurora's bedroom, sitting on the floor and using her seer's vision to try to get a glimpse of the battle to come. Though she wasn't all-seeing, her visions were the most reliable of any seer's. Though it was almost impossible to circumvent fate, Sofia believed in being prepared.

A moment later, Aurora appeared in the living room, three people at her side.

"Found them!" she said. "Loki and Sylvi were in Mnemosynia. Vivienne had to take me to get them."

"Mnemo-what?" Sofia asked.

"Mnemosynia," said the tall, dark haired man with a wicked smile. "A place of memory on the abandoned afterworld of Moloch. It's for lost souls waiting to be reincarnated. I'm Logan. Though everyone insists on calling me by my better-known name."

He stepped forward and extended his hand. She shook it.

"I'm Sylvi." The tall blonde at his side smiled, then tipped her head toward the statuesque brunette standing nearby. "This is Vivienne."

"Hi," Vivienne said. She extended her hand. "Nice to meet you. Sorry you're in a bind."

"I am. But if you're here, I assume you're willing to help?" Hope fluttered in her chest. Logan was a full god, Sylvi a demigod. They were *powerful*. And Vivienne—whatever she was—looked willing to help, and that's exactly what Sofia needed.

"Yes," Logan said. "Aurora helped us once. We're happy to return the favor. And I don't like what the High Witches are doing."

"Bitches," Aurora said. "Can't keep their greedy hands to themselves. That's the problem with Mytheans whose magic comes from destruction. They're wild cards. They play by the rules for a while, but eventually they pull something you don't expect."

"Thank you," Sofia said. "Really. Having a god and a demigod on our side will really help."

"Andrasta will help too," Aurora said. "And her man, Camulos. Ana and Cam, they prefer to be called. That's another god and demigod. Esha just told me the news. Ana is her best friend, so she's got pull there. And Vivienne here is a Sila Jinn. She can access afterworlds."

Ah, so that's why she'd been the one to get Logan and Sylvi out of Mnemo-wherever.

"I'm pretty new to the world of Mytheans, but I'm good with a sword and have some other nifty powers, like traveling to afterworlds. And frankly, I like a good battle." Vivienne grinned.

"Thank you, so much," Sofia said.

"Okay," Aurora said. "At least a dozen powerful Mytheans associated with the university have agreed to help. There's one more that I want to check with. I'm headed out to do that. I'll let you know if I have any luck."

Aurora left, along with Vivienne, Sylvi, and Logan.

Sofia was about to get a drink from the kitchen when Aleia appeared in the doorway to the bedroom, her face white and her eyes stark. She supported herself on the doorway.

Fear shot through Sofia. "What did you see?"

Aleia opened her mouth to speak, but no words came out. She tried again, whispering, "Your—your death. In the battle."

CHAPTER SEVENTEEN

Sofia's knees weakened. Kitty's warmth pressed against her calf, but it wasn't quite enough to keep her on her feet. She sank onto the couch.

"How?" Sofia had no voice. She cleared her throat and asked again. "How?"

Aleia came to kneel on the floor in front of her. Her face was still stark. "I couldn't see that. Just the moment right before. You're gasping your last breath, surrounded by sand. It's very strange. I didn't see after that, though."

"Oh my gods." Sofia gripped the couch cushions.

"They capture you during the battle. It's important to them. They get power from destroying the village itself, but more so from the deaths of the Mytheans who live there. It's a dark magic. The energy of your life fuels them, and you're the most powerful Mythean in Bruxa's Eye."

Sofia tried to control her breathing. This wasn't set in stone. It couldn't be.

But fate wouldn't be denied. She was grasping at straws.

Sofia reached for Kitty, sinking her fingers into her soft fur.

Dimly, Sofia realized that Aleia sat next to her and rubbed her shoulder.

"There will be a way out of this," Aleia said.

"You think so?"

"I do," Aleia said, but Sofia could tell she was lying through her teeth. Seers were good liars. They often saw things they knew people shouldn't hear. And Aleia subscribed to the school of *better to tell a white lie than hurt someone.*

"Would you mind giving me some time alone?" Sofia asked. "I just need to get my thoughts together."

"Sure. I'm headed back to the village. If you need me, you know where to find me."

"Great, thanks."

Aleia left. Sofia stared at the wall.

Her mother had foretold this. Being Protector ended in death. It was the way of things. She'd already lived over four hundred years. Short for a normal Mythean, but longer than her mother and grandmother before her, who'd died recovering tributes.

But she felt as young as any other immortal Mythean— invincible.

And now she would be cut down.

But she didn't have a daughter to whom she could pass on the role of Protector.

It didn't matter though, did it? This was to be the end of her village. The High Witches had been done with them for a while now. There'd be no need for another Protector. And she wouldn't wish this on a daughter anyway.

She sucked in a breath and stood up. She'd face this like she faced everything else thrown her way. She didn't have a choice.

She felt Malcolm's arrival, a warmth that was specific to their connection, and turned to see him, his dark hair windswept and some strange emotion in his eyes. Her heart thudded, trying to beat its way out of her chest.

He always did that to her. She was starting to think there was no escape from it.

"What's wrong?" he asked. He strode to her, then grasped her upper arms and stared into her eyes. "Tell me."

"Nothing." She didn't want to tell him. She didn't want him to look at her like her doom was imminent. Her death might come, but she wouldn't bear pitying looks until it did. "Just worried about the upcoming battle."

"We'll manage it."

She tried to take comfort in his certainty. It was a chore, but she forced herself to nod.

"Aurora has found more warriors for the battle?" he asked.

"Yes. More than a dozen. A couple are gods." They really did have a chance with their help. The High Witches were powerful, especially when together, but they weren't gods. "I think she's gotten pretty much everyone she knows."

"Good. Come with me, then. I have something you might like."

"All right." The agreement came immediately. She still hadn't forgiven him and their future was impossible, but she was still halfway to falling in love with him and she didn't want to think about the future right now. If he wanted to take her mind off of it, she would let him.

She wrapped her arms around his waist and called to Kitty. Once the warm little body was pressed against her leg, Malcolm aetherwalked them away.

When she opened her eyes, she stood in a small round room. A sitting room of some sort, with beautiful furniture and a dozen windows. The walls were almost entirely glass, with strips of wood between each window. Mountains stretched in all directions. The orange globe of the sun was approaching the mountain ridges.

"Are we in your home?"

"Yes. I had this room built for you. Not that I ever expected to see you again. But sunsets have always reminded me of you. I like to come up here sometimes."

Tears pricked at her eyes. He remembered. That night at Dartmoor when she'd accompanied him to pay his respects to his mother had been the night she'd fallen in love with him. What could their life have been if he hadn't made the choices he had?

She forced the thought away. She wouldn't spend the last days of her life mourning the past. She'd embrace what little future she had left until fate stole it from her. That included Malcolm.

If she had one night left, she wanted it to be with him.

His hand cupped her cheek. "You're sad."

"It's just worry over my village." She looked out at the mountains that were now washed in orange light. "Could we just talk? Distract me?"

"Anything." He walked to a sideboard and picked up a decanter full of golden whisky and tilted it toward her inquiringly.

"Yes, please," she said gratefully.

Kitty curled up on a chair and Sofia sank onto one of the plush sofas. The golden light of the sunset bathed the room in a soothing glow. When Malcolm brought her the tumbler of whisky, she took it gratefully and sipped. The burn down her throat made her feel alive.

Malcolm sat next to her and draped an arm over her shoulder, pulling her close. She stiffened out of instinct, then relaxed into him. Why not enjoy being with him during the few days she had left? He might have taken the dagger and started all of this, but he'd never meant to get her into this mess. Of course he'd thought they could handle the High Witches. *She'd* thought that.

Ugh. She needed to think about something else.

She glanced up at Malcolm. His gaze was grave as he watched the sunset. She didn't know where he'd gone today, and she didn't want to ask. Judging by the furrow of his brow and the worry in his eyes, it hadn't gone well. She didn't want more bad news.

She wanted a distraction, and talking wasn't going to do it.

Sofia set the whisky glass on the floor and climbed onto his lap, straddling his thick thighs. Out of the corner of her eye, she saw Kitty slink out of the room.

Fate, he was big. She gripped his shoulder and met his gaze.

"What are you doing?" His voice was rough.

"Distracting myself." She pressed her mouth to the side of his neck, dragging her tongue along the delicious expanse. His cock hardened beneath her as she bit his neck. Unable to wait, she climbed off his lap to kneel before him. Her hands found the buttons of his trousers and began to undo them.

He hissed in a breath. "Are you sure—"

She pressed a hand over his mouth. She'd had a hard day, but she didn't need his coddling. What she needed was a distraction, and his thick, beautiful erection was just what it was going to be. She hadn't really been able to spend much time on him before, and fates, how she wanted to.

With fumbling hands, she tugged his trousers and underwear down around his calves. His thick cock sprang free, thick and long. It was beautiful, with a tracing of veins and a pearl of fluid at the tip.

"You want this?" he growled.

She glanced up to see him watching her, desire and some darker emotion on his face. He looked at her like she held the last cup of water in the desert. Like he'd die if she didn't put her mouth on him.

It made her sex clench.

"Yes," she said.

He gripped his cock in his big hand. Veins stood out on the back of his palm, so masculine that she shivered. Those big, blunt fingers had been inside of her.

"Then take it," he said, and tilted the shaft toward her.

A groan tore from his throat as she darted her tongue out and lapped up the drop of fluid. Another lick to the tip.

His head dropped back on the couch and she thought she heard him say something like *fates, just once* but she was too busy with his taste.

Musky and dark, it was delicious. It made her breasts throb and her pussy ache. Wanting more, she took the crown into her mouth.

A groan tore from his throat. His hand threaded through her hair, squeezing gently. It was so dirty, the way he held her head and fed her his cock. The idea made her moan around his shaft.

He groaned.

He was too big to take entirely into her mouth, so she nudged his hand away with her own and gripped him in her fist. His shaft was so big that her hand barely fit around.

"Fuck, that's good, Sofia," he rasped.

She glanced up to see him watching her, his eyes bright and his cheeks flushed. His chest heaved. Fates, he was handsome. She raised a hand and waved it over his chest, making his shirt disappear.

The broad expanse of his chest and his ridged abdomen were enough to make her whimper. She couldn't even look at the muscles that roped his arms or the tattoo that wrapped around his shoulder without wanting to run her hands over him. Fates, she wanted to touch all of him. Trace his hard pecs and the swell of his bicep, the curve of his throat and his strong hands.

So many nice things to touch, but she returned to his shaft, the part that she most wanted to worship, taking him deeper. She pumped her fist in tandem, reveling in the silken steel beneath her palm. He shuddered, his fist tightening in her hair. The slight tug of pain sent a wave of dark pleasure through her.

With a gentle hand, she cupped his balls.

"Yes," he groaned.

She took him deeper into her mouth, straining to accept as much of him as she could. The head of his cock bumped the back of her throat. His thighs shook and she could tell that he was fighting not to thrust up into her mouth.

A soft touch at her cheek made her glance up. He cupped the side of her face and gripped her hair, cradling her as if he treasured her. The dark need in his gaze fought with tenderness.

"So bloody beautiful," he breathed.

Her heart fluttered and she returned to his cock. She sucked hard, wanting to taste his come on her tongue.

"Sofia!"

She picked up her pace, squeezing his shaft hard and taking him as deeply into her mouth as she could. He was far too big to take all the way into her mouth, but even that excited her. She was shaking with need. From just this?

But with him, it was different. The way he responded to her... His hands and the sounds he made, the way his hips fought not to thrust.

"I'm going to come," he ground out, tugging lightly at her hair to remove her.

She fought him, sucking the head of his cock deep while stroking the shaft with her tongue.

"Gods," he growled. "If you want it, I'll give it to you."

Yes. Give it to me.

She swallowed him as deeply as she could.

He stiffened, his back arching off the couch as his cock throbbed in her mouth. She felt it swell even more and his balls tighten up. His hips jerked. If he were inside of her, he'd be pounding into her, but she knew he didn't want to hurt her.

With a roar, he began to come, filling her mouth with his seed.

Pleasure sparked along every nerve ending in Malcolm's body. His cock throbbed, shooting jets of come into Sofia's hot little mouth. The way she sucked and worked his cock made him shudder violently as the orgasm tore through him.

The sight of her watching him, her pretty pink lips stretched around his thick shaft, had been what sent him over the edge. Now, with her silky tongue lapping up the last of his spend, he wasn't sure if he could bear to pull away from her.

When the orgasm faded, he collapsed back on the couch, his chest heaving. His entire body tingled as he pulled Sofia up onto his lap. She curled up, her face near his.

"Thank you." The words barely had any sound, he was so out of breath.

"I wanted to."

He knew she had. It'd been so bloody sexy, the way she'd devoured him. And the sounds she'd made... The moans that had vibrated his cock and sent pleasure shooting up his spine. Gods, how he wanted to eat her pussy while she sucked him off.

Her breath was sweet on his face and he leaned over to kiss her, tasting his own saltiness on her lips. He pulled away and set her aside on the couch, then stood and tugged his trousers up.

Without asking, he reached down and picked her up.

"Whoa!"

"I want you in my bed," he said. He didn't know what the future held. After talking to Corrier, he knew he couldn't be with her. Not after tonight and all that had happened.

When he'd left Corrier's, he'd told himself he wouldn't be like this with her again. No more intimacy. No more sex. That he'd make a clean break to try to protect her.

He'd thought he could handle the High Witches, and he'd been wrong. He'd wanted to be with her again so badly that he'd fooled himself into thinking he could avoid fate. But he couldn't, he'd realized. Their involvement would lead to tragedy. Likely one of their deaths. He didn't mind so much if it were his own—at this point, he'd risk his own life if it meant being with Sofia. But he couldn't bear it if something happened to her.

So he'd have one more night. *They'd* have one more night. And then they would part.

Warmth flowed through him when she wrapped her arms around his neck. Not wanting to waste the time walking across the castle, he aetherwalked them to his bed and laid her upon it. He flicked on the bedside light so that it cast a golden glow over her.

She was so slight that it was easy to push her toward the middle of the bed and then climb in after her. He pulled her into a sitting position and tugged gently at her blouse.

"I saw you the other night, but not as much as I wanted to. It was too dark." He wanted to worship her. To kiss every inch and memorize her for the future. To hold these memories close on a future lonely night.

Sofia raised her arms and he pulled the sweater over her head. Her full breasts were cupped in ivory lace, the dusky rose of her nipples showing through. He crouched over her like some great beast and gripped her ribs, lifting her so that he could take one of the small peaks into his mouth.

She fisted her hands in his hair and cried out as he sucked. The lace was rough against his tongue but her skin was sweet. The bud of her nipple hardened against his tongue and he bit down.

"Yes," she gasped.

"You like a little pain?" he asked.

"So far, I like everything with you."

Gods, how he wished they had time for everything. He thrust the thought away and turned his attention to her other nipple, sucking and biting until it too poked through the fabric.

Malcolm leaned back to look at her, at the way her skin flushed and her breasts swelled over the top of her bra. She was small, but so perfectly formed. Her dark eyes were steady on him as his gaze roved over her, from her trim waist and the sexy little swell of her belly to her full lips and dark, flowing hair.

"I've never seen anyone as lovely as you," he said.

She was a bloody dream come true. For the last four centuries, he'd fantasized about her, dreaming of what she'd look like without her clothes. He'd never seen her this way, but his imagination had been vivid. She'd been beautiful in his mind—beautiful enough that he'd spilled his seed countless times against the sheets—but those imaginings were nothing compared to the real thing. The way her skin was smooth as silk and her curves rounded and lush.

He reached around her back and unclipped her bra. Her breasts spilled free, full and sweet in the dim light. He groaned and pressed her back onto the bed, then loomed over her and kissed the side of her neck.

"I want to kiss every inch of you," he said against her throat.

"Do," she whispered.

He set to work—the most divine work he'd ever done—and ran his tongue along her slender neck. She shivered, gripping his biceps. Tiny goose bumps formed on her delicate shoulders as he ran his lips along the smooth skin. Her breasts were soft and smooth. Though he could have spent hours kissing them, he craved the taste of her pussy on his tongue. He wanted to tear her trousers off and bury his face in her.

Savor her. This would be the last time. He had to enjoy it. To burn the memory into his brain. So he slowed himself, tracing kisses and licks down her stomach. Her hands came up to grip his hair as he laved circles around her belly button.

When her back arched, he slipped his arm beneath her, supporting her and marveling at how much smaller she was than he. Finally, the temptation became too much. He knelt up and undid the button of her jeans. His hands trembled as he pulled the zipper down.

He tugged off her boots, then her jeans, leaving only her white underwear. White cotton with a border of lace. Her swollen sex pushed against the thin fabric, soaking it so that he could see the pink of her flesh through the fabric.

"Beautiful," he growled. His cock pulsed and pressed hard against his jeans.

Malcolm reached down and splayed his hand over her upper thigh, brushing his thumb over her core. Her hips jerked and he looked up to see her panting, her skin damp and her eyes wild. His kisses had made her mad for him, he could see it in her eyes and the way her hands gripped the comforter.

She was trembling, desperate for him to touch her. Her body vibrated with it.

"Shhh," he soothed. "I'll give you what you need."

His gaze returned to his hand, so big and rough against the pale fabric and her delicate sex. So badly, he wanted to tear the cloth from her and devour her. He shook with it, but forced it away. Though he wanted to gorge himself on her, he had to start slowly.

He dipped his thumb under the elastic between her legs, drawing it over the soft curls and down to the silken flesh that dampened her panties. She was wet and hot, the softest thing he'd ever felt.

She cried out, her back arching and her breasts trembling. He reached up to press his other hand against her chest and throat, making a loose circle around her neck, as if collaring her. He recalled doing the same the other night, unable to help himself.

He wanted to own her. To ensure she'd be with him forever.

It was impossible, but at least here, he could have the illusion that she was entirely his.

His gaze was drawn back down to her center. She trembled as he dragged his thumb through her slick folds, dipping slightly into her entrance and then rising to find her clitoris. He made tight circles, watching and listening to see what she liked best.

When Sofia started moving her hips against his hand, he could wait no longer.

"I have to have you," he groaned. He pulled her panties off and then spread her knees, his gaze riveted to her glistening pink pussy. Her labia unfurled like petals, her little clitoris revealed.

He gripped her ass in his hands and fell upon her, pressing his open mouth to her sex and plunging his tongue into her.

"Malcolm!" Her hands gripped his hair and her hips jerked.

Gods, she tasted perfect. He devoured her, lapping at her sex and thrusting his tongue into her heat. He knew he should focus on her clitoris, on the things that would make her come, but he was insatiably greedy. His hips ground against the bed as he lost himself in her. His face and neck were wet, his head full of her scent.

She shivered against him, pressing her pussy up against his mouth for more.

"Malcolm!"

The desperation in her voice pulled him out of his haze. His woman needed. He shifted to lave her clitoris, making small circles on the little bud.

"Yes, that's it, please," she gasped and gripped his hair.

He released her ass with one hand and pressed two fingers inside of her. She was so slick that she accepted him easily, a beautiful slide into pleasure. He thrust slowly as he licked her clitoris, listening to her moans and speeding up when she sounded close.

When he sucked her clitoris into his mouth, she screamed, gripping his hair and pulling his mouth against her. His cock grew unbearably hard at the feel of her forcing him against her pussy.

Inner muscles clenched around his fingers as she came, making him desperate to sink his cock into her.

The moment her orgasm ended, he used magic to remove his clothes and then settled over her. She spread her thighs to accept him. The acceptance, the quick willingness and trust, thawed something inside of him. Her pussy pressed wet and hot against his cock, a delicious brand.

He met her gaze. She blinked up at him, her chest heaving. "Now, Malcolm. Inside me, please."

He grasped her wrists and raised them above her head, as if he could keep her here forever, then reached down to adjust himself. His teeth clenched when he felt the heat of her entrance kiss the head of his cock.

"Yes," she breathed, and tilted her head back, closing her eyes.

"No," he growled. "Look at me. I want to see you."

She glanced back at him and held his gaze with her own as he pressed his cock into her channel. His whole body tightened as she accepted him. Gods, the pleasure was blinding.

Aftershocks of orgasm fluttered through Sofia as Malcolm's cock filled her. He was almost too big for her, pressing inexorably inside, but the pleasure still radiating through her made it easier to take him. She shifted, moaning at the stretching fullness as her muscles fluttered around him.

He loomed over her, his whole body huge and taught with muscle. His chest and biceps bulged as he held himself over her. When she glanced down to see his thick shaft disappearing inside of her, she could see the ridges of his abdomen and the neat black hair at his pubic bone.

She raised her gaze to his, remembering his command to look at him. His eyes were hot and desperate, his lips swollen and damp from her pussy, which he'd licked like he couldn't get enough.

Gods, he was the most handsome man she'd ever seen.

Sofia cried out when his thumb started to make circles on her clitoris. His other hand threaded through hers near her head.

"I want to feel you come around me," he said as his thumb drove her crazy. "I want to feel your little pussy clench on my cock."

She tried to speak, but he pressed his cock deeper, slowly. He shuddered, clearly resisting the desire to pound into her. When his thumb picked up pace, she felt another orgasm begin to coil within her.

"I'm close," she breathed as the tension increased, spiraling tight. She filled her gaze with the sight of his face and straining chest, imagined what his cock must look like thrusting into her, thick and slick with her juices, sinking into her soft flesh.

The visual was enough to push her over the edge, into a roaring climax that tore through her. As her pussy spasmed, Malcolm began to thrust, pushing her pleasure higher and harder. It felt as if every nerve ending inside her was alight, ten times as sensitive.

She could feel the ridge of his cockhead, every inch of every thrust. She writhed beneath him, out of her mind, but he never stopped stroking her, never stopped thrusting.

Finally, it faded enough that she could make eye contact again. Her breath caught at the look in his eyes. As if she were everything in the world that mattered to him.

"I want this to last forever," he ground out. "But I'm—so close."

She shuddered as he picked up his pace, thrusting harder and faster. His hand faltered on her clitoris and he gripped her hip, holding her steady. She didn't need any more sensation to come. Just the sight of him, his jaw clenched and his eyes fierce, every muscle tensed and bulging, was enough to send her over the edge again. The orgasm tore through her, this one harder than the last.

"Ah, gods, I can feel you." His brow furrowed as his fingertips bit into her ass and his hips lost their grace.

Malcolm shuddered and roared through clenched teeth as the orgasm wracked him. His cock swelled and pulsed as his seed shot forth, propelling her orgasm to the point that her vision faded and pleasure overwhelmed her.

Her head whirled as she came back to earth. Malcolm shook above her, his shoulders and chest heaving. He gently disengaged and collapsed beside her, then pulled her to him.

She curled into his side, exhausted and sated. At the edge of her mind, her impending death loomed. She'd accepted it, but in the meantime, she would enjoy every second with Malcolm. She wouldn't tell him, she'd just take what goodness she could get with him before it was all over. They had at least two days left and she planned to enjoy them.

CHAPTER EIGHTEEN

Malcolm woke early the next morning and extricated himself from tangled sheets. Sofia was draped over him, but he slipped out quietly. He turned to look down at her. Dawn light gleamed on her cheeks and the half-moons of her lashes. She looked so peaceful, so beautiful.

She looked perfect in his bed.

He brushed a hand over her cheek, regret washing through him. What could they have had if he hadn't botched it all? A long life together. A good one. She'd be with him always. Maybe bearing his children—something he'd never considered or wanted before her.

As it was…

He shook his head and turned from her, headed toward the bathroom, flicking on the light and revealing the white marbled space. His power had earned him ridiculous wealth that had bought this immaculate castle. He couldn't care less about it now.

A hot shower did nothing to help him find peace. They'd fight a battle in two days that might kill them both. If they lived, he'd have to leave Sofia.

He couldn't win this, no matter how he tried.

After he'd dried and dressed in clean clothes, he returned to the bedroom. Sofia was still asleep, but he couldn't bring himself to leave her. He went to stand by the window, gazing out at the mountains that had been his home for more than two hundred years.

The sheets rustled, but he didn't turn. A moment later, he felt Sofia's arms wrap around his waist. Longing suffused him, warm and cold at once. Like he was standing in the doorway of a warm cabin as the snow raged behind him, wishing he could walk in but knowing he couldn't.

His chest ached as he turned to her.

The sheet was wrapped around her and her golden skin gleamed. She was so beautiful.

Her gaze darkened. "What is it? You look upset."

The words scratched his throat on the way out. "You're right, Sofia. We can't make this work."

Her lips parted.

"I've been fooling myself," he said. "I've wanted to be with you so badly that I told myself I could avoid fate. But I was wrong. I recognize that now. I went to Corrier's yesterday. There's no way for me to stop being a warlock. This has to be the last time we're together."

Her shoulders sagged and a shining tear rolled down her cheek. "I know. There's no hope for us. For me."

For her? Of course there was. Did she think she would die in this battle? *The hell she would.* He'd protect her with everything he had. "Of course there's hope. I'll help you with your battle. You'll win this."

She nodded. The pain in her eyes made his heart feel like it was tearing itself out of his chest. He had to get out of here. This was too hard.

He squeezed her shoulders. "I'll meet you in Bruxa's Eye. I—I need to go now." He spun on his heel and strode into the hall, then down the stairs and all the way into his aether room.

When he reached the cool, dark room, he bent over and propped his hands on his knees, heaving. His whole body was rejecting the idea of pushing Sofia away. Gods, he felt ill.

But it had to be done. This had been wrong. He was a warlock. Love and life weren't in his future. He was destruction and he always had been. Great power at great cost, and he was paying it.

But Sofia shouldn't have to.

Malcolm sucked in a hard breath and straightened. He had to help her. To at least make up for part of this. Sofia would go meet her council in Bruxa's Eye. He'd follow, but first, he needed to fuel up on as much power as his soul and body could hold. A battle was coming.

He turned to the center of the room, taking in the space that was the epicenter of his power. This room's worth was immeasurable. Its enchantments made it strong enough to contain the portal to the aether that gave him unlimited access to power. He could fill up with almost as much raw magical energy as a *god*.

But without this room to contain the aether, he'd lose control. It'd go wild, an impossible flame that would devour everything in a forty foot radius. More, even.

This type of room was everything to a warlock.

And he hated it.

Didn't bloody well matter though, did it? He'd thrown away the one person worth anything, so now the least he could do was see to it that he protected her.

He focused on the air around him, and more importantly, on the aether. He reached out toward it, focused it on the center of the room and multiplied the aether he felt in the air around him, using it to tear a hole in space until he accessed the core of the aether. Like the darkness of outer space, but when accessed by a warlock, compressed into the brilliant white light of magical energy. He had to squint against it.

His skin prickled and his mind and muscles strained to contain it. Even with the room's protections, it took strength to keep it from bursting outward. He extended his hands, drawing energy from the aether, filling himself up with it until his muscles vibrated and his skin tingled. The power of the aether burned into him like the heat of the sun, and he embraced the flames because the pain that touched him now replaced that in his heart.

When he felt full to bursting, he cut it off, closing the aether until the room was dark.

He panted, his chest heaving. He could blow up a city right now, he had so much magical energy vibrating within him.

After his breath calmed, he checked his watch. More than an hour had passed. Sofia would be in her village, meeting with her council.

He aetherwalked there, sucking in the warm jungle air and realizing that the wild smell reminded him of Sofia. The screeching cacophony of tropical animals filled the air.

It was two hours earlier here than it was in Scotland and the early morning sun was just starting to peek over the top of the canopy. The buildings were quiet and the street was dead.

He made his way down the quiet street toward the bar where they'd first met the council and slipped in the door. He kept to the shadows, finding a spot near the door to watch.

The same half dozen council members were seated in the dim room. Sofia, cloaked in her Crone form, stood at the front with Aleia, who he'd figured out was her informal second in command. Inara stood with them as well.

Sofia glanced over at him, then quickly turned back to the burly Were who was giving his report on how many outsiders from different packs would join the fight.

It sounded dire. Though nearly all citizens were willing to stay and fight regardless of whether or not their ancestors had been cursed, the Were was reporting that less than a dozen Weres from outside the village were willing to fight to their potential death.

Not surprising really. Weres were loyal only to their packs, so getting others to help them was unlikely.

"Thank you, Alistair," Sofia said. She reached down to rest a hand on Kitty's back, who stood on the stool next to her. She glanced at the small female vampire who'd spoken at the last meeting. "Cora?"

The vampire rose and bowed low. "I have had better luck, Honored One. We have two dozen vampires willing to come to our aid, as well as all who live in Bruxa's Eye. Though they expect to be able to drink those they slay."

"Fair." Sofia nodded.

"They've agreed to arrive tonight to prepare for the High Witches' arrival tomorrow."

"Excellent." Sofia turned her gaze to the group. "In addition to our own citizens, it seems that we have approximately forty outsiders willing to come to our aid and most will arrive in two days. That's good. We may stand a chance. I don't know what's coming, but the High Witches will use dark magic and we need to be prepared for anything. Continue to seek out assistance from your kind and we will meet again this evening. We'll devise a plan for the battle tomorrow."

Everyone rose and bowed low, then began to leave. Malcolm slipped out the door before them. He couldn't speak to Sofia, but that didn't mean he wouldn't be here to keep an eye on her and fight in the final battle.

The moment he stepped into the sticky jungle air, he knew something was wrong. The air vibrated with a dark, unnatural power. It was too quiet, the jungle animals silent. It made goose bumps rise on his skin and his hands tingle to unleash destructive magic.

The council members who filed out behind him stopped short.

"What's wrong?" Cora, the vampire woman asked.

"The air's not right." The Were's burly voice was worried.

Malcolm walked farther down the street, dread coiling in his belly. He was being pulled toward the Amazon River that adjoined the north side of the village. When the street opened up to reveal the small wharf and the river, he pulled up short.

The waters were receding. The river was over a hundred yards wide here, a huge expanse of murky water that was now slowly drawing away.

Fear, an emotion he hadn't felt in centuries, skittered over his skin.

The High Witches were here. Or close.

Damn it, they should have had another day.

Footsteps sounded behind him then halted.

"Shit," a feminine voice breathed.

The bank was slowly being revealed, muddy and wet, as the waters disappeared. Boats of all sizes sank slowly and came to rest on the slimy surface. He'd been at the site of a tsunami once. It had looked exactly like this before the flood waters had begun to rise.

"The battle is starting," Sofia's commanding voice rang out behind him. "Early. Council members, wake the village. Gather whatever outsiders you can who will fight."

"That'll be hard," Cora said.

"I know," Sofia said. "Do what you can. Get a message out and see if anyone will come. But we're going to be fighting today. Soon."

Two of the council members raced down the boardwalk, shouting the alarm. The rest aetherwalked away.

Malcolm understood why she was the leader. Not just the Protector of Bruxa's Eye, but its commander. Pride welled in him.

Gods, how he wished that she were his.

Sofia's sharp gaze met his. "Get Aurora to rally the help she promised. We need them. Now."

He nodded sharply, and though he hated to leave her, he aetherwalked away.

Fear suffused the pain Sofia felt at watching Malcolm disappear. Kitty pressed up against her leg, but it gave her no comfort. Seeing him but knowing they couldn't be together felt like a burning knife in her chest. And it didn't even matter if he could stop being a warlock, because she was fated to die.

In the battle that was about to start. The High Witches hadn't given them until the end of the deadline. They were attacking now.

The air was deadly silent and now held an unnatural chill. The waters of the river were nearly half gone, receding in both directions.

"Why?" Aleia asked from her side. "Why the river?"

Sofia glanced at her friend. "I don't know." But it scared the crap out of her.

"It will come back," Inara said. "Stronger. More. It will flood."

Sofia whipped around to look at her. Inara's face was white, her fists clenched. "What?"

"I've seen this before. It will flood. And it will bring more than water."

"More?"

"Evil. But I don't know what kind." Inara was stepping slowly backward.

Sofia turned back to the river. The morning was bright, normal, except for the river and the unnatural chill of dark magic in the air.

The sounds of townspeople spilling out of their houses sounded behind her, breaking through the eerie silence. But her gaze was riveted to the far side of the river, over a hundred yards away. Morning mist still clung to the ground on that side, which was more shaded from the harsh rays of the sun.

From the ghostly mist, figures began to appear, walking from the jungle toward the bank. Their cloaks flapped around their feet.

Thirteen.

The High Witches. They would wage their battle from that side. The thirteen figures came to a stop at the bank, so far away that they appeared small and slight.

A lie.

A snarling wolf loped up to her side. Alistair, leader of the werewolves. Other wolves, all smaller but no less deadly, appeared next to him. Vampires armed with swords and speed came to a stop behind them.

On her other side, next to Aleia, a group of fae arrived, clutching bows and arrows. Their wings trembled in anticipation, their eyes gleamed with a feral hunger. Fae loved to fight, but Sofia was worried that they were biting off more than they could chew here.

Not that they had much choice. They were here to fight for their lives.

Sofia reached for Aleia's hand and squeezed it. She wanted to scream at the High Witches, curse them to hell, but they wouldn't hear her at this distance.

Her skin heated as the energy in the air shifted. Her gaze darted over the water, at the boats that rocked.

The water rose.

Slowly, but it rose. With it would come evil.

Her heart pounded. They couldn't wait here for it, not for whatever dark magic the High Witches would raise against them. But they would have to. Even now, she could see the shimmer in the air that denoted a magical barrier surrounding the High Witches. If they tried to aetherwalk, to attack directly, they would be blocked.

Cowards. They possessed immense power, but they were cowards.

"Bruxa's Eye," she called, her voice strong despite her fear. "The High Witches fight from afar for their own safety—to wield their magic to destroy our greater numbers. Our home. They are cowards. Whatever they bring us, we will destroy."

A cheer rose, vibrating through the village. The courage and willingness of her friends and neighbors emboldened her. She might be fated to die here today, but they would win. They had to.

CHAPTER NINETEEN

"Be ready," Sofia called. The water was nearer. Ever rising.

Four Mytheans appeared on the big dock that made up the main part of the wharf. Two figures she didn't recognize, but also a small blond woman and a tall red-haired man that made hope surge in Sofia's chest.

Ana and Cam, two Celtic gods who she had once helped and who Aurora had promised to find for her. In addition to being a Celtic god of war, Cam had been a riverboat captain on the Amazon for years, regularly pulling into Bruxa's Eye. Sofia was grateful they'd come to help and that they'd brought reinforcements.

Ana and Cam glanced around at the water, then raced toward them, their comrades at their sides. Bows and quivers were strapped to their backs.

They stopped before Sofia.

"I take it this is where the battle is going down?" the petite blond goddess asked.

"Yes. Thank you for coming."

Ana nodded. "You helped us when we were in trouble. We owe you."

"We've brought help," Cam said. He nodded at the strapping, dark-haired man next to him who clutched a sword in his big fist. "This is Cadan. A Mythean Guardian from the university." He nodded toward the red-haired woman. "And his mate, Diana, the reincarnate of Boudica."

Sofia's brow's rose. Boudica might be an ancient British warrior queen, but she'd been powerful enough that even Sofia knew of her. "Thank you for coming. The water is rising and bringing—"

The dark surface of the river began to bubble and clouds formed overhead, dark and ominous. The four additions to their army turned to face the water.

The roiling surface rose past the normal water line, drowning the docks. Horrifying figures began to rise from the water, bedraggled skeletons dripping with decayed flesh and river weeds. Some were more decayed than others. All were awful.

"Zombies?" Ana asked.

"The reanimated dead," Sofia whispered. The river had receded, picking up all those who had drowned and bringing them here. Breathing new life into them.

Ana and Cam drew their bows at the same time Sofia drew her wand. They fired arrows and she fired flame. The three monsters that they hit burst into a shower of water.

Hope welled in Sofia's chest. They could beat them.

A second later, others formed in their place. The same? Different? They lurched across the surface of the water, headed toward them. Others crawled out at the shore, some with gaping holes in their skulls searching sightlessly for targets. Others had decayed eyes that looked as if they no longer worked.

Would they come indefinitely or could they be defeated?

There was nothing to do but fight. As the clouds above cracked with thunder and rain began to fall, Sofia raised her wand and yelled, "Now!"

She charged toward the river, toward the enemy and certain death, Kitty at her side. Her comrades roared and followed. Sofia shot flames from her wand as fae arrows flew and wolves lunged at the corpses, tearing out throats and shattering those that were more bone than decayed flesh. They all splashed to the ground as water.

Horrified, Sofia watched the water flow back into the river and reform as a new corpse that climbed forth. Through it all, the water continued to rise, nearing the first row of buildings. Her boots sloshed in the water and rain soaked her cloak.

Sodden, she tore it off and flung it to the ground, revealing the black pants and shirt she wore underneath. Although she still looked like an old Crone, her strength remained normal.

A scream sounded to the right. Blood spurted from the shoulder of a tall male vampire. A bedraggled skeleton threw the vampire's arm to the side and fell upon him again.

They were strong. Desperately so, if they could tear the arm off a full-grown vampire.

And the water was rising.

Out of the corner of her eye, she caught sight of Ana and Cam, their bows now strapped to their backs and their hands outstretched toward the river. Light gleamed from their palms, spreading out to form a force field. The water receded from in front of them, extending out a hundred feet on either side.

It was working!

But not enough.

Where was Malcolm? Felix and Aurora? They needed more than field warriors, they needed big magic to help Ana and Cam. All around her, the battle was raging, her friends falling to the dirt beneath the hands of the wickedly strong, enchanted skeletons.

Something grabbed her from behind and Sofia whirled, breaking free of the grasp. A skeletal form lunged for her. Kitty leapt upon its chest and tore at its throat with her small fangs. Though unassuming in normal life, she was vicious in battle.

The skeleton collapsed as water.

"Sofia!"

Malcolm's voice. As soon as she heard it, she felt him. The connection Corrier had established. Thank fates.

She spun to see him racing toward her, Felix and Aurora behind him, the Norse gods Sylvi and Logan at their side, along with Vivienne, the Sila Jinn she'd met at Aurora's flat.

"Help Ana and Cam lower the river!" she yelled at them. It was lapping at the buildings now. The higher it got, the more corpses surged from it, lunging toward her comrades. Ana and Cam kept it back, but not everywhere.

"I can try," Logan shouted. He spun and sprinted to a spot farther away from Ana and Cam. Sylvi separated from him, her blue cloak swirling around her as she moved impossibly fast through the crowd, her wooden staff whirling around her, destroying opponents faster than they could reform. It was insane the way she moved. Sofia had never seen anything like it.

Felix and Aurora clashed with the nearest combatants. Felix tore the head off a corpse with his bare hands as a great silver wolf burst from his chest and lunged for a another one. Like Malcolm's. Sofia didn't know how she did it, but every time Aurora touched a dripping skeleton, it burst into ashes rather than melting into water.

Malcolm appeared in front of her and demanded, "Are you all right?"

Magical energy flowed into her, warm and powerful. Malcolm was transferring some of his strength to her, aiding her magic with his own. Thank fates, because she needed it.

"I'm fine," she said. "Help Logan and the rest with the river!" She pointed down to the east end of town where the river was still rising. The others were managing to hold the rest of the river back, though barely, and the buildings on the east side were swamped.

"If you come fight near me," he demanded.

"No!" She wanted to stay in the middle of it all.

He grabbed her arm, his gaze fierce. His face was wet, his hair plastered to his head. "Come. With. Me."

"Fine!"

They raced to the east end of town. Her boots sloshed in the water, sticking in the mud and rain poured from the sky, an awful deluge that make it hard to see which combatants were friend and which were foe. Kitty had had to turn to smoke just to travel. They stopped near the edge of the battle.

Malcolm threw out his hands and the water surged back, faster than even Logan had managed. He must have refilled his power, because it was immense despite the fact that he had given some to her.

At her right, five shimmery forms appeared, along with Vivienne. She recognized the shimmering white light immediately. Souls. They approached and she could make out their features.

Her mother. Her grandmother. Great-grandmother and the two who came before her. But not Oriva, the one who had started it all.

"What are you doing here?" she screamed as she fought off a corpse that had gotten her by the arm. "How?"

"They contacted me!" Vivienne yelled. "It's one of my powers. Told me to get Inara. We went to them and got them out. Temporarily."

"We cannot stay for long," her mother said. She looked like herself, only transparent and ephemeral. "But we can help, daughter. After what Oriva did, we must help."

Sofia's eyes teared up at the sight of her mother and the sound of her voice. "Thank you."

They floated off, then split into two groups. Though they couldn't really fight because they were incorporeal, when several of them surrounded a corpse, their energy destroyed it.

They were slow and not very effective, but just having them here made Sofia's heart swell. It felt like they had a chance.

She turned back to the battle, her gaze catching on Malcolm. He held the water back with his hands while his silver wolf lunged around him, tearing at any figure that ventured too close.

The battle raged around her as Sofia shot jets of flame from her wand, felling corpse after corpse. Though she couldn't see the High Witches, she felt their power. Dark and cloying, it wrapped around her. She fought harder, desperate to beat them.

To live.

Just as the river started to hold steady at its original water line and she thought they might actually have a real chance, the wind began to roar. Clouds swirled overhead, coalescing into a funnel over the river. A dark spot formed on the water, spiraling out and upward until a tornado of water rose to meet the cloud above. In the distance, the High Witches raised their arms and screamed.

The mutant waterspout surged toward them.

"We have this!" a feminine voice yelled. "Keep holding the river back!"

Sofia searched frantically and saw Aurora, Esha at her side. They raced toward the river and splashed in up to their knees. Their familiars followed. Fangs bared and coated in mud, they turned to smoke at the water and hovered by their mistresses. Aurora and Esha raised their hands, black hair and blond whipping in the wind.

A tornado formed in front of them, as big as the waterspout. They directed it toward the oncoming disaster. Wind shrieked and leaves flew through the rain.

Sofia fought a skeleton that went for her throat. She tore its slimy grip from her throat, then blasted him with fire from her wand. She whirled to watch the tornado. Wind and water clashed. The water poured back into the river as the waterspout was torn apart by the soulceress' tornado.

Hope flared in Sofia's chest. They were beating back the rising river and the waterspout. If they could hold them off, the High Witches would run out of magical power and the corpses would fade. Then they could kill the witches.

They could win this.

The waterspout flared back to life, bigger than ever. A second joined it. The air roared with the wind as the river surged forward. It broke past Malcolm's defenses, past Cam's and Logan's. Sofia was up to her waist in a second, her chest a moment later.

The High Witches weren't fading. They were destroying enough of her village that they were reaping the extra power. They'd be fueled until they destroyed them all.

She wanted to scream her despair to the sky, but she couldn't. That wasn't her role.

They weren't going to win. She was going to die. But she wouldn't go out like a coward who'd abandoned her people.

"To higher ground!" she screamed. "We fight from the roofs!"

She was about to aetherwalk to one of the gently sloping roofs when a great force picked up. Though it was invisible, it squeezed her chest and yanked her off the ground, like an angry child with a doll. The earth dropped away from beneath her and fear roared in her chest. She kicked and clawed, but couldn't break free as she soared through the air.

Malcolm roared as something squeezed his chest and lifted him into the sky. He thrashed, trying to see what held him, but it was futile. He could see nothing but the view below.

The floodwaters devoured the town as the enormous waterspouts overpowered the soulceresses' tornado. Mytheans had moved the battle from the wharf to the streets, where they fought in waist-deep water.

Whatever carried him dropped him onto the rooftop patio of one of the tallest buildings in town. He crashed to the ground next to Sofia. They scrambled to their feet.

The Salem Coven surrounded them. A quick glance revealed twelve of them. They were soaking wet, hair straggling around their faces and their grins manic. Had they come all the way from Massachusetts to join the battle?

Fuck.

He glanced at Sofia. She stood, bedraggled and wet, but straight and tall with Kitty clutched to her chest.

A witch wearing a green cloak waved her hand at Sofia and said, "You think we'd let you wear the guise of power in our presence?"

Sofia's Crone form and clothing disappeared, replaced with her normal visage and apparel.

"Didn't think you'd see us again?" The witch who spoke was the Salem Coven's High Priestess, if he recalled. She hadn't shown up that night in Salem until their escape because she'd been away. A crazed light gleamed in her eyes.

"Not particularly." He glanced over the side of the building. Every bit of help they could hope for was already engaged in a battle for their lives. He swallowed hard and looked back at the witches.

"We owe you one for destroying our Grimoire and half our house. We hadn't intended to pay you back so soon, but then we caught wind of this when the villagers were seeking help from outside Bruxa's Eye. Well, we couldn't let the opportunity—"

An icy chill formed at Malcolm's back and dark power prickled along his skin as a voice demanded, "How dare you!"

With dread rising in his chest, he turned to see the thirteen High Witches standing behind him. Malevolent power seethed around them. Their white cloaks were dry despite the rain and they were exponentially stronger than they had been when he'd first met them, no doubt from feeding off all the power caused by the destruction of Bruxa's Eye.

"They're our kill!" the High Witch bellowed. Her voice made the roof tremble. "Yet you encroach upon us?"

"We didn't start this." The High Priestess' voice was so dark that it chilled Malcolm's bones.

In a second, he knew it.

He and Sofia were going to die.

The village was drowning, their fellow warriors all engaged in battles for their lives. Even the backup from the university was occupied below.

And he and Sofia stood between twenty-five immensely powerful witches who would vie for the right to kill them. Rage at their fate overwhelmed him.

He deserved this, but not Sofia. Every terrible thing he'd ever done—the worst of it to Sofia—could land him here and it would make sense.

But not her.

Fighting their way out of this was likely impossible. The odds of rescue coming in time were slim to none

When the brilliant white forms of the souls of Sofia's ancestors appeared at her side, the answer hit him. They were creatures of the aether. What power they had was tied to it.

"What's this?" the High Witch yelled.

"Can you protect Sofia from an aether blast?" he hissed at the nearest soul. Her mother, he realized.

Her mother's eyes widened, shocked. "Y-Yes. I believe so."

"Then do it now."

She gasped, then whirled. In a split second, she and the other souls formed a protective circle around Sofia. Her mother and grandmother and those that came before. A dome of protective light surrounded her and Kitty.

He took one last look at her shocked face, his heart breaking, then spun away. He extended his arms in the opposite direction and focused on the aether, calling it forth.

Then he did what no self-preserving warlock would ever do and tore a hole in space that would spell his own death.

The brilliant white light of the aether radiated, growing fast. As the power sang up his arms and vibrated his muscles, he held fast, letting the aether grow.

"No!" Sofia's scream tore at his heart.

But it was the only way. He didn't have a chance to make it out of here, but she did. Even if he lived, he couldn't be with her. Fate demanded it. His past choices ensured it. She'd sacrificed so much for her village. And he'd been the one to set them on this path by stealing the dagger.

It was only right that he do this.

He could see to it that she escaped. That what was left of her village survived.

Pain sang along his nerves as the energy of the aether began to spiral out of control. The witches shrieked, falling to their knees. He could hear Sofia crying behind him, screaming at him to stop. He forced the sound away.

Peace suffused him. Though it meant his death, he'd been given a gift when the Salem Coven had arrived. In their rage and desire to be the ones to kill Sofia, the High Witches had left their protective circle.

And he was now close enough to kill them all.

As the white energy of the aether consumed him in unbearable heat, his last image was of Sofia.

Sofia fought against the souls containing her, shrieking as a blast of pure magical energy consumed Malcolm. It radiated outward, immolating the witches who surrounded her and destroying the building beneath her feet.

She stayed suspended within the protective bubble created by the souls of her family, the world now eerily silent. It only emphasized the pain ripping through her heart. She had felt him go. The warmth of his presence was gone now.

She felt so alone.

Tears blurred her vision. The witches were dead, but so was Malcolm.

He'd sacrificed himself.

The area around her was chaos. The entire building was destroyed. Forty feet across at least. In the street, the flood waters had receded immediately and the waterspouts had disappeared.

Her friends were scattered in the street, some standing but not all, the battle stopped mid-fight. It was chaos still, but tragic and silent.

The souls of her ancestors lowered her to the ground. She nearly collapsed to her knees when she felt the solid surface beneath her, but forced herself to stand.

Her mother stood before her.

"Why?" Sofia whispered.

"Of course we had to protect you," her mother said. "Of course. I love you daughter."

With a last smile, her mother disappeared. Sofia wanted to scream her grief to the sky, to tear at her hair.

Her people turned to look at her, but it wall all she could do not to scream. Through blurry vision, she saw Felix and Aurora approach.

Felix. A timewalker. Of course.

She ran to him. "Felix. Malcolm is gone. You have to take me back in time. Back to before he did it."

Grief crumpled Felix's brow and his fists clenched. Aurora clutched his arm and Sofia was struck by envy that she could do that. That her man was still alive.

Why hadn't she tried to be with Malcolm sooner? She should have taken what she could get.

"I can't do that." Felix's voice was rough. "It's against timewalker law to change such a big piece of history. And even if I could, I wouldn't."

"What?" she gasped.

"Malcolm chose that fate. If he hadn't, you would be dead. He chose your life over his own. Malcolm was the smartest man I've ever met. He knew it was necessary or he wouldn't have done it. It was his choice and I'm going to respect it." His voice was nearly gone by the time he stopped talking.

"No! You have to!"

"I won't." He shook his head. "I'm sorry."

"I'm sorry," Aurora said, her golden eyes sad. "We have to go."

They disappeared, no doubt returning to their lovely home.

The rest of their help from the university approached: Vivienne, Sylvi and Logan, Cadan and Diana, Esha and Warren. All had survived, though most were dripping blood or limping. They were too powerful to kill, but not powerful enough that any had made it to Malcolm in time.

"Thank you," she choked out, forcing away her grief. "For helping. We wouldn't have—wouldn't have—"

"We understand," Diana said, her voice kind. "We'll send back healers from the university to help your wounded. Call upon us if you need anything else."

Sofia nodded blindly, barely noticing when they departed. Kitty pressed against her leg and Sofia reached down and picked her up, holding her to her chest. She looked out at the remnants of her town.

Her people staggered in the street, helping the injured to their feet. The building Malcolm had destroyed still smoked. The street was mud and littered with debris. The tornados and waterspouts had destroyed several buildings near the wharf.

In the distance, she saw Aleia helping Inara walk.

The sight of her friend—of her village and her people— hit her in the chest. She sucked in a ragged breath and pushed the near-crippling pain down deep inside her.

The High Witches were dead, destroyed in the aether blast, but she was still the Protector of Bruxa's Eye. And her job wasn't over yet.

CHAPTER TWENTY

Sofia staggered down the street, so filthy and exhausted she could barely see straight. It'd been nearly six hours since Malcolm had died and the battle had ended.

Every muscle hurt, and with the oncoming dusk, it was becoming harder to see the street and debris in front of her. If she tripped and fell on her face, she'd probably just stay there. Kitty would probably sleep on her back.

She hugged Kitty closer. Normally she didn't carry her, but everyone was exhausted after the battle this morning.

"It does look better," Aleia said from beside her.

"Yeah, much." Inara's voice sounded as exhausted as Sofia felt.

Sofia glanced around at the main street. At least there were no more bodies amongst the debris. Their dead—over a dozen in all—had been sent to their afterworlds. The afternoon had been a time of mourning and goodbye. Though the loss of her people—of Malcolm—stabbed her like a dagger through the heart, they'd been lucky. As bad as what the High Witches had thrown at them, that hadn't been the death blow.

Losing only fourteen wasn't so bad.

Except that they were her friends. Other Mytheans' loved ones.

Like Malcolm.

She tried to force the thoughts away. There was so much left to do that she couldn't collapse. She had to focus on the good. Only fourteen. It was terrible to think *only* in front of that number, but she'd been a Mythean long enough to know the nature of their world. They'd have lost more if the university hadn't sent healers. The gravely wounded were too many for Cata, the healer of Bruxa's Eye, to handle. Sofia had been able to lend a hand, as had others, but they'd needed more.

The university had stepped up and she'd been grateful. As the healers had swept through town in their white cloaks—so different from the white cloaks that the High Witches wore—she'd realized that they were going to recover.

"We'll rebuild," Sofia said. "Though I want the building that was destroyed turned into a park. A memorial." Her throat burned at the thought, tears trying to escape.

Aleia squeezed her shoulder. "That's a great idea."

Sofia nodded. They could move the three-story bar that had been there before. The village had loved it, but they'd understand.

"And I think we should loot the High Witch's afterworld." Vindictiveness seethed pleasantly in her belly. Thinking of it pushed away the hurt. "We'll take back every tribute I ever gave them, every piece of gold, then burn the place to the ground."

"*That* is an excellent idea," Inara said.

Sofia nodded. If she were going to keep it together, she had to focus on duty and vengeance. Duty had to be done, but vengeance would keep her spirit from sinking into oblivion.

They reached Aleia's apartment over the apothecary and stopped in front of it

"Are you sure you don't want to stay over? Inara's in the second bedroom, but my bed is big enough to share," Aleia said.

Sofia shook her head. Though it was tempting, she wanted to force herself back into normal life as soon as possible. Malcolm had only been back in her life for less than a week. So short a time. She could get over that if she tried.

"No, but thanks," she said. "Kitty and I are headed back to mine to check it out."

"All right. I'll see you in the morning. The rebuilding won't be so bad."

Sofia glanced down the street towards the wharf. A whole row of buildings had been destroyed by the waterspout. Piles of timber and debris stood along the front of the river.

If Aurora and Esha hadn't been here to help, would all the buildings have been destroyed?

Probably.

Grateful. Be grateful. It could have been worse.

But the worst did happen, part of her whispered.

To her, yes. Losing Malcolm had been the worst thing that could have happened to her. Worse than her own death, even, because feeling like this wasn't something she wanted to live through.

But she had more than her own problems to worry about. For over four hundred years, she'd been the Protector of Bruxa's Eye. Just because the High Withes were dead didn't mean she could throw away that mantle so quickly. She had to be grateful that more of her village hadn't been destroyed, that more lives hadn't been lost.

"I'll see you tomorrow, okay?" Sofia said.

"Yeah." Aleia started to close the door.

"Hey, wait," Sofia said. "Your premonition of my death—was it me on the roof with the witches?"

Aleia nodded. "I guess so. I didn't see much detail. Malcolm must have saved you from it."

Sofia nodded and managed to squeeze out a weak, "Thanks." She turned away before they could answer and headed down the street. It was almost full dark now, the night animals waking up, screeching and howling. It felt hotter, unusually so, and the sweat dripped down her spine. Probably just misery. Her mind was miserable, her body too.

She just wanted to fall asleep. To forget all of this for a while.

Her house, at the far end of the village away from the river, hadn't sustained any external damage that she could see. Just water and mud on the walls about three feet high. She pushed open the door and stepped into the same mud that covered the street.

It was quiet and dark inside—lonely—but she could make out the puddles and mud. The walls were wet all the way up to her waist, furniture and rugs soaked and dirty. It barely registered on her scale of bad things. At this point, she couldn't care less about the damage to her home.

She reached out a hand for the light switch and flipped it.

Nothing.

She sighed. No surprise after the damage to the village. She drew her wand and lit the end, heading for the stairs.

All she really wanted was a shower. Didn't even matter if it was hot. Her footsteps thudded heavily upward. Every bone in her body felt as old as her Crone form normally looked. A form she'd no longer be required to take every day, she realized. With the High Witch's death, her job as Protector was over. Bruxa's Eye was free. Though she'd be able to use the form when she needed the power, she'd no longer be expected to appear as the Crone in everyday life. Her job was done.

She had no idea how that made her feel and didn't plan to explore it.

When she reached the top floor, she turned into the bedroom.

"Here you go, Kitty." She set Kitty on the bed.

Kitty looked up at her with her good eye and her squinty one. Sofia reached out to scratch her head, then turned and went to the bathroom. A thudding sound indicated Kitty had hopped off the bed. Sofia glanced behind her to see Kitty following her.

Tears welled in her eyes. "Thanks, Kitty."

In the small bathroom, she set her glowing wand on the sink and held her breath as she turned on the shower. It creaked, then water poured forth. Muddy at first, and then clear.

Her shoulders sagged in relief. It didn't get hot after a minute like normal, but she didn't care. It took only seconds to tear off her clothes, and then she was standing under the spray.

Immediately, tears started to roll down her face again.

Kitty meowed—more of a meep, really—then hopped in the shower with her. Water soaked her fur and her ears flattened. She looked like a fat, bedraggled rat and Sofia laughed pathetically.

Count on Kitty to try to make her feel better like this.

Kitty loved her.

Like Malcolm had clearly loved her. The tears came again, this time harder. She stood in the shower, weeping as Kitty rubbed her wet little body against her calf. Sobs wracked her as she leaned her head against the cold shower tile and curled her fists.

Malcolm had sacrificed himself for her village. For her.

He'd known what he was doing when he'd opened the channel to the aether. It'd been genius. Selfless. The High Witches were too powerful for other Mytheans to kill—as least as long as they'd been protected on the other side of the river behind their barrier.

Even outside of their barrier, it would have been almost impossible, given their numbers and the amount of power they'd already reaped from the destruction of Bruxa's Eye.

But an aether blast... that would destroy anyone. The High Witches, the warlock who opened the portal and inevitably lost control. Malcolm.

But not her. Through a dumb stroke of luck, her ancestors had been there. Souls. Creatures of the aether— pretty much the only thing capable of protecting her.

And Malcolm had orchestrated it all, pulling the trigger on the bomb when the remote option hadn't worked.

And now she was free of the High Witches. Her life was her own. She could look like herself when she walked the streets of Bruxa's Eye, take the Crone form only when necessary, and not have to spend her entire year searching for tributes and going through the hell of delivering them.

Malcolm had saved her from that. Set her free.

She knew she should be grateful, but as sobs tore themselves free of her throat, she realized that the only thing she cared about was Malcolm.

And he was gone.

She felt empty. Lost.

Ever since he'd come back into her life, she'd told herself that they didn't have a future. But now she realized that she hadn't really believed that at all. She'd thought it would work out—somehow.

She scrubbed her hands over her face. It was time to get out. Kitty was soaking and probably miserable. Sofia turned off the water and stepped out. First thing, she grabbed her wand and waved it over Kitty, drying her immediately.

Kitty started purring. Normally, it would make Sofia smile. But not now.

She grabbed a towel and wrapped herself up, then dried her hair with her wand. Kitty hopped onto the bed and Sofia followed, falling asleep almost immediately.

The dreams came slowly, through the dark exhaustion that dragged at her. As they coalesced in her mind, Sofia found herself standing atop the Sorcerer's Tor on Dartmoor.

Malcolm kissed her as the sun set around them, shining its golden rays over the hills and valleys of Dartmoor. Desolate and beautiful.

It was the day they'd gone to pay their respects to his mother and he'd just told her that he wanted to be with her forever.

She fell into the kiss, immersing herself in the dream. If it was going to be the last time she kissed him—even if it was a memory—she wanted to memorize every part of it.

Malcolm was so warm and alive under her hands, strong and powerful and vital. She gripped his big shoulders, pressing herself close, as his mouth took hers.

When he pulled away, her head was spinning. His gaze met hers as he said, "I love you, Sofia."

Joy suffused her.

Then she woke up, gasping.

The pain hit immediately.

Just a dream. Malcolm wasn't back with her.

But he'd loved her. He'd probably never stopped loving her, just as she'd never stopped loving him. warlocks shouldn't love, but fate had been put on hold when he'd tossed her aside in the past. After he'd sought her out again, the wheels of fate had begun to turn.

This had been inevitable.

But it didn't have to stay that way. Fate could be fought. She might not win, but that didn't mean she wasn't going to try.

Ten minutes later, as the dawn sun peeked over the canopy, Sofia pounded on Aleia's door. She pounded until it cracked open.

An exhausted-looking Aleia pulled it open, scrubbing a hand over her eyes. "What's the matter?"

"Inara. I need to see her." She stepped into the apartment, which was still in good condition because it was on the second floor, and yelled for Inara.

Her new friend stumbled out of the bedroom, dressed in shorts and a t-shirt, her short hair sticking up everywhere. "What?"

"I need your help. I know where the entrance to the sorcerer's afterworld is. I want you to get me in. I'm going to find Malcolm."

Inara's eyes widened. "I can't. And you couldn't get him back out anyway. He's dead."

"I can try. And even if I can't get him out, I have to see him." Her voice broke. "One last time."

Inara's face softened. "I'm sorry, Sofia. I'm just a world walker. I can't bring people to afterworlds or release souls."

Panic beat in Sofia's chest. She wouldn't let this chance escape. "What about my ancestors?"

"That was Vivienne—and she could only get them out for a short while. I was just here to help."

Sofia nodded. "Vivienne. All right. She lives at the university, right?"

"Yeah," Aleia said. "I talked to her during cleanup after the battle. She mentioned that she lives in a small yellow cottage on the east side of campus. Purple shutters."

"Thank you." She met Aleia's sympathetic gaze. "Take care of the village, okay? I've got to do this."

Aleia nodded and Sofia didn't wait for her to speak. When Kitty pressed up against the side of her leg, she aetherwalked to the university.

The ground was white and the trees topped with snow. More fell from the sky. Kitty turned to smoke and hovered at her side. Sofia shivered and used her wand to conjure a jacket, then set off toward the east. Her feet sank into the snow as she cut across the rolling hills. She ignored the big stone buildings to her left and kept heading in what she hoped was the right direction.

Finally, a small yellow cottage appeared. Purple shutters were cheerful in a way she wasn't sure she'd ever feel again. She knocked on the matching purple door, praying that Vivienne would be home.

When it swung open, she almost sighed in relief.

Surprise flashed across Vivienne's face. She was dressed for lounging at home—leggings and a loose sweater draped with a colorful scarf. Her wild dark hair was pulled up in a knot atop her head. "Sofia. What's wrong?"

"I need help."

Understanding dawned on Vivienne's face. "Come on in. Have a seat."

Sofia followed her into a colorful living room scattered with Persian rugs. Art from around the world hung on her walls, including a striking engraved platter over the fireplace.

"You want me to take you to Malcolm's afterworld," Vivienne said.

"Yes. How did you—"

"I've only been in this world a little while. I'm a half-blood and spent most of my life mortal. But what I can do is rare and valuable and other Mytheans figured that out pretty quickly. So when someone who has just lost someone they love comes to me, I know why they're here."

"Can you take me? Will you?"

Vivienne's visage was solemn. "Yes. But just for a little while. To say goodbye. I don't have the power to bring him back from an afterworld. Once he's there, he's there forever."

"If you get me there, can I stay? Forever?" That the question entered her mind didn't shock Sofia. It meant death, leaving earth and her village and her friends, but she'd do it in a heartbeat.

"No. And I know you know that, deep down. The only way to get to an afterworld is death, and only if you believe in that religion. If you die, you're going to the same place your ancestors would go, I would guess."

Sofia nodded. Of course. She'd just been grasping at straws. "But you'll take me?"

"Yeah. We can go now. I'm sure you want to do this right away."

More than anything. Sofia stood. "It's on Dartmoor, in southwest England."

"All right. Let me get a coat. I'm not used to this cold." Vivienne pulled on tall boots and wrapped up in a puffy black coat, then held her hand out to Sofia. "All right. Take us there."

Sofia gripped her hand and, once Kitty had pressed herself up against her leg, aetherwalked them to Sorcerer's Tor.

The wind was howling today, the sky overcast. The granite stones tumbled over the hilltop in massive disarray, just as she remembered it. She pointed to the larges pile, to the large crack that cut through the middle of the biggest rock. "There."

Vivienne nodded. "Looks about right."

To a mortal, it would appear as just a shallow fracture. It even looked that way to Sofia. But Vivienne seemed to know what she was looking at.

"Come on," Vivienne said, and led the way over the tumbled stones and spongy ground. They stopped right in front of the fissure. Anticipation sang through Sofia. Fear as well.

"Take my hand," Vivienne said. "Normally getting to an aetherworld requires aetherwalking, but I think we can just go through this portal."

Sofia gripped her hand and followed her through the opening. Dark cold surrounded her and fear gripped her throat, but the next step took them into the light.

A village sprawled before her, sun sparkling down on the white streets. The buildings were all pale stone with slate roofs, immaculate, but cold. Even the flowers that spilled from window boxes were faded blues and pinks. Like a ghostly version of one of the villages at the edge of Dartmoor.

"How do we find him?" Vivienne asked. "Because from here, I've got no idea."

"Ask around," Sofia said.

A woman in a cloak walked out of one of the houses. She was as faded as the cottages. Sofia ran to her, anticipation and fear and hope all fighting in her breast.

"Excuse me!" she called.

The woman glanced up, startled. She was so pale that Sofia couldn't determine the color of her clothes or eyes or the hair under her cap. "An outworlder?"

Sofia guessed that was their word for Mythean from earth. "Yes. Could you tell me, where is Malcolm the warlock? He would have arrived yesterday."

Confusion flashed across the woman's face. "Malcolm? No, he's not here. I would know."

Fear and panic welled in Sofia's chest, like acid eating away at the hope that had bloomed there. "What? How would you know? Maybe he's elsewhere and you haven't seen him.""

"I'm his mother. We always know when a member of our family has arrived." She shook her head, disgusted. "But perhaps its better he didn't come here when he died. He's not living up to his potential as a warlock, is what I hear."

Sofia stumbled back, horrified. His mother didn't care about him. Not at all, from the look on her face. But that's how sorcerers from his clan were. They all aspired to be warlocks, so they trained the emotion out of themselves in preparation. His mother was only concerned with his reputation and whether or not he'd fulfilled their expectations.

"You're sure?" Sofia breathed.

"Of course I'm sure."

"But then where could he be?"

His mother shrugged. "He was never much of a wulver, so I doubt he's there. If anything, it sounds like his soul wouldn't leave earth. Perhaps he's waiting to be reincarnated. That's usually why souls don't show up in their afterworld after death. Something ties them to earth and they refuse to leave."

Sofia stepped back blindly, shaking her head.

"Go on with you, now." His mother shooed her hands. "Outworlders shouldn't be here."

Sofia spun blindly and returned to her friend.

Reincarnated? But that could take centuries.

But did that mean he wasn't trapped in this afterworld for an eternity? He might live again. His soul hadn't been able to leave earth.

What did this mean?

She glanced up at Vivienne, whose brow was crumpled in confusion. At the sight of her, the memory hit Sofia.

"Mnemosynia. You've been there," Sofia said.

"Oh, shit," Vivienne said. "He's not here, is he? You think his soul is going to be reincarnated."

"Yeah. Yeah, I do." It felt right. Or she was grasping at straws. She didn't know, but she sure as hell wasn't going to give up. She was going to chase clues of him until she found him. "Take me there."

"Whoa, that place is different. There are rules. It's only for the souls of reincarnates who are waiting to be reborn."

Sofia shook her head, frantic. "That's why I have to go there. If he's not here, then there's a good chance he's waiting to be reincarnated. You have to take me."

"Sofia, it's not a normal afterworld. It's special. Until recently, it was an awful place. A labyrinth of misery. It only became Mnemosynia and a place for reincarnates once Sylvi and Logan destroyed the sickness in the labyrinth. Now it's overseen by various gods. We can't just break in. We're not souls waiting to be reincarnated—I don't know what happens to live Mytheans."

"Just take me then. Drop me off and go."

"I can only take you to the desert outside of Mnemosynia. The souls are within the city walls. You might not be able to get back. You might not even be able to get inside the city to find Malcolm."

"I don't care." Tears stung her eyes.

Vivienne's brow creased. She was torn, weakening. Sofia grabbed her jacked lapels. "Please, Vivienne. Just drop me off and go. Your skills are so valuable to the university. They won't punish you. Tell them I threatened you. I am stronger than you. Tell them you had to or I would have killed you."

"Would you?"

"No." As much as she wanted to see Malcolm again, no way would she hurt Vivienne. "No way. But they don't have to know that. Just drop me off and go. I'll figure it out from there."

"Once you're there, you really might not be able to leave. You could be punished with death. I mean, no one is allowed there without permission. I was only able to go get Sylvi and Logan because it was an emergency, and I didn't actually enter Mnemosynia. I just went to the desert outside."

"But if you took me to the desert, I could enter?"

"Maybe. There's a gate. But if you can't get through, you're trapped in the desert."

"I'll do it. I don't care." She glanced down at Kitty. "You don't have to come. It's risky. You could live with Aurora and Mouse. Mouse likes you."

Kitty hissed at her, obviously not impressed with the scenario. A teary smile tugged at Sofia's lips.

"Thanks." Sofia looked back up at Vivienne. "Please. I want this. I know the risks."

Vivienne nodded. "Fine. We go now, and I leave you at the entrance."

"Thank you. Thank you so much. I owe you."

"Big time," Vivienne said, then aetherwalked them all to the desert.

The sun beat down mercilessly and sand stretched out in all directions. Sand whipped on the wind, making Kitty turn into smoke for protection. Behind Vivienne loomed a huge city, ornate and whimsical.

Vivienne squeezed her arms. "Good luck."

She disappeared, leaving Sofia and Kitty standing in the middle of the desert.

CHAPTER TWENTY-ONE

Sofia stared at the great city looming before her, hope and dread welling within her. This was it. If she was wrong, she could be trapped here forever—without Malcolm.

The city was far away, but enormous. Sections of shimmering gray stone walls dotted the periphery, but parts were missing, as if they'd fallen. The buildings that peeped above the walls were beautiful and fantastical, turrets and spirals. It was gorgeous—such a contrast to the desert outside.

"Come on, Kitty." She set off across the sand, shedding her jacket as she walked. It was hotter than the jungle. Stifling, with the sun beating down mercilessly.

The wind began to pick up. It howled and shrieked, blasting in her ears and picking up sand that hurtled through the air like minuscule bullets.

Kitty turned to smoke and Sofia tried to conjure a pair of goggles and a handkerchief for her mouth. It didn't work. Like the High Witch's afterworld, her magic was blocked here.

So she squinted and pulled her shirt up over her mouth, then moved forward. Her skin stung wherever the sand hit her. She pushed on, fighting the wind and heat and sand. It was as if the desert were trying to keep her from reaching Mnemosynia.

When the wind hurtled even faster, pushing her back a step for every two that she took, fear started to claw at her.

She was making almost no progress—the city was still desperately far away. Her eyes burned and sand was getting in her mouth. In her smoke form, Kitty pressed against her, trying to give her strength, but it wasn't enough.

Sofia stumbled to her knees. The hot sand burned. Gasping and choking on the grit, she scrambled up and pushed onward. She fell every ten yards, probably more often. Any idea of distance was eclipsed by the sand that now blocked her vision.

Her hope was dwindling when a figure appeared before her. Through the hurtling sand, she could make out a tall person dressed in white. Any other details were obscured by sand and the grit in her eyes.

"Sofia Viera, turn back now. Aetherwalk from this place." The woman's voice radiated power. Sofia's skin tingled with it.

"No." The words scratched her sand-coated throat. "Malcolm is in there."

"You do not know that. You are not meant to be in Mnemosynia. Only the dead tread there."

"I have to find him, and this is the last place I know to look." She continued to push her way through the sand, which had become even more difficult to walk through. As if it were sucking her down.

"The journey will only become more difficult. Impossible. You can aetherwalk away and live a happy life. Continuing on means certain death."

Sofia had nearly reached her on trembling legs. "Who are you?"

"Mnemosyne. The Titaness for whom this place was named."

A Greek Titaness, of course. Not a goddess, at all. Even more powerful than a goddess. Through burning eyes, Sofia could make out her dark hair, piled high on her head in an elaborate configuration, and a white dress that looked like something carved on a classical statue.

"I'm going to find him," she gasped as she pushed past Mnemosyne.

"So be it, though it spells your doom."

Sofia shivered as the words rushed over her. She looked at Kitty. "You can aetherwalk to Aurora. She'll take care of you."

Kitty hissed at her, then continued on, stalwart by her side. Thank fates she could take her smoke form and be safe from the sand. If only she were that lucky.

Endless moments passed as she made her way, praying she was going in the right direction. The sand was so thick in the air that she couldn't see more than a few feet ahead of her.

When the warmth of Malcolm's presence hit her, she jerked. She was close enough that their bond allowed her to *feel* him.

This was the right direction. It had to be. She would make it.

The earth below her trembled and surged, sand shifting and parting. Figures crawled up from the ground, but to Sofia's nearly blind eyes, they weren't remotely human looking. Rather, they looked to be made of sand and rock.

One grabbed her ankle and she kicked, trying to break free. She tried to draw her wand from the aether, but her magic was still blocked.

"Fuck!" She tore at the sand figure's hands, but they were made of stone. Kitty jumped on him, but could do no damage to his stone body.

No longer able to hold her shirt in front of her face, sand began to choke her, filling her lungs. Her fingertips bled from where she dug into the sand man's hands, but she couldn't make him budge. A shriek tore from her lungs as he began to pull her into the sand.

Suddenly, a surge of magical power filled her, warm and strong.

Malcolm. He must be able to feel her and was giving her what strength he had. She grasped it like a lifeline, drawing her wand from the aether and sending lightning at the sand man who held her.

He fell back, releasing her ankle. She scrambled to her feet, digging her way out of the sand, and ran. More sand men clawed at her, dragging her down. Gasping and choking, she used her wand, throwing them back with the force of her lightning, but they were unending.

"Go back. Aetherwalk away." Mnemosyne's voice sounded through the roar of the wind.

"No," Sofia choked, blasting another attacker. She'd been right. Malcolm was here and she could feel him.

But her power was waning, which meant his must be too. After he'd sacrificed himself at Bruxa's Eye, she had no doubt he'd fuel her with as much power as he had until he'd run completely dry. What would happen to him then?

She shook the thought away, fighting onward. He would be okay. He *had* to be. But would she? Her breath was now almost gone. She hacked and coughed as she crawled along the sand, no longer able to rise to her feet. Kitty had turned herself corporeal and was tugging at her sweater with small teeth.

"No," she gasped. "Turn back, Kitty."

Her body felt heavy, her mind leaden. Through near-blind eyes she could see the open gates of Mnemosynia. No need to close them if outsiders went through this. She wouldn't make it.

Kitty pulled her onward and Sofia clawed at the sand, dragging herself inch by inch along its burning surface. Every breath burned on its way in and tore at her as she coughed it out. She was strangling on sand, drowning in it as it filled her lungs. There was too much in the air.

But she was so close. Only feet now. With a last surge of strength, she collapsed on the threshold of Mnemosynia. Kitty curled up beside her, licking her hand to try to revive her. Sofia blinked burning, teary eyes and saw Malcolm, collapsed on the other side of the gate.

She tried to sob, but was too weak to do so. He'd given her all his power. But that was what kept his immortal soul alive and in Mnemosynia. Without it, he would fade away.

Was he fading even now? His big form lay collapsed on the ground. She reached toward him, weeping.

This was what Aleia had prophesied. Her death, strangling in the sand. She hadn't escaped it after all. And now Malcolm's soul would perish as well.

"I told you to turn back." Mnemosyne's voice boomed. "But you did not."

"Couldn't," Sofia gasped.

"Wouldn't. There is a difference. You could have left Malcolm, but you would rather have choked to death on sand."

Sofia had nothing to say to that. Physically, she couldn't say anything. Through her grief and pain, she recognized that it was true. But it hurt too much to say the words that would confirm it. And what did it matter? Mnemosyne was the Titaness of memory and this place was named for her. She knew all. Sofia didn't need to confirm it.

"I suppose it changes the situation," Mnemosyne said.

What?

Warmth suffused Sofia's cold limbs. Slowly, her breathing became easier and her lungs began to clear. She still hurt, but eventually she was able to drag herself to her knees. Mnemosyne had healed her?

Out of the corner of her eye, she saw Malcolm sit up. She clambered to her feet, her legs still leaden from exhaustion. Kitty stood beside her.

"Malcolm!"

"Sofia." Relief echoed in his voice. "I felt you. But you were in danger."

He was at her side in an instant, sweeping her into his arms. He felt as whole and vibrant as he had been in life, his arms strong and real. Not ghostlike as his mother had been nor faded from giving her all his power. Warmth filled her.

"You gave me all your power," she said. "You were fading when I got here."

"I had to." His gaze burned with conviction, and he pressed a hard kiss to her mouth.

Joy surged in her chest. He felt so strong and warm and real. This was worth any cost.

She leaned back and looked up at him, cupping his face in her hands. His golden eyes were bright with unshed tears, his gaze devouring her. He looked so handsome and familiar that she felt hot tears begin to pour down her cheeks.

"Why are you here? You should be on earth, alive." Anguish resonated in his voice.

"I had to find you. Vivienne brought me here."

"You need to leave. More than anything, I want to be with you. But this is a half-life, just a waypoint. You need to live. You need to go."

"I'm not leaving you." She gripped his shoulders. "I don't care what's here. I love you, and I'm not leaving."

"But you—"

"Silence," Mnemosyne's voice resonated with power.

Sofia whipped around to look at her, dread sinking her heart. The sight of Malcolm had made her completely forget about Mnemosyne.

She was even more beautiful than Sofia had realized, regal and elegant. Only now did Sofia see where they stood—in a beautiful courtyard that was paved with the same glimmering gray stone that made up the walls. Colorful flowers bloomed everywhere, in beds and pots. Two-story buildings with balconies surrounded the courtyard and fountains burbled in the middle.

Beautiful.

"Malcolm the warlock and Sofia the Bruxa. One of you should be here, but the other should not," she said.

"I'm sorry I broke the rules, but I want to stay with Malcolm. Please," Sofia begged.

"I know. I saw what you went through to get here. Do you know the story of Orpheus and Eurydice?"

"The Greek myth?" Malcolm asked.

"Yes. But as with all myths, it was true."

Sofia nodded. "Orpheus went to Hades to try to save Eurydice when she died. He was allowed to lead her from Hades, but she would only make it out if he didn't look back at her." Sofia could see how it was a bit similar to her circumstance.

"Yes. And you are a bit like Orpheus. Coming to the afterworld to find your beloved." A small smile curved her mouth.

"If you let us leave, I swear I won't look back at Malcolm," Sofia said.

Mnemosyne shook her head slowly and Sofia's heart dropped. "No. That will not happen. You don't want that. You see, Plato had it right in his version of the story. Orpheus never really had a chance to save Eurydice. He was a coward, unwilling to die to be with his beloved. He mocked the gods by attempting to steal her rather than by having the courage to join her."

"I can't say I wouldn't try to break Malcolm out if I could. I'd do anything to be with him."

Mnemosyne nodded. "I know. You faced death to be with him, as he died to save you. And then he gave you all of his power through the bond you share. He would have faded to the unknown."

Sofia swallowed hard, fear still beating in her chest. Could Mnemosyne do that to them? Make it so that their souls faded into nothing?

"Your commitment—your love—is rare. You have done what Orpheus should have."

Sofia gripped Malcolm's hand.

"Malcolm is here because his soul refused to leave you. He should have been sent to the sorcerer's afterworld, but his soul refused to be parted from yours. So it lingered as a reincarnate. And you are here because you refused to leave Malcolm. But I can't allow a still-living Mythean to stay in Mnemosynia. And after I healed you both, you are still alive."

Sofia nodded, not daring to hope but unable to help herself.

"Therefore, I am going to let you both leave."

Sofia gasped. Malcolm's hand tightened in hers.

"Malcolm, you no longer bear the warlock's curse. As your mentor Corrier told you, the greatest sacrifice will break the curse. You made that sacrifice. And because Sofia came to find you, I've decided to give you both a second chance at love."

"Thank you." Malcolm's voice was rough. "But how did you—"

"Know? I know everything about the reincarnates in Mnemosynia." She tapped her temple. "My mind is vast and memory is my gift. My curse."

As a Titaness and the primary goddess of memory, it would be.

"So we can be together?" Sofia asked, her heart galloping as if it would break free of her chest. "Without fate conspiring against us?"

"Yes. You can."

"Oh, fates, thank you," Sofia said. She wanted to hug Mnemosyne, but resisted. The Titaness didn't seem like the type.

"Thank you," Malcolm said.

Mnemosyne inclined her head. "And as a gift to celebrate what I presume is your coming union, I thought you would like to know that the fourteen friends you lost in the battle of Bruxa's Eye were all given the option of reincarnation as a reward for their bravery in fighting the High Witches." Mnemosyne scowled. "They really were a blight upon the earth. Better that they are gone."

"And?" Sofia asked.

"They all chose their afterworlds. Fortunately, they all subscribed to belief systems with afterworlds that they found favorable. Each one chose that over reincarnation. They all seemed happy. They'll be joining old friends and family."

Relief washed through Sofia. "Thank you so much. It does help to hear that."

"Indeed." She ran her hands over her skirt, smoothing the unlined fabric. "Now, it is time for you to go."

She waved her hands at them and Sofia felt the aether drag her away.

A second later, Malcolm stood with Sofia in the middle of Bruxa's eye. Damage was everywhere. Mud and debris in the street, storefronts damaged. The whole front street on the wharf had been demolished, but dozens of Mytheans were working on it, clearing away the debris. The building that he'd blown up was a gaping hole in the street.

"Bloody hell," he breathed. He looked down at himself, then at Sofia. They were both solid and whole. "We're alive."

Sofia nodded and flung her arms around his shoulders. "Thank fates." She laughed. "And Mnemosyne."

"No, thank you. Thank you for coming for me. I could see the sand from the gates, though I couldn't see you. But I could feel you. I know what you went through." He pulled her to him and kissed her hard. "Thank you for coming for me."

"How could I not, after what you did for me? You sacrificed yourself for me. For my village. I can never thank you enough."

"I owed it to your village after what I'd done. Taking the dagger was idiotic. And to protect you, I'd do it again in a heartbeat."

"Don't you dare. I'll never forget what it felt like to watch you die."

He pulled her close and kissed her forehead, then pulled away and looked around at the damage to Bruxa's Eye. "And we'll fix this."

"We will. But for now, let's go to my home. We'll help clean tomorrow. For now, I just want to look at you."

He leaned down and kissed her, then swooped her up into his arms. She laughed, then wrapped her arms around his neck. He made his way into her house, then upstairs to the dry part. Thank fates this part of the house had escaped the water.

He set her on the bed, then knelt down before her.

"I made a mistake, Sofia. I never should have chosen power over you. I love you. I've loved you for centuries, I was just too stupid and stubborn to realize it."

She leaned over and kissed him, drawing him up to sit next to her. "You were stupid and stubborn, but you've more than proven yourself." She kissed him again as if she couldn't get enough, holding her face near his. "And I love you. I know that now. I was just fighting it because I was scared. But I think maybe we've always loved each other and that the battle—and your death—were part of fate's curse."

"But now we have forever, with nothing standing in our way. We'll rebuild your city. You're free of the High Witches. You can do anything. We can live here or in Scotland. Anywhere. Felix and Aurora spend half the year on holiday traveling around in a big motor home. We can do that if you like."

She grinned and pressed her lips. It sent a burst of warmth through him.

"I know I want to be here part of the time. But then, let's just see."

"Excellent."

She reached up and played with the hair at the base of his neck. The gentle touch—and the knowledge that there would be more—felt like heaven. There'd been no time for touches like these before. And she'd been too angry and afraid to touch him like this.

"I swear, Sofia, I'll make you trust me again. I'll make it all up to you."

"I do trust you. After what you've done, how could I not? Things are going to be great from here on out. I'm free of the High Witches and we're free of your curse. And I'd say that your sacrifice more than makes up for whatever happened in the past." She grabbed his shirt, then pulled him down on the bed on top of her. "But I can think of a way you could continue to make it up to me."

He grinned and kissed her, running his palm down her side to her hip. "I'd be delighted to."

EPILOGUE

Malcolm's Home in Glencoe
December 23rd

"I'd say it turned out all right, what do you say, Kitty?" Sofia looked down at Kitty, who wore a festive red bow around her neck.

Kitty meeped and Sofia nodded her agreement, then sipped her mulled wine and looked toward the fire.

Malcolm's library was decorated for Christmas with every strand of garland and ornament that she could find. Red and gold, silver and green—it really was a bit gaudy, but she loved it. It was their first Christmas together—and the first Christmas she was able to spend outside of the jungle—and she wanted to enjoy it.

They'd debated spending the holiday in Bruxa's Eye—which was now entirely rebuilt after a solid month of reconstruction—but had decided it would be nicer to spend it in the cold. This way, all the Christmas songs about snow didn't make her long for it, because she could go right out into the stuff and roll around.

Which she wouldn't be doing tonight, because they had guests. Everyone from the university who'd helped them in Bruxa's Eye had been invited over for a thank-you dinner. They all sat around the fire now—Felix and Aurora, Andrasta and Camulos, Diana and Cadan, Warren and Esha, and Vivienne. Inara and Aleia were pouring themselves wine from the table and gossiping, as they'd gotten into the habit of doing.

Mouse and Chairman Meow, the two other familiars, lounged in front of the fire. If she wasn't mistaken, Mouse was sitting a bit closer to the Chairman now. He looked pleased. And festive, in his green bowtie.

Everyone was laughing at something Vivienne had said. Snow fell outside the window and holiday music drifted out of discretely placed speakers. The smell of the turkey was making her mouth water.

In short, everything was perfect. She almost couldn't believe her luck. But life had been so good lately that she was starting to accept it.

She glanced at the door. Malcolm should be here by now. He'd gone to his aether room in the basement to make a last minute gift for Inara—who they'd thought wouldn't be here.

He appeared in the doorway.

"Finally," she said as she went to him and kissed him. His mouth tasted of wine and spices. Divine. "What took you so long?"

"A letter arrived. Shot right out of the aether when I opened a portal."

"From Corrier?" Nerves danced in Sofia's stomach. For an unknown reason. Malcolm's warlock powers, and his ability to access the aether, hadn't disappeared with his death. With the curse gone, they'd assumed his powers would go too. When they'd first realized it, she'd been worried that the curse was still upon him. Though Mnemosyne had said it wasn't, they'd gone to Corrier to confirm.

But he hadn't been there. They'd left a message with his apprentice. Hopefully this was the answer.

"It was," Malcolm said.

"And?"

"It's fine. Death broke the curse, but I'd already learned the skills required to be a warlock. Hence, I keep the power. He said that some warlocks believe you're more powerful after death. It's a transition. A magnifying glass."

Her brows rose. "Wow. That makes sense though. You have to refuel your power so much less often, even when I siphon some off you for my own use."

He pressed a quick kiss to her mouth. "Which you're welcome to do anytime you like."

She grinned and pressed another kiss to his mouth, squeezing the shoulder that bore her tattoo.

She couldn't get enough of kissing him now that he was back with her. The last month and a half had been divine. They'd settled into their routine—which wasn't very routine at all—and it was like slipping into a comfortable chair.

A sexy, comfortable chair.

"Have you brought the gift for Inara?" she asked.

He nodded and held up the bag. "Good. We'll put it with the others. And the turkey should be done soon?"

"Twenty more minutes." He'd started cooking from scratch lately instead of using his magic, and she couldn't wait to see how the turkey came out.

"Perfect." Her grin was so big that it hurt her face. Fates, she loved this life. It was more than she'd ever hoped for.

"You know you're everything to me, right?" he asked. His golden gaze was intense, devouring. It made her shiver.

She was damned grateful for what fate had finally given her.

She wrapped her arms around his neck and met his gaze. "I love you—"

"More than life." He finished her sentence for her. It'd become their thing, and though it was a bit morbid, it suited them. Because she did love him more than life, as he did her. And that's what had saved them.

THANK YOU FOR READING!

Reviews are *so* helpful to authors. I really appreciate all reviews, both positive and negative.

If you'd like to know when my next book is available, you can…

- Join my new release newsletter at http://linseyhall.com/
- Connect with me on twitter at @HiLinseyHall
- Or find me on Facebook at https://www.facebook.com/LinseyHallAuthor

Author's Note

Hey, there! I hope you enjoyed Witch's Fate as much as I enjoyed writing it. As with all of the books in the Mythean Arcana series, I drew from history and mythology to enhance this story.

For one, I didn't make up wulvers. They're actually a type of werewolf from Scottish folklore who live in the Shetland Islands and are generally peaceful, though the ones in my world are not. The wulvers of Scottish folklore are men with the heads of wolves; they are not shapeshifters. However, in the world of the Mythean Arcana, they are the more traditional sort of shapeshifting wolf (though I loved the thought of wulvers, I quickly discarded the idea of having a hero with a wolf's head).

When I thought about Sofia having to save Malcolm from an afterworld, the first myth that came to mind was that of Orpheus and Eurydice. I always thought it was one of the saddest myths, but reading Plato's take on it had me rethinking. It's still a sad story, but Plato's version (written about in his text *Symposium*) has Orpheus painted as a coward who was unwilling to die to be with Eurydice. Because he was unwilling to die for his love, it was not true love. So the gods punished him by presenting him with an apparition of Eurydice (she was never really behind him holding his hand). This version of the myth is somehow less heartbreaking (to me, at least) and I thought it suited Witch's Fate best.

The inspiration for the stone circle outside of Bruxa's Eye came from another stone circle that has been found in Northern Brazil. The circle is located in the Amapa state and consist of 127 pieces of granite, some of which are four meters tall. As with other stone circles, the exact purpose is unknown, but it is believed that it may have been used for ceremonial or astronomical purposes.

Of the names of Sofia's ancestors, only Oriva was invented by me. The other names—Laís, Karajá, Nauquá, Panenoá, and Aparai—are actually the names of indigenous groups in Brazil. When I thought about who Sofia's ancestors might be, I realized that none of the Protectors would be Portuguese because the Portuguese did not arrive in Brazil until 1500 AD. Sofia, who was born in 1586, was the only Protector with a Portuguese parent—her father. Her mother and the rest of her ancestors would have been the indigenous people of Brazil. Because I couldn't find the first names of some of the indigenous people of Brazil from the period 0 AD - 1500 AD (I doubt they were recorded, particularly women's names, and it would take far too long to delve into the literature), I gave the Protectors names of the indigenous groups. I can't guarantee these groups were around when Bruxa's Eye was created, but they might have been.

In the first draft, Sofia almost cursed in Portuguese, but after careful thought, I also realized that she likely wouldn't do this. If anything, she'd curse in the native language of her ancestors—but I have no way of knowing how indigenous Brazilians cursed. So, unfortunately, she still curses in English, a language in which she is fluent because modern day Bruxa's Eye is home to so many species and nationalities. Her species of witch—the Bruxa—is actually a Portuguese name. Had I been able to find a name for witches in one of the indigenous Brazilian languages, I would have used it.

For this book, I went to Salem to learn a bit more about witches and to also learn about the history of the town. The history of witchcraft in Salem is very sad—it's primarily a story of greed and patriarchy. Because of this, the witches in this book have nothing to do with the women who were accused of witchcraft between 1692 and 1693. But I highly recommend you visit if you have a chance—it's a really fun (and educational) place.

And last—you might have noticed my reference to House Elves and Diagon Alley. This is of course an homage to the inestimable J.K. Rowling.

GLOSSARY

Aether - The invisible substance that connects the afterworlds and earth. It is both nothing and everything.

Aetherwalking - A method of traveling through the aether to access the afterworlds or different places on earth. Some Mytheans have this power and can bring another person with them.

Afterworld - A heaven or hell created by mortal belief. Mortals can access them only through death. Some Mytheans can aetherwalk to them.

Bruxa - A Brazilian witch. They use wands to focus their magic and have familiars.

Immortal University - An organization created thousands of years ago to protect Mytheans and keep them secret from mortals. It was initially founded as a true university, hence the name, but over time it morphed into an institution with greater power and responsibility. The university's primary goal is to maintain the secrecy of Mytheans and to keep the gods from warring to obtain more followers. They do this primarily through diplomacy. The university also provides services to Mytheans that they can't get elsewhere, lest mortals figure out that their clients never die. Things like education, health services, and banking.

Mortals - Humans. They are unaware of the existence of Mytheans or that all heavens and hells truly exist. They are immortal in the sense that their soul will pass on to whatever afterworld in which they believe.

Mythean - Supernatural individuals created by mortal belief. They are gods and goddesses, demons and monsters, witches and other supernatural creatures. They are immortal in the sense that if they live on earth, only beheading or grievous injury from magic can kill them. If they are killed their soul will pass on to an afterworld. Secrecy from mortals is one of their highest priorities. Some Mytheans, particularly species of demons and some gods, are trapped in their afterworlds. Others have access to both earth and the afterworlds.

Mythean Guardians - Powerful mortals made immortal, or other supernatural beings who serve at the Praesidium. They protect those mortals and Mytheans who are important to the fate of humanity.

Sila Jinn - Derived from Arabian mythology, a Jinn is a supernatural spirit in a class below that of angels and devils. A Sila is a female Jinn who can shapeshift, aetherwalk between all afterworlds, and manifest some types of magic.

Soulceresses - Mytheans who fuel their power by draining the immortal power of other Mytheans' souls. When fueled by the power of others, they can manifest their magic with a thought. They are hated by other Mytheans because of this. They also have the ability to see the evil in a person's soul.

Vala - A Norse sorceress who uses Seidr magic. Vala use a staff to channel their magic and when they are threatened or fighting, an apparition of a blue cloak appears around their shoulders. The first Vala, Sylvi, was trained by the Norse goddess Freya. All other Vala were trained by Sylvi.

Warlock - Immensely powerful Mytheans, also known as Oath Breakers. They specialize in magic that is destructive and are capable of the greatest magic, but they pay a great price by becoming Oath Breakers (any oath or promise they make will be torn apart by fate). They can draw unlimited magical power from the aether. They are made, not born. To qualify for the apprenticeship, one must be a Mythean with enough magical ability to be accepted by a master warlock. If one passes the apprenticeship, they must break their greatest oath to transform into a warlock/Oath Breaker. They cannot love because they are Oath Breakers.

ACKNOWLEDGMENTS

It takes so many people to create awesome books, and mine are no exception.

Thank you, Ben, for everything you've done to support the creation of this book and all the others. Thank you, Emily Keane Smith, for reading every story I've written and for sharing your great ideas. As always, your comments have improved this story. Thank you to Carol Thomas for sharing your thoughts. The book is better because of you! And Doug and Veronica, for helping me with the historical details for Hatshepsut.

Thank you to Jena O'Connor for various forms of editing. Thank you to Emily Murphy for being an awesome beta reader.

ABOUT LINSEY

Before becoming a romance novelist, Linsey Hall was a nautical archaeologist who studied shipwrecks from Hawaii and the Yukon to the UK and the Mediterranean. She credits the historical romances of the 70's, 80's, and 90's with her love of history and her career as an archaeologist. After a decade of tromping around the globe in search of old bits of stuff that people left lying about, she settled down and started penning her own romance novels. Her debut series, the Mythean Arcana, draws upon her love of history and the paranormal elements that she can't help but include. Several books may or may not feature her cats.

Copyright 2016 by Linsey Hall
Published by Bonnie Doon Press LLC

Linsey@LinseyHall.com
www.LinseyHall.com
https://twitter.com/HiLinseyHall
https://www.facebook.com/LinseyHallAuthor

ISBN 978-1-942085-60-7 (eBook)
ISBN 978-1-942085-61-4 (Paperback)

Printed in Great Britain
by Amazon